TEEN DUN

PRICE: $20.00 (3798/tfarp)

izzy + TRISTAN

izzy + TRISTAN

BY SHANNON DUNLAP

POPPY

LITTLE, BROWN AND COMPANY

New York   Boston

Copyright © 2019 by Shannon Dunlap

Cover art copyright © 2019 by Indigo O'Rourke. Cover design by Marcie Lawrence. Cover copyright © 2019 by Hachette Book Group, Inc.

Poppy
Little, Brown and Company
Hachette Book Group
1290 Avenue of the Americas, New York, NY 10104
Visit us at LBYR.com

First Edition: March 2019

Poppy is an imprint of Little, Brown and Company. The Poppy name and logo are trademarks of Hachette Book Group, Inc.

The publisher is not responsible for websites (or their content) that are not owned by the publisher.

Library of Congress Cataloging-in-Publication Data
Names: Dunlap, Shannon, author.
Title: Izzy + Tristan / by Shannon Dunlap. Other titles: Izzy and Tristan
Description: First edition. | New York ; Boston : Little, Brown and Company, 2019. | Summary: In this modern retelling of the tragic romance of Tristan and Iseult, two teenagers fall in love even though family, friends, and society threaten to keep them apart.
Identifiers: LCCN 2018020159| ISBN 9780316415385 (hardcover) | ISBN 9780316415408 (ebook) | ISBN 9780316523110 (library edition ebook)
Subjects: | CYAC: Interracial dating—Fiction. | Love—Fiction. | Triangles (Interpersonal relations)—Fiction. | African Americans—Fiction. | Brooklyn (New York, N.Y.)—Fiction.
Classification: LCC PZ7.1.D8637 Iz 2019 | DDC [Fic]—dc23
LC record available at https://lccn.loc.gov/2018020159

ISBNs: 978-0-316-41538-5 (hardcover), 978-0-316-41540-8 (ebook)

Printed in the United States of America

LSC-C

10 9 8 7 6 5 4 3 2 1

*To those who understand
that love can collapse time*

Then while we live, in love let's so persever,
That when we live no more, we may live ever.

—Anne Bradstreet, 1612–1672

PROLOGUE

THIS IS NOT A NOVEL. IT'S A ROMANCE.

A *romance*—Mrs. Dwyer taught us this in sophomore
year English class, when I was still going to my old school—
a romance is more like a fable. It traffics in ideals, mysteries,
and obsessions. Grasp too hard at the characters in a romance,
and they'll float away from you, become abstract, drift in the
direction of myth.

Believe me, I don't feel mythic at the moment. Sisyphus
aside, my unchanging daily routine, here at this desk, is the
opposite of mythic. My *narrative perch*, Mrs. Dwyer might
have called it, and I do feel perched here in time, a bird at rest
without an impulse to migrate farther.

Back then, though, everything was different, I was

different, and I suppose I did feel *romantic*: in the common, everyday use of the word, red roses and poetry, but also in the academic sense, wrapped as I was in the myth of my own story. Tristan always felt that way to me, too. Tristan, so beautiful his edges were blurred, like he didn't quite exist in reality. Tristan the Ideal, Tristan the Mystery, Tristan the Obsession. I saw it all in that very first moment I set eyes on him, when I wanted to swallow his pain, hold it in my mouth like a hard candy, let it melt until it was part of me.

Maybe that is what happened. Maybe that was the cause of all the trouble that followed.

I'm getting ahead of myself.

Mrs. Dwyer also taught us that the word *novel* comes from the Italian for "new little story," something fresh, something that, at the time the word was coined, no one had ever tried before. So you see, this can't be a novel, because it's not about anything new. It's about the oldest thing in the world. It's about love.

PART 1

THE KNIGHT

MARCUS IS SITTING A FEW YARDS BEHIND ME ON A park bench, and even though my eyes are focused on the board, I know exactly what I'll see if I turn around. He's stretching out those long arms, taking up the space because he can, letting his lackeys cling to the edge of the bench or skulk around behind it. Tyrone, K–Dawg, Frodo—less charismatic than the pieces on the board and with about as many brains. I hear Marcus yawn and know that he's making a big show of adjusting his lid, closing his eyes like he couldn't care less about what is going on in the match.

"Yo, T, this going to take much longer?" he asks. When I first moved up to Brooklyn and in with Auntie Patrice two years ago, Marcus took to calling me Lil' T, because Tyrone was already called T. But that was before I started making money for Marcus at the chess tables.

"Not over 'til it's over," mutters Antoine. I can see him out of the corner of my eye. He has his arms crossed over his chest. He's nervous. He should be, too, because his man, the fat Puerto Rican kid sitting across the table from me, is running out of options and trying to sidle his rook into a better position. Bad move.

"Not over 'til it's over," I say without lifting my eyes from the board. "That is what they say. But it's almost over. Check."

I can feel the slow spread of Marcus's grin behind me.

From that point on, it's standard procedure, all over but the shouting, if you will, which the three stooges provide a few moves later when I announce checkmate. (And I always have to announce it, because it's not like they could see a killer move if it was mooning them in the face.)

"Way to go, Lil' T," Tyrone says, punching me on the shoulder.

"Ain't so little these days, is he, Tyrone?" Frodo says. Frodo is so short and ugly that his only real joy in life is trying to feel more important than Tyrone.

I ignore them all, ignore Antoine walking over to pay Marcus, too, and focus on shaking the fat kid's hand. I don't like to know the dollar amount that Marcus has riding on these matches. It messes with my game.

"Good game," I say, looking fully into the fat kid's sweet face for the first time that day. He's young, maybe only fourteen, and his emotions are wallpapered all over him, tip to toes. He tried tripping me up with a strange opening called the Orangutan. Kid's got guts, if not the experience to back them up.

"Yeah," he says, "maybe for you."

"Hey," I say, lowering my voice, "you shouldn't hang with Antoine. He's bad news, man."

The fat kid smirks. "Yeah. And Marcus isn't?"

And then it's time to go, time to leave the park, ditch the lackeys, walk home with Marcus, maybe smoke a joint with him to come down from the adrenaline of the match, and leave that poor fat kid to get knocked around a little by Antoine.

———————

There's a chill in the air tonight, the first little dip into fall that we've had this year, but as we amble down Eastern Parkway, Marcus is still wearing short sleeves, and I know he probably will for weeks yet. He doesn't like to cover up his tats, which cost a fortune, that's the real reason, but when the girls, the girls with the lip gloss and tight jeans and low-cut tops, when they squeal and ask, "Aren't you cooooold?" he flashes them his thousand-watt smile and says, "Hot-blooded."

Sometimes, looking at the raw strength knotted up in Marcus's biceps, I marvel that we could be related or even of the same species. We are, though, and by blood, no less; his father is my mother's brother ("God rest her beautiful soul," Uncle Sherwin always says to me through tears when he's had one cupful of rum punch too many), and Auntie Patrice is aunt to both of us, even though I'm the one who lives with her. Marcus lives with his mother and his baby sister, Chantal, on the same block. Officially, that is. In reality, Marcus lives everywhere and nowhere: on the basketball courts down on the piers, on the benches outside the TipTop Social Club where the old men roll dice, at Patrice's table, where he often slides into a chair at dinnertime, unannounced, and at the corner of Fulton and Nostrand, where he has various business ventures that he insists I don't need to know too much about. I never argue that point.

There are people out there who are scared of Marcus, and they're not all as helpless as the fat chess player, either. I've seen a few things, hanging out with Marcus, things that make me wish that my brain had a delete function. But on whatever scale I want to weigh it, my loyalty to Marcus is always the single heaviest stone, and not only because he's the best insurance policy against getting beaten up that someone like me could ever have. He's blood, pure and simple, and we start from the same side of the board, always. Marcus can be impulsive, and I don't want it to get him tangled in serious trouble. Most of the time, though, he seems too perfect for anything to go wrong.

When we get back to the block, he starts jogging up the steps to his door, and I say good night, but then Marcus says, "Wait," and sits down on the top step, nodding to the empty space beside him. My mouth is dry, that weird postmatch headache starting to creep in around the edges of the faint buzz from the weed, and I want to go home and try to catch a nap before dinner, but instead, I sit, one step below him, telling myself it's to give us both more room.

"That was some solid shit you were working today," Marcus says.

"It was nothing," I say. "Kid was scared from the beginning. Of Antoine, not me."

Marcus smiles and stretches back, leaning his bare elbows against the concrete of the stoop. "You gotta learn to take a compliment, little cuz."

I shrug. Marcus doesn't know a thing about chess, and I'm not in the habit of accepting empty praise.

"School next week," he says.

"Yup."

"You wanna know something crazy?"

I turn toward him slightly, raising one questioning eyebrow. "Frodo might actually graduate this year?"

Marcus smiles, a small reward for my lame joke, so many gleaming white teeth. "Naw. It's like this: I feel like this is my year. My year to be on top. My moment. That sound crazy?"

It does, but only because, from my vantage point, Marcus has always been on top. This will be his senior year; he made it this far largely because of his mother's pleading (with both him and the school administration) and because he likes the reinforcement that school gives to his place in the social hierarchy. I'm only a grade behind him, but a full two and a half years younger, and I look it, too. Some advice: Skipping a grade is not a route to respect and admiration from one's peers.

"Nope," I say.

"Things are changing, T," he says, with that distant, pitcher-winding-up-on-the-mound look that he gets sometimes. "I can feel it."

"Mmmm." I'm having trouble focusing on anything but the dry patch at the back of my throat. That and the image of the fat kid with a black eye and a swollen lip. Dragging himself home to practice chess problems. Maybe masturbating out of loneliness if he can get the bathroom in his tiny apartment to himself for a few minutes. And the thought that the only difference between him and me is a handful of losses, lighter than the fluff of a dandelion.

"You're a million miles away," Marcus says coolly, and I snap back to attention, afraid that I've pissed him off. "But that's okay, T. All that stuff going on up here." He taps his temple. "It's what makes you a winner." Then he smiles that smile, which makes me as weak in the knees as one of the girls who are always following him around, and he cuffs me on the back of the head, a little too hard.

That's the thing about Marcus: He's so beguiling that sometimes even I forget how powerful he is.

———

The lock in the front door is tricky and it always requires a few moments of fooling with the key to make it work. This gives me enough time to sniff at my jacket for any trace of smoke and become adequately paranoid. If Marcus is a force to be reckoned with, then Auntie Patrice is a straight-up force of nature. She's stirring a saucepan of something on the stove when I reach her fourth-floor apartment, but she's typing, too, with one hand, an email on a laptop that is propped on the counter and also talking to someone on her phone headset, most likely a distant relative in Trinidad.

"Hold on," she says to the distant Trinidadian when she sees me come in. "Tristan just walked in."

"Tristan," she says, clucking the word like an agitated hen. She is one of the only people to use my full name, this crazy German name, and I know it's out of loyalty to the person who gave it to me. She sniffs the air delicately, like a bloodhound, and says, "You been hanging out with Marcus?"

There is never a point in lying to Patrice. "Yeah. But it's okay. Nothing bad." And that's true enough, I guess, that she buys it.

"Marcus," she says, shaking her head. "That boy is nothing but trouble." And that's true enough, too, but I know she loves Marcus fiercely, probably more than she does me. "Is he coming for dinner?"

"Not sure. I don't think so."

"Okay." She hasn't stopped stirring the entire time we've been talking, but she still looks restless, as if her other hand is annoyed that it isn't doing anything. "Dinner in forty-five minutes. You can't water the coriander in the evening, baby, it will bring in the bugs. You gotta do it early in the morning." It takes me a beat to realize that this last directive is meant for the faraway relative, not me, and by then, Patrice has already turned away and is reaching for her laptop again. "No, that's not early enough."

I trail down the hall to my room, or the room where I sleep, at least. It still looks mostly like a guest room, even though I have been living here for two years. It's easy to have gratitude and respect for Aunt Patrice, since she is easily the most sensible person in my family, and I have plenty of affection for her, too, but she isn't the warmest person, and the truth is, there are days when I feel like an intruder here.

I flop down on the bed and shut my eyes, but now that I'm here, I can't shake the feeling that something is closing in on me, a suffocation so subtle I'll be dead before I put my finger on it. Eyes open. Eyes closed. Monster easing itself down onto my chest. Eyes open. On the bedside table, there's a framed wedding photo of my parents, and I've never known if Patrice put it there because she thought it would be comforting for me or because she wanted it in here, out of her sight.

In the photo, they're cutting a cake. She's wearing a white suit and laughing and saying something to someone out of the frame. I have my father's light skin, but the rest of me is so completely my mother that it looks like we were cast from the same mold. My father's head is tilted down, but you can tell from his dimples that he's smiling, too. (Dimples! I can't think of the last time I saw his dimples in real life. Do they still exist? Can you age or grieve your way out of dimples?) The photo is black-and-white, which I've always found confusing, since it's not like it was all that long ago. In fact, I'm pretty sure I'm in the photo, too, under the buttoned coat of my mother's white suit. No one has ever mentioned it to me outright, but it doesn't take a genius to count the seven months between the day this photo was taken and the day my mother died.

"Bianca was a wild child," some of the relatives will say, shaking their heads, smiling at the memory of her. When I was small, I would snatch at the words people used to describe her: beautiful, crazy, fun, charming, impulsive. I would take them and try to roll them together into my own memory of her. But it's not an easy thing to do, building a person from scratch.

I reach out and turn the frame facedown on the table, and then I search for my phone in my backpack. I want to hear my dad's voice, even though I know he won't pick up the phone. He's a concert promoter, and he works strange hours. I listen to the recorded message on his voice mail, and then I redial and listen to it again. He'll see that I tried to call, obviously, but a lot of people call him. He'll make a mental note to call me later and then he'll forget.

If that makes me sound like a big puddle of self-pity, I don't mean for it to. I'm not tearfully waiting for my dad to come reclaim me, nothing remotely like that. Before I moved to Brooklyn, my dad and I were living in McAdams, a suburb of Atlanta, in one side of a little ranch double house that was always dark and usually smelled bad, like dirty feet and a half-hearted punch of cheap cleaning products. It took me a long while to figure out that it wasn't normal, having a father who could barely make himself get out of bed to pay the guy who delivered our groceries. At seven, I went over to my friend Benji's house for the first time and marveled at the fact that his mother seemed to have a vested interest in knowing where we were, what we were doing, whether we were hungry, whether we were safe. When she brought his laundry into his room, all fresh and folded, I think I stared at her as if she were a unicorn. I had figured out how to use the washing machine when I was five, and folding the laundry seemed entirely unnecessary. I was pretty afraid of lighting the finicky gas stove in our kitchen, but sometimes I did it anyway to make us macaroni and cheese. Most of the time, though, we ate peanut butter and jelly sandwiches and salad out of a bag and pretzels.

I got really good at school. For one thing, I liked being there, because no matter how dumb the classes were or how mean some of the kids could be, it felt so much less lonely than my house. But also, I knew that the better I did, the less likely anyone was to interfere with my life. I wasn't stupid; I knew what sort of shit happened when teachers started to notice that someone was having "trouble at home." Ace every test and you're suddenly way down on any potential do-gooder's list of meddling priorities. So I got good grades, joined a couple of clubs in middle school, like chess club, because it seemed so laughable that you could play a board game for a few hours and get praised for it.

Maybe this all sounds sad, sad, sad to you, but it wasn't. Life is made of comparisons, after all. In school, from the time you're small, they teach you about wars and more wars, diseases and famines and still more wars, and I would sit there in the back of my social studies classes, marveling at the boring era I'd been born into and feeling relieved. I think a lot of people have the opposite reaction, and those are the people who start new wars. Not me. I was too busy flying under the radar.

That's how it was, with me knowingly and expertly avoiding attention for over a decade, while the twin gargoyles of grief and depression sat on my father's chest, suffocating him.

And then, everything changed. I'm still not sure how, exactly. My father had always gone through periods of feeling better, when his mood would lift and he would hire a cleaning service and ask me what I was doing at school and even call his colleagues at the PR firm that he still technically co-owned. My best guess is that during one of these periods of relative okay-ness he went to a doctor and got some pills, because almost overnight, he became frantically, manically busy. He went back to work and pounded the pavement the way he did when he was a twenty-year-old kid just starting out. He said that all the time, that he felt like a kid again, cigarette in his fingers, leg jiggling, a glazed expression that said that he did not, necessarily, remember that he was speaking to an actual kid, his kid. He started working late, and I was home alone a lot, and even though it shouldn't have made that much difference, since it was similar to him being asleep in the next room, I admit that this is the part of the story where I started to feel kind of abandoned. And offended, maybe, that after all those years, I hadn't been the thing to get my father out of bed.

Then he sat me down one day and told me that I was going to go live with my aunt Patrice.

"But I barely know her," I said. That was true. Auntie Patrice was a name that I mostly recognized from birthday cards, and I wasn't certain that I could pick her out of the crowd of Mom's siblings in the old photo albums piled in the hall closet.

"What do you mean?" he asked, fidgeting in his chair. "You lived with Patrice until you were almost two."

"In Brooklyn?" This was all news to me. "Where were you?"

My father sighed. "This isn't a life, T. It's my fault, but still."

"It's *my* life," I said.

"Patrice will know what to do. She always knows what to do. And things will be fine." I think I started to protest, to list some pretty valid reasons for not wanting to go live with a virtual stranger, but he got distracted by something and walked out of the room, and left me there, trying to remember something, anything, about Patrice.

So my dad fumbled the opening move a little, but the thing is, he was right: Moving in with Patrice was probably the best thing that could have happened to me. Suddenly, there were Patrice and Marcus and the wonderland of Brooklyn. There were chess tables in the parks and beautiful, worldly girls on every block and big, extended-family parties on holidays. School is even more laughably easy when someone else is making the macaroni and cheese. It was an entirely new point of comparison.

My father works all the time, and sometimes I see the uncles shaking their heads and *tsk*ing about that, saying that he's just a different kind of crazy now, but he sounds okay when I talk to him on the phone or when he comes up to visit every few months, happier than I've ever known him to be. It's like he finally decided to come back from the dead and live a second life, and I'm not mad at him about that. Those words that he said to me haunt me sometimes, though. *Is* this a life? If it is, can I legitimately call it my own or have I merely been letting the circumstances wash over me? My dad, he's had two lives already, but have I even started my first?

"Dinner!" Patrice shouts from the kitchen.

———

Marcus doesn't show up for dinner, and there's a little pop of relief in my chest, along with some nervous anticipation. Sometimes it can be awkward when Patrice and I are left alone, like we don't quite know how to talk to each other. I ask her polite questions about her job at a bank in Manhattan when, really, I'd like to ask her about my mother or what it used to be like when she took care of me as a baby or why she never goes out on dates, even though she's still pretty, in her no-nonsense, often-frowning way. But it feels like all of these topics are off-limits.

"It's good spaghetti," I say, but it comes out almost apologetically.

"Labor Day this weekend," Patrice says. "That means the block party on Saturday." Patrice helps to plan the neighborhood block party every year, and I know she puts a lot of time into polishing every detail. But I've learned from the past two block parties that it's one of those things where the whole neighborhood seems to be having more fun than I am and I don't know what to do with myself.

"Oh, yeah," I say. "I have to work in the morning, but I'll come straight home afterward. I should be able to catch a lot of it." I have a job as a summer math tutor at one of the branches of the library. I took it so that I could hang out in Brooklyn for the summer instead of going back to Atlanta like I did last year. I barely know anyone there anymore, and besides, tutoring is not terrible money compared to flipping burgers. Marcus, though, didn't agree. "You're worth more than that, fam," he said. But I couldn't give up the job and play chess for Marcus all day long; I knew enough about Patrice to know that wouldn't go over well. "One of my last shifts," I finish, as a sort of explanation.

"Maybe you can help with the activities for the children when you get home," Patrice says. "There's a new family up the block, and the lady wants to do some kind of arts-and-crafts thing." Patrice shrugs and rolls her eyes, so I know she's talking about the white family who moved in a few weeks ago. They renovated one of the oldest houses on the block, and now that corner, without the overgrown yard and rotting porch, looks completely different. "Buddhist sand sculpture or something. I don't know."

"That sounds...interesting," I say cautiously. It's way different up here, the whole race thing, than it was in Atlanta. Personally, I like the way everybody's so blasé about it here, the way people try their best to get along because there's not enough room not to.

Patrice makes a noncommittal *hmm*ing noise. She's been living in this neighborhood since she was younger than I am now, and she can definitely be a little territorial when it comes to our block. She's seen a lot of changes, and any newcomers get put through a long probationary period while she decides if she likes them or not. This is especially true if they look like they might not fit in. If they make Buddhist sand sculptures, for instance, and wear flamboyantly tie-dyed scarves, like I've seen this woman wear.

"Well, I'm glad you think it sounds interesting," Patrice says. "You can help her, then."

If Marcus were here, he'd make some joke about crazy white people and their crazy schemes and make her laugh. He can be a harsh judge of people when he wants to be, but maybe that's just another form of being territorial.

I get uncomfortable making jokes like that, though, so I act terrifically interested in my spaghetti and nod. I compose my face into a blank that says: You know me, I love Buddhist sand sculptures.

"Good," she says. "It's settled, then."

THE QUEEN

I'D SPENT MOST OF MY TIME THAT SPRING AND SUMMER dwelling on the possibility that my parents might be idiots. I was tired of their relentless optimism and their matching sandals and their boring, overeducated friends and their pretending that musical history stopped with *The White Album* and their community co-op bulgur wheat and their organic but ineffective toothpaste. The sixties were half a century in the past, but somehow, they hadn't gotten the message. Hell, they had barely even been *alive* during the sixties, but that didn't stop them. Living with people like this would have been irritating under the best of circumstances, but it was particularly infuriating when they decided that the Lower East Side, where my twin brother, Hull, and I had spent our entire young lives, didn't have enough *soul* anymore, and we needed to uproot our comfortable existence and move to Brooklyn at the end of our sophomore year of high school. You should have seen the shade of purple that my brother turned when they dropped that piece of news during the family dinner at Shah Jalal, their favorite Indian restaurant. Is it easier to imagine if I tell you that he was yelling "Fuck this stupid family" at the same time?

They say that round parents have square children, and you couldn't find a more apt illustration of that axiom than the Steinbach clan. We were five when Hull created his first Excel spreadsheet. (Its purpose was to keep an inventory of his stuffed animals, which he was certain that someone was pilfering. I was.) Starting in fifth grade, he insisted on wearing collared shirts, even on the weekends, and got his hair trimmed every three weeks in a style that my mother called "the Mitt Romney" with an exasperated sigh. He ran for student council every year under the slogan "Hull Steinbach, the Responsible Choice." And it was unusual enough at our small, experimental school that he always won, too. Hull could be hard to take, a little prickly. People thought he was arrogant, but the truth was that he really was smart and special, and he wasn't into pretending that he didn't know it. I loved him dearly, in spite of and because of all of this.

As for me, I was as distinct from my kooky parents as Hull, but in different ways. I spent most of my childhood curing my family of imaginary diseases. My dad, a professor of Renaissance drama at NYU, couldn't keep anything that had "Dr. Steinbach" printed on it because I would spirit it away to add to my doctor kit. "Why do you have them anyway when you're not a real doctor?" I would ask him, a question his friends always found precocious and extremely funny when it was related at dinner parties. When my mother made me go to stupid weekend classes with her, pottery-making or painting or interpretive dance, I would sullenly pore over *Gray's Anatomy of the Human Body* for the entire subway ride. She was a jeweler who made large, elaborate pieces that only eccentric wealthy people could afford, and she simply couldn't believe that she'd birthed a daughter with so little artistic aptitude. *Believe it*, I'd think as I was half-heartedly pretending to be a tree in dance class. *Believe it.* When I broke the news, at age nine, that I had my sights set on med school, my parents tried to take the news bravely.

"Well, William Carlos Williams was a doctor," my dad said hopefully, "and so was Chekhov!" And then my mother said, a little too brightly, "That's great, honey!" and lit some sandalwood incense, which is what she does when she's stressed.

But I'm already getting distracted from the point, which is that my parents' big announcement that we were moving to Brooklyn and that we would be enrolling in a public school there didn't go over so well.

"It will be amazing," my mother trilled. "The house we found is a gem. Haven't you guys always wanted a real backyard? And Brooklyn is where all the really interesting stuff is happening these days. We'll be in the middle of it!"

"What kind of interesting stuff?" Hull asked. He was angrily ripping his naan into bits and compressing them into round pellets, an arsenal of doughy BBs rolling around his plate. "Artisanal pickles and ironic facial hair?"

While Hull and my mother went mano a mano on wide-ranging social issues, I chewed a forkful of biryani and considered. Here are the things that occurred to me, in the order in which they did: 1) I didn't want to leave my friends and teachers at Hope Springs Day School. Some of my friends, like Alma and Philip, had been in my class since kindergarten. 2) HSDS didn't have the strongest science program, and there was a chance the new school would have AP Biology. 3) Hull was not going to stop freaking out about this, not for a long time. Hull had spent years laying the political groundwork to be both junior and senior class president, and he was enraged. He actually pounded his fist on the table, knocking over a little bowl of mint chutney.

"Don't I have some kind of legal recourse?" Hull shouted, which made my father laugh, which is what made Hull drop the f-bomb, which is when the diners at nearby tables started to give us the side-eye.

"I think that in just a few months, you're going to love

it there," my mother said, and then burst into tears. Dinner was over.

———————

The house my parents bought was old, very old, and it used to be a farmhouse when Brooklyn was full of rolling, grassy fields and stately vacation homes, though now it was squashed improbably onto the end of a row of brownstones. I wouldn't call it a gem; I would call it more of a fixer-upper. But it did have a wide porch and a big living room and a pretty curved staircase that led up to an entire second story, the sort of comforts that most Manhattanites teach themselves to live without. And my parents, to their credit, are good at fixing things up, so they hired Nicolas, a soft-spoken contractor, to do the more serious repairs while they sanded floors and stripped wallpaper and painted and landscaped and varnished their little hearts out. This was in the late spring, as school was letting out for summer break, and sometimes they managed to drag me along to help, but Hull was steadfast. He didn't even want to set eyes on the place.

Eventually, he had to, of course. The co-op that my parents had owned for almost two decades sold quickly to a young investment banker and his aspiring actress girlfriend, and moving day was set for early July. "It's not that bad," I tried to tell him a week or two before. "There's a lot more space." He looked at me sadly, as if even this simple statement of fact was a deep betrayal, and shook his head.

Hull and my mom and I piled into our aging Volvo and drove to the new place behind my dad in the moving truck. Over the river and through the woods, I thought, as we crossed the Manhattan Bridge into our new borough. When we got there, Hull slid out of the back seat with a duffel bag and a box of his stuff, and disappeared inside to lock himself in his empty new room, completely shirking any other moving responsibilities. "I think he's grieving," my mother said to my father and me as we dripped sweat onto box after box. "We should respect his emotional journey."

"I think your son doesn't like Brooklyn so much," Nicolas said solemnly as he helped her maneuver a dining table through the front door. "Maybe it is not the place for him." Nicolas almost never said anything that was superfluous and, consequently, anything he did say seemed like a grave and irreversible proclamation. My mother dropped her end of the table and knocked it against the doorframe, causing a gouge on one of the legs that could never be repaired.

We were all so focused on Hull and his wrath that I think we may have overlooked some of the other difficulties of the move until we were in the thick of them. The house was in a section of Bed-Stuy that was pretty cool, but a little rougher around the edges than our neighborhood in Manhattan. One night, some people who were drunk (or angry) trashed a bunch of the landscaping my parents had put in, and they had to do it all over again. The empty lot at the other end of the block always smelled like urine, and used condoms appeared there overnight like fungi. My mother made me start to carry a tiny can of mace in my backpack. She looked sheepish when she gave it to me. "Not that anyone will bother you," she said. "But it's good to be safe."

I was a New York City kid, so it wasn't like I didn't know plenty of black and Latino and Asian people. What I wasn't used to was being so obviously, attention-grabbing-ly white in a neighborhood where most people weren't. What's more, it was a summer full of problems that I'd thought were solved decades before I was born; the newspapers carried grim stories of black people shot by white police officers, and the headlines flashed through my head every time a police cruiser glided past. Most of the neighbors, Nicolas had informed us, were longtime residents of the block and most were Caribbean, immigrants from decades before or their first-generation children, and I could feel them giving me the once-over whenever I walked by. Slightly farther from home, on the way to the hardware store or the grocery store, I got called Snowflake once or twice, and another time I had to pretend not to hear a very drunk homeless guy yelling down the block, telling me what all white girls liked to suck. But mostly I got along just fine.

The situation was far worse when I was with my parents. My mom wanted to engage with everyone she saw, trying to make new friends, but it was painfully awkward. "My family is from *Ireland*," she would say whenever we met someone new, running a hand through her curly red hair, "though I was born in *Illinois*." When I asked her why she kept saying something so stupid, she told me, "I'm sharing something of my background so they can feel comfortable sharing theirs with me. That's how people learn about each other, Izzy." Honestly, it was mortifying.

I spent a couple weeks at the house after the big move-in, helping my dad stain a new deck that Nicolas had built in the back and counting down the days until I could leave for my summer job as a counselor at Camp Timbuktu in the Catskills. I'd gone there every summer as a little kid and had adored every second of it. It was kind of a nerdy version of camp, lots of learning in addition to the usual swimming and capture the flag games. I'd already missed the first six-week session because of the renovation and move, but my parents had promised me that I could work the second one.

"You should come with me," I told Hull on a rare occasion when I wheedled my way into his room. "You know they hire any former camper who applies. Especially one with grades like yours. You could teach debate tactics or run a political science seminar or something."

"Can't," Hull said. We were sitting in the mess on his floor: unpacked boxes and strewn clothes. His mattress was still on the floor because he hadn't bothered to put the bed frame together and had ignored my parents' offers to do it for him. Even his hair looked longer and messier than usual.

"Why not?"

"I'll be too busy convincing Mom and Dad to sell this

dump and move back to Manhattan," he said, but then he gave me a small smile that reassured me that he was not completely out of his gourd.

"You know it's not a bad view, if you would ever open your window blinds. Mom and Dad are almost finished with the back garden."

"Oh, Izzy," he said. "I love that you think the view could really fix what's wrong with this place."

If I had known how much more would be wrong by the time I got back from camp, I might have responded with more than an eye roll. I might have begged Hull to be more open-minded when it came to approaching a borough as vast as Brooklyn. I might have warned him that some actions have consequences that go on and on and on. Instead, I said, "Bork," which was the tiniest scrap of our infantile twin-speak that we had left and which we used to mean whatever needed to be said at any given moment. This time it meant "Everything will be okay. You'll see."

"Bork," he said, but I couldn't read the tone in his voice, and it made me nervous.

THE KNIGHT

THE ENTIRE TIME I'M TUTORING ON SATURDAY, TRYING to get poor Tomaso to finally, finally understand the difference between sine and cosine, I have a weird jitter in my stomach, and sure enough, when I get back to the neighborhood for the block party, things are beginning to come off the rails. In spite of the crepe paper and brightly colored signs and the puffs of smoke from the charcoal grills that have been wheeled onto the sidewalk, everything feels wound tight. There are dark clouds speeding in, and it's airlessly hot, a final throwback to stormy summer. It's that point in the afternoon when adults have had too much beer and are feeling lackadaisical and sleepy. The kids have been riding their bikes up and down the blocked-off stretch of street since early in the morning, and they're sweaty and cranky, and everybody's beginning to grate on each other's nerves. But that isn't even the main problem, at least from where I'm standing. The main problem is that Marcus and his lackeys are sitting on his stoop, gathered like a pack of wolves, and like any good pack, they have their eyes trained on easy prey. Some white kid, dressed real nerdy, has set up a table across the street from them with a sign that says LESSONS IN CHESS AND POLITICAL STRATEGY—$10. A groan vibrates in my chest, knowing already that I'm going to get dragged into something here, but I try to pretend that I don't notice anything—the kid, the sign, Marcus's evil eye, nothing.

"What's up?" I say to Marcus, hoping it will be taken as a mere greeting, not as a question that needs to be answered. All of them smell of the malt liquor that Marcus has gotten somewhere and barely bothers to conceal behind him on the step. K-Dawg looks stoned beyond speech, but the others are whispering to each other and laughing.

Marcus looks up and gives me a nod. "T, the man of the hour. We've been waiting for you to show up so this dog could give you a *chess lesson*." He says this last part loud enough for the white kid to hear. He's doing his best to not glance in Marcus's direction; the antelope has smelled the predator but knows it is suicide to look him in the eye. "Big man on the block over there, he's gonna teach us a thing or two."

Frodo smirks. "Even his ma tried to get him to take it down." He gives a quick chin jerk toward a woman standing at a folding table a little way down the street. She's playing with her frizzy hair nervously. The kids near her are shooting each other with Super Soaker water guns, ignoring both her and her sand art.

I'm about to say that I'm supposed to be helping her, but before I can, Marcus takes my arm and says, "Hey, T, let's go talk to this cat. Welcome him to the neighborhood." There is nothing that I would like to do less than go over and confront this kid who's asking, with that smug expression alone, to get his ass beat, but there's iron in Marcus's grip, and so I let myself get pulled alongside him. I fold my arms and look down at the table and hope that this will be over swiftly.

"Hello," White Boy says. "How may I help you?"

"What's your name, son?" Marcus asks, smiling that killer smile.

"I'm not your son," White Boy says, with his own wide politician's grin. "But if you're interested, I might be able to provide you with some useful advice." He nods at his sign.

"Ohhh," Marcus says, pointing at the sign as if he's reading it for the first time and then putting his hand to his mouth as if in wonder. "I see. A chess master, right here on our block."

White Boy doesn't say anything, but he doesn't drop his eye contact, even when Marcus leans in closer.

"Turns out, though," Marcus says, "that my boy T here is actually pretty good at chess already."

"Mmmm," White Boy says, and his eyes relax a little. Do

I know him? He looks like a lot of people I've played at school tournaments.

"'Cause, see, I think you have the wrong idea about your new neighborhood. We could probably offer you some lessons about that. Right, T?"

I clear my throat and try a different angle. "Man, it's really not cool to sell stuff at the block party. It's kind of a situation where everyone shares what they can. You know?"

White Boy smirks, and I recognize that feeling sorry for someone and liking him are two different things.

"So maybe you two should have a friendly chess matchup at the park tomorrow. You know, to welcome you to the *hood*," Marcus says. Then switching to a goofy British accent: "Wouldn't that be a sporting way to pass an afternoon, Mr. Strategy? As long as we have a little wager going, that is." The uneasy jitter that's been there in my stomach all day is now scratching and biting, a squirrel in a bag. I'm pretty sure I can beat this kid, but there's always the fear.

"And what are we wagering?"

"I expect you could pay me a C-note when T beats you, and we'll call it even. For now."

"And if I win? You'll pay me a hundred dollars?"

Marcus leans across the table slowly, and for a sickening moment I half think that he's going to kiss this kid and make him shit himself right there on the pavement, but instead he says softly into his ear, "You win and I won't make you regret the day you were born." Then he pats White Boy on the shoulder so hard that the kid almost topples over sideways, and bursts into laughter. "I'm just joking with you! You should see your face!" White Boy manages a weak smile. Marcus sticks out his palm for a handshake. "We got a deal, son?"

"It's Hull," White Boy says, and puts his hand in Marcus's. Something clicks in my brain at the name.

"Marcus," Marcus says, and I can tell by the twitch of pain in Hull's cheek that Marcus is squeezing his hand harder and harder. "Two o'clock in McNair on Eastern Parkway. It's not hard to find, Mr. Strategy. Don't be late."

The first rolls of thunder break as he's saying this, a cartoonish premonition, and you can hear little squawks of alarm go up and down the block as big, fat raindrops begin to fall. The women hustle to cover up the trays of jerk chicken and rice. The children run in crazed circles, letting the rain soak their T-shirts.

"Two o'clock," Hull says. He picks up his table without bothering to fold it and walks toward the newly renovated house on the corner.

I start to jog to get out of the rain, but it's clear that Marcus isn't about to hurry, so I slow my pace and we walk toward Aunt Patrice's building. At the door, she loads our arms with food to take inside and put in the refrigerator. "And take your shoes off!" she yells as she runs back to the picnic table to collect more items.

Inside, I get two towels for us and throw our T-shirts in the dryer. Then I stand in the kitchen with Marcus, who is dripping water onto Patrice's floor and brooding, forearms leaning on the counter, popping his knuckles one by one.

"I shoulda smacked that loser while I had the chance."

"Oh, come on, Marcus." I toss him the towel. "Why's this kid getting to you? He's nobody to you." Marcus can get angry quickly. My guess is that it's because he's quick to get his feelings hurt, too, but that's not a theory I'd ever share with him.

Marcus glowers. "It rubs me the wrong way, T. Him looking down on all of us." Then something in his face breaks open, and he gives me a wry smile. "Doesn't matter. You'll show him what's what tomorrow. I had a dream last night that you turned into a champion pit bull, that you tore apart the competition."

I cover my head with the towel and rub my hair dry. I'm not interested in hearing Marcus's dreams right now, especially if they involve me being a dog. "You know that kid's not bad at chess, right? I recognized him. His name's Hull, and his team finished, like, fifth at the citywides last year, mostly because of him." I don't like the way Marcus is looking at me when I pull the towel down around my shoulders.

"And how did you do at citywides, my man?"

"We won."

"That's what I thought. So tell me you're going to beat this kid tomorrow."

I shrug. "I'll win."

"That's what I thought," Marcus repeats, and he opens his mouth to say something else, but Patrice comes bustling in, arms full of wet tablecloth. I take it from her, glad to have an excuse to dodge Marcus's gaze.

"What a mess!" she says in that voice that lets you know that she could plan the weather far better than whoever is currently in charge.

"Sorry your party got rained on, Auntie," Marcus says, and leans down to kiss her on the cheek as I leave the room.

"It's okay," I can hear Patrice say. "You staying for dinner, Marcus?"

"Naw, I got some errands to run. I'm on my way out."

"Marcus, you're not wearing a shirt!"

Whatever Marcus says in response is muffled, but I hear Patrice laugh girlishly in response. "See you tomorrow, T!" he calls out, right before the door bangs shut behind him.

I dump the tablecloth in the big utility sink and lean against the washing machine. I don't want to play tomorrow. I don't know why it's different than any other match that Marcus has set up for me, but it is. It feels more personal, and the little facts that I usually brush away are more pressing this time. Like the fact that Marcus has never offered to give me a set percentage of the winnings. Sure, most of the time I roll with it, chalk it up to honing my skills with a few side benefits. But right now, it feels more like licking up the scraps that Marcus deigns to throw my way.

I've been on a winning streak lately, picking up speed all summer. Last summer, when Marcus and I first started this racket, I played mostly old guys from around the neighborhood, guys who spend all day shooting the shit and playing chess. They were tough at first, but then I came to realize that they relied too much on a pretty small pack of tricks that they'd picked up over the years. Catch on to the tricks and you can take them down. That's what I did, gradually. Now the old guys won't even play me; they just wave Marcus off, say they'll keep their cash, go back to drinking their afternoon beers. This summer I've been playing younger guys, recruited by Antoine or some other tough. These kids play a looser, more creative game than the old-timers, but they're also green, lacking in methodology. I can sense the moment when they start to panic, can almost feel my reputation taking on weight as I lay them down gently. These past few weeks, winning has started to feel like an inevitability.

So I think I can beat Hull, but it's not a sure thing. He's good, and all streaks come to an end, even mine. I do have an advantage, though: I recognized Hull and I can look up his stats online tonight, maybe even find lists of moves from some of his matches. He could, theoretically, do the same for me, but I don't think he recognized me. Probably because Marcus always calls me T instead of Tristan and because we didn't go head-to-head at citywides last year. I already know, though, what Marcus would say if I mentioned this to him: "Asshole thinks we all look alike." And I don't know. Maybe Marcus would be right.

THE ROOK

So I'm drying off the outside tables, or more like shoving the water off of them with an already soaked rag, when Marcus appears in front of the restaurant and, oh God, he's not even wearing a shirt, and, as usual when he shows up, my heart refuses to beat for a full minute, maybe longer. I'm sweaty to an embarrassing degree because I've been working all afternoon in this humid weather, but I don't think I smell bad and besides, *Cosmo* says all the time that men like women who are natural and earthy, so I put my hand on my hip in a way that I hope looks fun and flirtatious and say, "How's it going, Marcus?"

Marcus smiles. He's wearing spotless red basketball shoes, a pair of athletic shorts riding low on his muscular hips, and nothing on top but that thin rope of gold chain that I like, the one with a pendant shaped like a house dangling from it. My brain sends a signal to my body to walk over and lick his glistening bare chest, but I don't.

"What's going on, Caballito?" he says. That's his nickname for me. Unfortunately, it's not because I look like a beautiful prancing pony. It's because my worthless older brother's nickname is Caballo, and thus I became Little Horse. "Is your brother around?"

I try to think of something fascinating, something witty, something just the right degree of playful to say to him, but my brain has short-circuited on his perfection, so instead I say, "I think he's inside."

"You going to tell me my future sometime, like you promised?"

"I'd love to," I squeak. I'd die to do a tarot reading for Marcus because it's intimate, tapping into the unexplained with someone else. I've done his astrological chart a million times already (of course I know his birthday, he's a Leo, he even has a lion tattoo on his right arm and I'm pretty sure that's why), but I would never let him know that I'm a total stalker.

"Good. 'Cause you got the gift. Everyone says that's the truth." Then he smiles and disappears behind the namesake yellow door of *La Puerta Amarilla*, my parents' café.

Be still, my heart.

What is it about Marcus? Honestly, that's like asking *What is it about oxygen?* It's been there always, and without it, you'd suffocate and die. For as long as I can remember, Marcus has had a role to play in my life: joke-cracking little boy, jumping around and doing spot-on impressions of the adults in the neighborhood; then athletic middle school kid, the first one in our circle to get muscles and a voice like hot chocolate; and then handsome and powerful heartthrob always one degree cooler than everyone else in the room. A portrait of my soul mate, no matter what age we happen to be. Before I go to sleep at night, sheets wrapped tightly around me, I think of what it will be like the first time we kiss, the surprise on his face when he finally understands, marveling that he didn't know it all along, the way I have. It's me who's a step ahead on this one.

Anyway, I barely have time to silently thank the stars, the fates, the mysterious forces of the universe for Marcus's scrap of a compliment before he's gone. Coming up short on a reason to follow him, I move toward the open window so I can at least eavesdrop.

"Evening, Mrs. Gutiérrez," Marcus says. "Is Hector available?"

I can't hear how my mom answers, but her voice is curt, so sharp that it makes me cringe. She doesn't like Marcus. She thinks he's "a bad element," but that's a laugh since, in fact, it's my brother who supplies Marcus with weed, not the other way around. Anyway, it doesn't matter what Mai says because Hector has come downstairs, I can hear his voice, and the two of them walk back out onto the patio, so I go back to looking busy.

"Scram," Hector says to me.

"It's cool," Marcus says. "It's just Brianna." I'm not sure if I should be elated because of the "cool" or mad because of the "just."

"You two need to come up to the park tomorrow afternoon. I got a little thing going, and this time I want people there to watch." Instead of betting on horses or football like everybody else, Marcus bets on chess. He's always different. One more reason to love him. He looks at me now and smiles and says, "You'll be there, won't you, Caballito?"

I've never been brave enough to ask him where he got that necklace, and when I've heard other people ask him about it, he only says it's a good luck charm. But to me, it's always been a symbol, a tiny gilded home for the future Marcus, the future Brianna. I nod. Of course I'll be there.

That night, I consult the I Ching about how many of Marcus's children I'm destined to bear, but the results are inconclusive.

———

The park: a patch of concrete and dried-out grass and a single statue of a long-dead astronaut, wedged in between the Brooklyn Museum and a school for deaf kids, largely overlooked by everyone except for the old guys who play chess there and certain high school kids whose pastimes make it advantageous to adopt the spaces that are overlooked by everyone else. Today, though, it's packed. I'm not sure what Marcus did to get all of these people here or why he would go to the trouble, but there's at least thirty or forty people, talking and messing around with their phones and generally goofing off. The crowd is loosely gathering around one of the granite chess tables at the front edge of the park. Hector has reluctantly agreed to come with me. I like having Hector with me because when I'm with him, Marcus has to notice me.

Marcus didn't mention who was playing, but I knew it would be T. T's in my grade. He's Marcus's little cousin, super smart, but also kind of a drag, always looking past you, like you don't exist in the same world as him, or looking too hard at you, like you're an alien species. He wins Marcus a lot of money with his crazy chess habit, though, so you won't find me saying a wrong word to him. When we arrive, T is shaking hands and sitting down with some white kid (dorky type, shoes like my dad wears to church), and Marcus and his friends are there, too, perched at the next table over. He's wearing a loose cotton shirt, buttoned halfway, almost as if he were getting dressed up for this occasion. When he leans forward, toward the game, I can see the curve of his chest muscle, the glimmer of his necklace.

Everyone pays close attention to the first few moves, but watching a chess game gets pretty boring when most of the crowd doesn't know what the hell is going on. People keep talking and making noise, but if someone gets too loud, Marcus throws him a look and then things get quiet again fast. A front row forms, made up of kids from our high school chess team, younger than T and worshipful of him, and since they actually know what's happening in the game, everybody else looks at them for cues as to when to cheer and clap. It's pretty obvious that everyone's rooting for T—no one cares about this other kid—but the chess geeks go *oooh* and *aaah* over some of the moves that Church Shoes makes, so that's how I know it's a close game.

It goes on like this for a while. Hector gets restless and wanders around the park, talking to someone on his phone. I pull out my tarot cards and do a quick whispered reading for Bethany Jones, who wants to know if she should have sex with her boyfriend, Saeed. Then I hear the row of chess geeks bubble and squeak, and by the time I look up, Church Shoes has gone red in the face. T slides a piece into place, coughs politely, and says, "That's checkmate."

"I *know* it's checkmate!" Church Shoes says, and he's so angry that I can see the little flecks of spittle flying from his lips, gleaming in the sunlight. I scoop up the cards and dump them back into my purse in a hurry, feeling a disruption in the afternoon's vibrations, and I'm right, because Church Shoes sweeps the pieces off the board, a little burst of chess shrapnel that bounces off the pavement. "How could I possibly concentrate with this *riffraff* making so much noise?" He sweeps his arm out to indicate us, the crowd. It's quiet for a second, and then somebody lets out a big, amused laugh. Marcus, I realize. Like a current is passing through the crowd, we all start laughing at the fit this pathetic kid is throwing. It always feels good to be in a position to laugh, rather than be laughed at. Church Shoes is turning a hot fuchsia.

"Riffraff!" I hear Tyrone Hill crowing. "Riffraff!"

Church Shoes walks over and pushes Marcus right in the chest. The laugh in me flickers and goes out, and the crowd noise breaks into a static of incredulous whistles and mutters. What's *with* this kid? Does he have a death wish?

But then the planets spin, things get weird. Before Marcus can punch this kid in the face, Church Shoes reaches in the back of his pants and pulls out a wicked-looking knife. It's not a switchblade; it's not like anything I've ever seen someone carry. It's curved and has its own leather cover and scary notched teeth on the blade, like something out of a horror movie. Somebody *actually* screams in horror at the sight of it, if that tells you anything. He swings the knife in wide, crazy arcs before pointing it right at Marcus, and I choke on my heart.

"Stay back!" he shouts.

By now Hector is at my side again, and then he's past me, stumbling through the crowd, because even though Marcus irritates him sometimes, there's no question about whose side he's on here, and I use his momentum to push closer to the front, too.

T, in that weird, flat voice of his, says, "Hull, man. You don't want to do this."

Church Shoes whirls around to face Tristan. He stabs the air and when he yells, it's high and jagged and crazy, a perfect match for his weird-ass knife. "How do you know what I want to do?"

But to say this, he's had to turn his back on Marcus and Hector, and in that moment, they jump him and tackle him to the ground, face-first. Marcus is pounding the kid's hand against the pavement so that he'll let go of the knife and Hector has his spine pinned beneath his knees, and that's the moment when the cops show up. Two in a patrol car. One fat, one skinny, and both of them looking like they arrest teenagers as a hobby. Their hands are on their holsters and they're running straight for my brother, straight for Marcus, and the crowd panics, a tide of arms and legs. Marcus looks around, wild-eyed, and for a second I think he's searching for me, but no, he's looking for T. "Get out of here!" he yells at him.

Hector pulls a Ziploc freezer bag out of his pants and throws it to me. "Run, Brianna! Go!"

I'm not exactly a track star, but I can move when I have to. I hike my skirt up and run for the edge of the park, stuffing Hector's weed into my purse as I go. The crowd is scattering in all directions. I feel someone running close to me, and I'm sure it's one of the cops, but when I glance back, I see that it's T. There's a fence on this side of the park, and we're going to have to hop it. I use my momentum to swing myself up and over, even though *crap*, I rip the hem of my skirt in the process, and it's one of my favorites, a pink paisley. T's right beside me, but I guess he's not the most practiced at running from the police, because his feet get tangled on the top of the fence, and he tumbles to the ground on the far side. I know I should run, leave him there to solve his own problem, but something makes me reach down and haul him to his feet.

"Thanks," he says, and he's limping, but at least he's up and moving, and we're running again. Then he turns a corner while I'm running straight, and that's the last I see of him. A block farther on, I see another cop car driving toward the park, and I pull up short, change direction again. I'm worried the cruiser is going to follow me, I'm waiting to hear it turn on its siren, because surely those cops in the park saw Hector toss me the bag, but a block later, I look behind me, and it's all clear.

I don't slow down until I've made it all the way home, and I bound up the stairs to the apartment and sit on the floor of my bedroom, waiting for my breath to settle. I had an inhaler when I was a little kid, but I'm determined not to use it these days. Mind over matter. I bury the bag in a drawer beneath my underwear and light a purifying candle. I'm worried about Marcus, and I'm especially worried about Hector, because he's not a minor anymore and that can spell serious trouble. He owes me one for saving his ass, that much is for sure, and that's not a terrible position for a younger sister to be in.

THE QUEEN

LONG, HOT DAYS OF SUNBURNS AND POTATO BATTERIES
and litmus solution made from red cabbage: The job at camp
passed in a comforting blur. When it was over (when the last
small camper had hugged me and sworn to never forget me
and departed, probably to forget me immediately) my parents
drove to Camp Timbuktu to pick me up, even though I told
them I wasn't nine anymore and could take a bus back to the
city. They were in a sunny mood on the drive home, and they
chattered to me about the house, about all the work they'd finished while I was away.

"What about Hull?" I asked. "Why didn't he come with
you?"

"Too busy acting like a jerk, I guess," my father said, sort of under his breath but sort of not. "*Most ignorant of what he's most assured.*" (My father was always spouting Shakespearean quotes like this, and yes, it was as annoying as it sounds.) My mother, seated in the passenger seat, swatted his arm, but she didn't contradict him. So I already surmised that Hull hadn't come around to my parents' point of view, and I knew enough about my brother to have an idea of what that might look like. I don't think any of us, however, could have foreseen the shitshow that we were, even at that very moment, driving toward.

I was curled up in the back seat, reading a thriller about a viral outbreak, and my parents were singing along to a staticky classic rock radio station (as they had been for over an hour—barf) when my dad's phone rang, and since he was driving, my mom answered. We were almost there, already passing green highway signs for the George Washington Bridge, and I was hoping to burn through a couple more chapters, so I started to tune her out. I snapped back to attention when I heard her say in a business voice, "Yes, this is Maura Steinbach speaking," as she clicked the radio off. I leaned forward for a better sight line and tried to interpret her expression. It looked surprised and pained, like a scene from a soap opera in which someone is receiving bad news.

"Is he all right?" she said. "Is he hurt?"

Hull. It had to be. I tossed aside the book, unfastened my seat belt, and inched forward until my head was in the front seat.

"I'm sorry, can you explain exactly what happened?" my mother said, and her voice had a trembling edge to it. My father rested his right hand on her leg, but she jerked it away. "Okay. Yes, Officer. Yes. We'll be there as soon as we possibly can. Can you give me the address, please?" My mother hung up the phone and turned to look at us, stunned. "That was the police. We have to go pick up Hull. He's been arrested."

"That's not possible," I said.

"What happened?" my father said.

"They couldn't tell me anything over the phone. They said they'd explain when we got there."

We passed most of the next twenty minutes in stunned silence. Here are the things I was thinking during that long, weighted pause: 1) While I was building baking-soda volcanoes in the Chemistry Cabin, I must have missed a few things. 2) An arrest record is not the best asset for an aspiring politician. 3) Hull must be freaking out right now.

My parents are pretty big on the whole family-acting-like-a-team thing, so I could barely process it when my dad took the exit off the BQE and said, "We have to drive right past the house. I'm dropping you off, Izzy."

"No. No! I'm coming with you."

"I think your father's right. We can handle this one ourselves." My mom shot my father a sideways glance, and I marveled again at how scrambled the household dynamics must have gotten in my absence.

They unceremoniously dumped me and my bag by the

curb and took off down the street. I knew where the spare key was hidden, but I was indignant and worried and I didn't feel like looking for it yet. Instead I wanted to sit on the porch step and breathe and try to think. I watched one of the stray neighborhood cats stalk across the yard, pause with one foot in the air, scratch at its mangled ear, then continue on its mission. Up the block, some younger kids were playing with a remote-control car. There were still a few scraps of damp crepe paper tacked to the trees from the block party I had missed the day before.

I'd only been sitting there brooding for a few minutes when I looked over at the run-down playground that sat diagonally across the intersection from our house, and my eyes snagged on something unusual. A person was sitting on the low crosspiece of a set of monkey bars, hunched over and rocking back and forth. I crept closer, snooping a little. I could see that it was someone my age. A boy. Holding his ankle like he was in pain.

On a different day, maybe I would have been too shy to say a word. Here's the thing, though: I always wanted to be the one to save the day, be the hero. And in that particular moment, I was right in the middle of not saving Hull. I walked a little closer.

"Hey," I said. "Are you all right?"

He looked up, looked me in the eye.

It's tempting, in retrospect, to say that it was love at first sight, but that's not exactly the truth. I've had a lot of time to think about it since then, and I'm still not sure I believe in love at first sight. Or at least, I think it's a much easier concept to swallow if you're expecting it to happen. When Cleopatra went sailing down the river in a golden barge full of rose petals in order to seduce Marc Antony, I'm sure she believed that love at first sight existed. The future of Egypt depended on it. I think most people, though, fall in love slowly, and then much later change the details of their first meeting to better suit the instantaneous-love story line. I'm a woman of science, so I'm not going to try to pull any of that stuff here.

I have to admit, though, that there are moments, and I think you'll know the ones I mean, when time collapses on itself, and you get this glimpse that someone or something is part of your future, good, bad, or otherwise. There, in the playground, I had one of those moments, but more jarring than I'd ever felt before, a thunderclap compared to the sound of a book closing. We both looked at the other's face for a few long seconds. It wasn't like looking at just anyone's face. I felt an urgency to remember the details of his features, a sudden need to be clearheaded and pay attention to what was happening.

As for Tristan, I don't know what went through his mind at that precise moment. Later, of course, I would ask him if he believed in love at first sight, and he would laugh and say, "How could I not?" But as I said, memory is fickle, and by the time we talked about it, everything had changed, so I'll never know for sure. All I can do now is pause the video of my memory right there, at that suspended moment, over and over again. Strangers studying each other in a playground at dusk. Lovers embracing their fate. You can choose the kind of story you like best.

Finally, Tristan nodded at his leg and said, "I busted my ankle pretty badly, but I'm not sure how you can help. Nice of you to ask, though." He pulled up the leg of his jeans, revealing an ankle swollen to the size of a grapefruit, and I made that sucking-in-air noise that you make when it looks like something hurts.

"Hold on," I said, and I jogged back to the porch and retrieved my counselor's first-aid kit from the end pocket of my duffel bag. I always made sure to have impressive first-aid kits, though the only time I'd cracked this one in the past six weeks was to give one of the older campers some Midol for her cramps. So it was kind of exhilarating to rummage through it as I crossed the street until I located an ACE bandage and one of those self-cooling ice packs.

"May I?" I asked my patient, and he managed a small smile and made a "be my guest" motion toward his ankle. I popped the inner bag of the ice pack to activate it, felt that magical kindling of cold, and then bound it to his ankle with the bandage, tight but not too tight. I concentrated on wrapping it evenly and perfectly, trying to cover up the fact that I was nervous to be touching a stranger. Caring for someone is intimate, even if it's only an ankle, and the crystalline stillness of that moment of eye contact had evaporated. I was self-conscious Izzy again. "What happened?" I asked.

He shook his head. "Long story. I twisted it down by Eastern Parkway."

"You walked all the way from there? Ouch. That probably means it's not broken, though." I was talking too much, I could feel it, but I couldn't stop myself, and, in fact, started speaking faster, making it worse. "Sprained, or maybe just bruised. Um, here." I handed him a little paper packet. "Ibuprofen will help with the swelling. You should probably go to the doctor, though. Get a second opinion."

"You live there?" he asked, nodding toward the house.

"Yeah, we moved in a few weeks ago," I said, and it almost seemed like he was cringing at that fact, but at the time I chalked it up to the pain in his ankle.

"I live up the block," he said, sort of somberly, and then he looked at me again. He had this way of tilting his head away from you and looking at you from the corners of his eyes. He did that, and then he smiled and shook his head and made an "ohhh" sound, like someone had told him a bad joke. And then he let his head fall back against one of the rusty metal bars and said, "Have you noticed the sky?"

I hadn't noticed the sky. But when I followed his gaze, the clouds were on fire from the setting sun, stripes of hot pink and lavender. "Oh, it's so pretty!" I said, then felt stupid for saying something so obvious. And then I felt doubly stupid that I was still kneeling in the dust at his feet, so I stood up and he stood up, too, gingerly, on his good leg, but then I felt stupid for not being able to think of something interesting to say, so I said, "I'm, uh, Izzy," and stuck my hand out for a handshake. Still more stupidity. I could see that, behind the lenses of his glasses, his eyes were light brown with little threads of gold.

"It's so cold," he said when he took my hand.

"Um, yeah, sorry. Ice pack," I said, trying to withdraw it. But he held on to it and rubbed it between both of his, warming it up. And then he turned it palm down, and bowed over it dramatically, and kissed the back of it. I could feel my face getting hot, and I was hoping he wouldn't notice the way my sweat was making my hair stick to my forehead.

"Izzy," he said. "Thank you." And then he started slowly limping toward the playground exit.

"So I'll see you around, I guess," I said, wishing my voice didn't sound so high and so much like a question.

"Sure. You couldn't not see me around if you tried." I think he was smiling when he said that, but it was hard to tell.

"Wait. You didn't tell me your name."

"Everybody calls me T," he said, and then he was limping away from me, down the block, and I was left to stand there and wonder if any of it had really happened. I snapped the first-aid kit shut and walked back to the house.

Looking back, I can see that I was acting willfully naive about what had transpired. Someone more self-assured might have already begun to scheme about how to see him again, maybe even how to seduce him. But for better or for worse, I was, and perhaps still am, a person of reasonable expectations. I had always been a nerdy science girl with a chubby baby face, so casting myself as a romantic lead, even in my own daydreams, wasn't something I was accustomed to doing.

Even so, I admit that after I retrieved the spare key from the geranium pot and let myself into the house, I spent some long minutes assessing my best and worst features (round eyes and wavy dark hair versus freckled nose and fat cheeks). Standing in front of the bathroom mirror, I wondered when and if anyone else would ever study them so closely: a teenage girl's preferred form of exquisite torture.

I was lying on my bed, pretending to read my novel but really bouncing between thoughts of the mysterious stranger with the injured ankle and visions of the nearly unimaginable moment when police put my brother in handcuffs, when I heard someone fiddling with the lock and raced to meet my family at the front door. The grim expressions on all three faces made me pull up short at the bottom of the stairs. Hull's eyes looked red and swollen, but when I reached out to touch his arm, he brushed past me and went to his room. I looked at my parents disbelievingly, and my mother said, "Please, no questions tonight, Izzy. Okay?" Her voice sounded so small that I didn't say anything as they, too, climbed the stairs and went into their own bedroom.

I spent a few minutes eavesdropping on the soft voices behind my parents' door. "I can't believe the lack of empathy," I heard my mother say, but I couldn't make out my father's muttered reply. Nothing but silence from Hull's room. I knocked softly on his door, then more loudly, but got no response.

I went downstairs and, since it seemed like everyone else had forgotten about dinner, ate some cheese and crackers while standing over the kitchen sink. Then I climbed into bed and went back to reading the same page of my book over and over. Typically I have a lot of thoughts spinning all at once or in quick succession: a mind like a Swiss Army knife, my dad calls it. But that night, lying in the unfamiliar house and ignored by everyone closest to me, I was consumed with thoughts of only one thing, and it wasn't a contemplation of how to help my twin brother. It was the conversation in the playground, playing over in my head on repeat. *He's not thinking about you, Izzy,* I told myself, *so stop it. Stop it right now.*

THE KNIGHT

I SURRENDER. THOSE ARE THE WORDS I CAN'T SHAKE this morning, the ones I can't stop repeating to myself. You can surrender in chess; it's called resigning. People will advise you never to do that, particularly when you're first learning, because there might be some way out that you're missing, some advantage that you can't yet see. But this time, I *know*.

Maybe I knew when she first offered to help me, when her sweet voice flooded into me like a cool gulp of lemonade. Maybe I knew when I saw her beautiful face lit up by the setting sun, when I got lost in the sympathy of her gaze. Or maybe I knew when I realized she was Hull's sister, when it dawned on me that it was just like fate to screw me over like this. Regardless, I'm certain by now: I'm powerless. My own fortune has checkmated me. I surrender.

It's the last day before school starts, and I'm considering burrowing down into the covers and hiding from the world for the rest of the morning, but a few minutes after I open my eyes, there's a sharp rap at the door. Aunt Patrice can sense when I'm awake; she can smell it, like a dragon.

"Tristan, I need to talk to you," Patrice says, and her voice has a hot edge of irritation. "Come out to the kitchen, please."

My brain was so capsized by meeting Izzy that I nearly forgot about the bigger picture: the chess match, the cops, leaving Marcus there to fend for himself. I hop out of bed and an arrow of pain shoots through my ankle. Still, upon further inspection, it looks remarkably better than it did yesterday. There is magic in her touch. I order my thoughts as best I can, trying to figure out a way to spin the previous day's events to Aunt Patrice, readying myself to do battle with the dragon. She's waiting for me, sitting on a kitchen stool, arms folded over her chest. I try not to limp.

"Were you involved in this fight?" she snaps before I've fully entered the room.

"Not really," I mumble. "And I swear to you that it wasn't Marcus's fault."

"Sure it wasn't," Patrice says. "Trouble has a way of finding Marcus, but he never has anything to do with it. Go on. Tell me exactly what happened."

So I give her a version of the events, omitting some selected details, like the fact that Marcus had money riding on the game, because she'll disapprove, and the particulars of what the knife looked like, because she'll get worried. "And when the cops showed up, Marcus kept yelling at me to run, run, run, and I guess I panicked, because I did. But I'm not lying: He didn't start the fight." And that was the truth, sort of, if you ignored the fact that Marcus started messing with Hull in the first place.

"So if no one was doing anything wrong, if everyone was perfectly on the up-and-up, why did you run from the police?" she asks me.

Why *did* I run? He had been looking at me in that forceful way that he has, screaming at me to get out of there, and I'd fallen into the habit of doing whatever Marcus told me to do.

"I don't know."

"You don't know?" Patrice shakes her head, her lips pursed so tight that they turn into a little lipstick-colored mark on her face. "Honestly, Tristan, I expected more from you when you came to live with me. 'Tristan is special.' That's what I kept saying to all the people who kept calling me crazy for moving you up here. And now you're hanging out with Marcus all hours of the day and night, sneaking around like a common criminal. You think I don't know what marijuana smells like? And now the cops." She blows her breath out in a long stream through those angry lips. Patrice knows everyone around here, even the cops, especially the cops, and she doesn't like anyone giving our block a bad reputation. That goes double, maybe triple, for me. "These days, those same people are saying, 'Oh, he's being an ordinary teenager.' But that's exactly the opposite of what I thought you were."

Her words carry a burn. But this isn't the first time I've seen Patrice angry, and I can tell that a lot of what she's saying is because she's worked up. Once she calms down, she'll see that it's not such a big deal. No one is dead, no one is hurt. You can always count on Patrice to be practical.

"And that's not even touching on the fact that you abandoned Marcus while he was getting arrested. If there was a problem, I should have heard about it from you."

"Arrested?" Maybe it sounds stupid, because it's not like the cops around here hold the most charitable view of kids like Marcus, but he has always seemed so untouchable that I thought he could wriggle his way unscathed out of the situation at the park. A thick lozenge of guilt lodges itself in my throat.

"I was playing cards at Ramona's last night, and Cherry gets a call on her cell phone in the middle of the game." Cherry is Marcus's mom. You might think it's weird that Patrice hangs out with her brother's ex-wife, but they've both lived around here for so long that no one blinks an eye. "You should have seen her face when she learned she had to go get Marcus at the police station." She makes a disapproving clucking sound with her teeth. "And I was so worried about you, because I knew there was no way you weren't with him, and I come home, and lo and behold, there you are, already fast asleep." That's true; when I got home, I felt so wrung out from the pain in my ankle and the encounter with Izzy that I collapsed on the bed and fell asleep.

"I should go see Marcus," I say. When Patrice raises one questioning eyebrow, I quickly add, "I'm sorry that I worried you. I didn't think Marcus was in trouble. Really, he shouldn't have been, because he didn't do anything bad." *Or nothing worse than every other day of his life*, I think to myself.

"I think you've seen enough of Marcus this weekend," Auntie Patrice says, finally uncrossing her arms. "I think you should stay here today and make sure you're ready to start school tomorrow." The way she says it, I can tell it's not a suggestion.

"Did they charge him with anything?" I ask.

"I haven't heard yet," Patrice says, but she's already standing up, doing dishes, making it clear that the conversation is over.

Back in my bedroom, I pull my phone out of my bag and call Marcus. It's strange, but I hardly ever call him; I see him almost every day, so there's no need. Just when I think he's not going to pick up, he answers.

"What up, T?" he says, and I already feel a cascade of relief at hearing him say my name.

"Not much here," I say. "Look, Patrice told me that the

cops got all over your ass yesterday, and I'm sorry. I should have stuck around to make sure you were okay."

"Nah," Marcus says, chuckling. "You're my golden boy. Can't let them mess with you."

"Did they charge you?"

"Nope. Except maybe Hector, since he's nineteen. You can bet that they don't want to mess around charging Mr. Strategy with anything. You should have seen his parents in the police station yesterday, panicking and wringing their hands." I realize he's talking about Izzy's parents, the nice sand-art lady from the block party, and nausea tiptoes through my stomach. "Anyway, best believe I'm not going to let that little weirdo forget that he brought trouble down on me. And shit, he still owes me a hundred bucks."

"Look, I can play him again if he disputes the win...." I would throw the game in an instant if I thought it would keep the peace.

"Not necessary, T."

"Okay," I say. And then, like a sudden case of Tourette's has come over me, I blurt out, "He has a sister. Hull does." Why on earth would I say something like this? But she's been there, fighting to the center of my mind, the entire time I've been talking to Patrice and now Marcus. And some part of me wants Marcus to know that everything—north, south, gigantic tectonic plates—has shifted for me.

"Huh," Marcus says, and there's a calculating note in his

voice that makes me wish I'd never brought it up. "What's she look like? She hot?"

"She's okay," I say. There's some noise in the background, and I'm eager to change the subject anyway, so I say, "Where are you right now?"

"Down at the TipTop. You want to come meet me here?" Of course Marcus isn't under house arrest like I am. It isn't his style.

"I don't think I can. Patrice is on the warpath today."

"K. I'll catch you later, then, T." And he hangs up before I have a chance to say goodbye.

Whenever Aunt Patrice is angry at me, I have the vague and probably irrational fear that she'll ship me straight back to Atlanta at the first opportunity, so instead of pushing my luck and lurking outside of Izzy's house, panting beside her door like a lovesick dog, I cool my heels in my bedroom all afternoon. That doesn't, however, keep me from pulling out my laptop, the one my dad sent for Christmas last year, and trying to find out more about her. There's not much online, except for some science awards listed on the website of her old school. Be still my nerd-loving heart. I try to find her profile on Facebook or Insta or Snapchat, all the usual social media sinkholes, but I can't turn up anything at first. Hull is much easier to trace (he has his own YouTube channel about political science, though he hasn't posted to it in a while) and finally, by poring over his Facebook page, I figure out that she's listed under her full name, Iseult. I close the computer and repeat it to myself a few times. Iseult, Iseult, Iseult, like the petals of a rose unfurling.

It doesn't matter how well you do in school, how easy it is for you; getting ready to go the first day each fall feels like dressing for a funeral. The death of summer, with her lazy evenings and icy drinks. May she rest in peace.

The period of mourning starts to drop away as I feel again the rhythms of the morning hallway rush, as I remember that this isn't such a bad place. People really dog the New York City schools, and lots of them, like Carl Sagan High, are big, a lot bigger than the suburban middle school I went to in Georgia. You could get swallowed in a place so big, but also, if you're lucky, you can find a niche and hold on tight. A lot of my classes are AP classes, and the same faces tend to repeat themselves in my schedule. It's not like I hadn't considered the possibility that Izzy might now be one of those faces, but even so, my heart does a stutter step when I see her sitting in my first-period AP Literature class. She's trying to lean back casually in the metal desk, but I can tell she's nervous, not knowing anyone here, and she's wearing a gray dress that's hard to imagine anyone else at this school wearing, sort of old-fashioned, verging on Amish-looking. I don't care about her clothes. I want to run to her, drink in the sight of her here, revel in the miracle that we're in the same room. All the seats next to hers are taken, though, so I drop into a seat near the door right as the bell rings. She glances over and we make eye contact, and there's a flicker of joy that lights up her face before she gives me a more composed smile. So I haven't been making it up; it's real.

Mr. Berger takes attendance, and I notice that even though Hull is on the class list, he isn't in the room. Then Berger stumbles over Izzy's full name badly, and she blushes, says that Izzy will be easier, and glances over at me again. My heart is pounding so hard for the next fifty minutes that it's hard to concentrate on Mr. Berger discussing the wonders of American literature. Melville and Hawthorne, Steinbeck and Hemingway, all of these long-dead guys running together in a slurry.

We meet up outside the classroom door.

"Tristan," she says. My blood prickles cold for a second, because I realize she's picked up on my real name, maybe when Mr. Berger said it, maybe when she was doing some online snooping of her own. I don't know, can't even begin to guess, really, what Hull might have told her yesterday. But then she says it again: "Tristan. I like that better than T." And there's such warmth in her voice that it's like I've never heard my name before, not the way it's really supposed to sound. "How's your ankle?"

My ankle seems like the least important thing that has happened to me in the past few days. Even so, it's healing much faster than I thought was possible. Like I said before: magic. Everything right with the world and a current of that rightness drawing us closer and closer together—who could care about a stupid ankle? But trying to sound less like the head case I am, I say only, "You were right. It's only a bad bruise. It'll be fine." She has very faint freckles high on her cheeks, and a dimple on the left side. Eyelashes for days. "You have Trigonometry next period?" I ask, because everything is going so well that it seems impossible that we won't spend the entire day gazing at each other.

"Ah, no," she says, pulling her schedule out of her bag. She fusses with her hair while she reads it, the only tell that she's the scared new kid, and it makes me want to protect her. Nerd turned chivalrous guardian. "Rathscott for Government, I think."

"She's nice," I say, giving her schedule a quick scan. No overlap until the afternoon. Not even the same lunch period. Eons without her, the suck of time a swirling black hole. "I'll see you in AP Physics, though."

"Right. I look forward to it. Physics, I mean." And even though I've barely noticed my ankle all morning, I feel it throb now, the dull pulse of it matching her departing footsteps as she drifts away with the crowd.

———

The rest of the morning is, predictably, interminable. I notice during the requisite first day roll calls that I'm scheduled to spend far more time each day with Hull than with Izzy, but each time it's spoken, his name is met with a span of silence, a scratch of the teacher's pen. Hull Steinbach is nowhere to be found today.

Lunch is the only period that I share with Marcus, and when I enter the cafeteria with my tray of overcooked spaghetti, he's already holding court in one corner, his lackeys gathered around him. They are not the cool kids, or rather, they are cool only because of their association with Marcus. Tyrone, Frodo, K-Dawg: They've been his best friends since elementary school, and I've never been totally clear whether it's because he's loyal to a fault or because their presence makes him shine more brightly in comparison. He raises a finger to acknowledge my presence but he's too busy relating the story of what happened at the police station to say hello, so I squeeze into a seat between Tyrone and Frodo and listen.

"The cops are so worried that we're going to eat White Boy alive that, check this out, they put him in his own holding cell until Mommy and Daddy can come rescue him. You can bet Hector and I didn't get our own cells. We got shoved in a pen with every smelly junkie who'd been caught shitting on the sidewalk that night."

The peanut gallery chuckles at this, even me, a little, except for K-Dawg, who keeps repeating, "It ain't right, man. It ain't right." He's on his second bag of Cheetos, eyes glazed over as usual.

"But the cell is right next to ours, and we can see right in through the wire mesh. So Hector keeps messing with him, growling at him like a dog, telling him he's going to find out where he lives—the kinda trash talk we been ignoring since kindergarten. But White Boy is huddled in the corner with his arms wrapped around his head, rocking back and forth like a mental patient. Hilarious."

"Yo, I heard from Roxanne that White Boy didn't even have the balls to show up to school," Tyrone says. Roxanne is Tyrone's long-suffering, on-again, off-again girlfriend. She once broke up with him because he said that American Indians arrived on this continent after enslaved Africans did, but then she felt bad for him and took him back. She's a smart girl with a Tyrone-shaped stupid spot on her brain. "She says that he's not in any of his classes."

"Do we have to call him White Boy?" I ask, dragging the lurid spaghetti around in circles on my plate. "I mean, Frodo is white." I'm agitating needlessly now, and I know it, but I'm in a contrary mood. Three whole periods since I've laid eyes on Izzy, and it's eating at me.

"That's different," Frodo says, shoving my shoulder, making the fork fall from my hand. "I'm Cuban."

I hold my hands up and shrug.

"You feeling bad for White Boy, T?" Marcus asks, his voice deadpan.

"It's not that," I say, crossing my arms. "But I guess I don't get why you're wasting your time on him." I glance up at Marcus, and his jaw looks hard, like he's grinding his teeth. "I mean, he looked like a mental patient because he probably is an actual mental patient. It's like picking a fight with a moron." This isn't true; I don't think Hull is crazy, knife or no knife, and he's definitely not stupid, but the comment makes Marcus give a reluctant snort of laughter, and the other guys follow suit. Bomb diffused, I think. Now we can talk about the sneakers that Frodo is flipping on eBay or some other dumb topic of the day. But instead, Marcus looks hard at me, like he's trying to read something on my skin.

"Hey, T, what about this guy's sister? Didn't you say you met her the other day?"

I shouldn't have said the first thing about Izzy to Marcus, but what's done is done. I take a big bite of garlic bread like it's no big deal, even though it immediately becomes a gagging clump that I have to work to talk around. "Yeah, I ran into her on the block."

"And?"

"And what?"

"What is she like?"

"I don't know. She seemed...nice. Not an arrogant ass like Hull, if that's what you're asking. I don't know if she even plays chess."

"She in school today?" Tyrone asks. "Or did Marcus scare the whole family out of Brooklyn?"

I am steadfastly determined not to answer this question, so I concentrate on swallowing the bread, but the table is quiet, and when I look up, they're all staring at me. "What?" I say. "How am I supposed to know?" At this, I think I see a muscle twitch in Marcus's cheek.

"You know," he says, "maybe you're right. Maybe I'm going about this thing with Mr. Strategy all wrong. It's all about the long game, right, Chessmaster T? I should have learned that by now from watching you play. So maybe I should be focusing my attention on his sister."

Cold sweat, spaghetti bile rising up in my gut. "Aw, come on, man. She never did anything to you. You're going to torment this girl because her brother's a jerk?"

"Tormenting? Did I say anything about tormenting? Nah. But I don't think Hull's going to like it too well when I'm banging his sister." Marcus studies me while he says this. It's a test, I think, some kind of loyalty test.

"Aw, damn," K-Dawg says. "That's straight-up brilliant right there."

"Do whatever you want, Marcus," I say, putting on the same poker face that I use for tough matches. "I think you're crazy for wasting your time on this shit. But do whatever you want."

"What *I* want?" Marcus says, giving me that beautiful crocodile grin. "I think it should be what *you* want, too, seeing as how I kept you from getting arrested the other day. You're going to help me with this girl." He reaches across the table, and for a second I think he's going to reach right inside my rib cage and tear out my telltale heart. But he's only extending a fist for me to pound. And I do, weakly, because I don't have a clue what to do instead.

THE QUEEN

BEING THE NEW KID DOES NOT EXACTLY PLAY TO MY strengths. I think that people who are truly great at the new-kid game are some combination of these things: 1) radiantly self-confident, 2) easily adaptable to shifting social situations, 3) a little dumb. You surely know someone who has all of those qualities, and you understand in your heart that that person would make a great new kid. I am none of those things.

I say that only to highlight my own surprise that the first week at the new school went mostly smoothly. The teachers seemed okay, a little less personable and generous with their time than the teachers at my old school, a little cagier, maybe, but not mean. And a lot of the kids were nice to me, nicer than I might have been if this was my longtime turf. I even made a friend on the first day, though it was cheating a little because I'd met her a few times before. The Brooklyn Central Library periodically offered free interpretive dance classes that my mother liked to drag me to, and Brianna had been one of the most enthusiastic participants. She recognized me immediately in Government class. It took me a second longer to place her, but then it came rushing back: Brianna in the basement community room, wearing a tank top and running pants, crawling like a turtle and leaping like a stag to the jangly live percussion provided by a jolly European named Vincent. What are the odds?

"Your mom was so awesome!" she said. "She was so good at waving around those scarves!" And then she laughed at the face I made in response. Weirdly enough, there were quite a few similarities between Brianna and my mom. They both wore wild combinations of colors and long, funky skirts. They both had a habit of closing their eyes whenever they needed to think really hard. They both talked incessantly of moon signs and mysticism. Brianna was fairly certain she was a Wiccan, though she was "still thinking that through" and hadn't yet mentioned it to her Catholic parents. She struggled with subjects like composition and history, but she was in the highest math and science classes, and I teased her that it was because she'd spent so much time working on complicated astrological charts. She nodded and said that was probably right. She was like a hippie love child with an undercurrent of Brooklyn tough girl mixed in. It made me sad sometimes to think about how much my mom would have loved having a daughter like her.

But mostly, I liked being around Brianna's quirkiness, her enthusiasms and obsessions. She was so different from me, and particularly that first week, she was a good distraction from some other stuff in my life that wasn't registering high on the sunshine scale.

For one: Hull. The day after I came home from camp, I'd been desperate to hear his side of the story, and by the time I woke up the next morning, I could already hear him arguing with my parents in the kitchen. Creeping down the stairs, I managed to catch a few snippets of the conversation:

"Don't think that you're going to magically get exactly what you want after the stunt you pulled yesterday. That's not the way the world works, Hull."

"Oh, so you don't think I mean what I said?"

"That's not what Dad is saying, Hull. Of course we're going to get you help for as long as you need it. But I'm surprised at the lack of remorse you've shown. You don't seem willing to—"

My mom stopped there because I accidentally stepped on a particularly creaky floorboard. I hadn't yet learned the landscape of the new house's sighs and groans.

"Izzy?" she called.

I waltzed into the kitchen casually, not at all like a person who had been eavesdropping on them. "Hey," I said. Hull had a big bruise on his face, and he looked older than when

I'd left for camp. I walked over and kissed him on the cheek. "I missed you while I was gone." Sometimes siblings have to support each other in the face of the powers that be, especially, but not limited to, parents, so it didn't matter at that point that I didn't have all the details.

My father sighed. "I'm going to go get bagels," he said, which was his typical code for *I don't want to be around any of you right now.*

"I'm not hungry," Hull said. "Can I go to my room?"

My father didn't even bother responding. Finally, my mother said, "Go on," and Hull went upstairs without looking at me or either of them. Dad made a noisy show of putting on his shoes and going out the front door. When they were both safely out of the room, I asked my mom to explain what was going on.

"Oh, Izzy," she said, scrubbing the counter down with a dishrag. "It's complicated." She walked over and put her arms around me and rested her head against mine. My mom is a hugger, and I'm not, but I let her get away with it this time because she seemed so sad. "The police claim that your brother was threatening people with Grandpa's hunting knife. And then he was saying some pretty strange things after we picked him up at the station last night. Stuff about wanting to hurt himself."

"What?" I wriggled out of my mother's grasp. "What exactly did he say?"

She was still holding the rag, and while she looked for the

right words, she twisted it, hard, making her hands splotchy with white and pink.

"He said..." She hesitated, and I wondered if it was because the words were hard for her to say or if she was trying to choose the version that would provoke me the least. "He said something like, 'It would be so convenient for you if I disappeared. So maybe I'll eradicate myself and tidy up your lives for you.'"

"Are you serious?"

"And then something about getting that for us as an anniversary gift. You know how he can be."

"Wait." She was still working that dishrag over, and I suppressed an urge to snatch it out of her hands. "So Hull is threatening to off himself, and Dad's wandering around the neighborhood buying bagels? Aren't you guys going to do something about this?"

Mom kind of puddled onto a kitchen stool and rubbed at her temples. She was doing that noisy diaphragm breathing she does when she wants to stay calm. "And what would you suggest we do right now, Izzy?"

"Um, I don't know. Take him to a hospital?"

"We've already looked into a couple of treatment options, but Labor Day isn't really the best day to get someone into one of them. I'm driving him up to Columbia tomorrow to see if we can get him into a special youth-counseling day program."

"Terrific." I'm not entirely sure why I was so flooded with rage in that moment. It wasn't fair, and it's not as if I had a better plan than she did. But I still believed at that point that my parents' love was so boundless that it could protect us from anything: the world, ourselves. It largely had up to that point. The illusion would be shattered soon enough, but as with so many fractures, the first fissures hurt the most.

My mother sat up straight and looked at me sharply. Even she had her limits. "You haven't been home dealing with this every day, Izzy. Your brother has been...very difficult lately."

This is completely mental, I thought as I stomped up the stairs to Hull's room. I pounded on his door, put my ear against it, couldn't hear anything inside, and promptly started to panic.

"I will kick this door down if you don't open it right now!" I shouted, with eighty-four times the bravado that I actually felt. "I've been leading nature hikes for the past month! My legs are strong."

A heavy pause the length of a breath. Two breaths. Three. I heard the latch turn on the other side of the door, then his footsteps as he retreated. I let myself in. The room was still a wreck, virtually unchanged since the day I left for camp, except now there were more books and clothes strewn everywhere. Hull was sitting on the floor, knees up in front of him. He looked skinny.

"What's going on, Hull?" I demanded. "This is crazy."

He looked at me, cocked one eyebrow. "No, I'm the one who's crazy."

"Did you really get in a fight yesterday?"

"Yep."

"With?"

"Just... cretins. Just the dregs of this illustrious borough."

"And you're totally cool with Mom and Dad shipping you off to the loony bin tomorrow? Instead of going to school?"

"I am not going to that school tomorrow," Hull said slowly, deliberately. "That much is certain."

I paced, frustrated. "What about your grades? What about everything you worked for?"

He shrugged. I couldn't quite fathom what was happening here. Either my brother was mentally ill or playing some kind of game. As angry as it had made me to hear about my father's reaction, it wasn't totally out of the realm of possibility that Hull was manipulating my parents. But I wasn't certain either way; it was like I couldn't recognize him with that bruise around his eye.

You could be forgiven, I guess, if you're not finding Hull to be very likable. In this story that I'm telling you, he's the troublemaker. You'll have to take my word for it, then, that in the story of my life, he was more than that. He was a fun-maker when we would hold daylong tournaments, involving board games and feats of strength and constantly shifting rules, every time school was canceled during a snowstorm. He was a loyalty-maker when I would disagree with my parents and he would think of the perfect point to back me up. He was a comfort-maker when I would sit in his room in the evening and feel completely myself and tug on that waning but still palpable thread of twin-ness that stretched between us and feel someone on the other end of it. Even now, writing this, I can whisper our twin word and feel the physical presence of him, something I've never had with anyone else.

"Bork," I said to him that night, but he wouldn't answer me. He curled onto his side on the floor and went to sleep. I picked up a book I found lying on top of one of the piles, *White House Years* by Henry Kissinger, and spent the rest of the last day of summer vacation sitting on the floor of his bedroom, keeping a silent and stubborn watch.

———————

If Hull had been my only problem during that week, it would have been bad enough, but there was something else, or rather someone else, constantly staking a claim on my thoughts. I had told myself, of course, the night we met that I shouldn't think about him, shouldn't entertain the possibility that something could happen between the two of us. And I know what I said earlier about love at first sight. Even so, I was still a sixteen-year-old with a hopeless crush.

When I finally fell asleep the night after meeting Tristan, I had a scorchingly embarrassing erotic dream: a sunlit clearing in a forest, the warmth of the sun on our bare skin, the soft, almost trampoline-like quality of the grass as we tumbled to the ground. The whole nine yards, basically. I woke up hot-faced, cringing on two levels: 1) that I was so quick to obsess over someone who showed me the tiniest bit of attention, and 2) that my sleeping brain couldn't come up with anything better than a romantic cliché. Nevertheless, I spent a long time lying awake in the tangled sheets, trying to breathe around a newfound knot of desire that rested right below my ribs, drawn so tight that it was almost painful.

And then the first day of school, when I saw him in our homeroom class, he smiled at me, and his face was so open and joyful, and my blood thundered through my love-addled head the entire class period. I watched him out of the corner of my eye, and when he raised his hand and made a comment in AP Lit, my heart did a tap dance. He wasn't just a pretty face; now I had evidence that he was smart, and the knot pulled tighter.

He waited for me outside the classroom. I know he did. He could have left, but he was waiting there, and he pointed out another class we had together, and he smelled like peppermint soap, and I almost reached out and squeezed his hand because it felt that right. And I guess I let myself hope for... what exactly? Something easy, I guess, like you could put on a love affair in the same way you'd slip on a clean shirt.

Stupid. Because it was the very same day that Brianna, unwittingly, brought these daydreams to an abrupt halt. It started in Trigonometry, not even four full class periods since she and I had figured out that we knew each other. We were supposed to be doing a review problem set with a partner, and between the two of us, it was so easy that we finished it with plenty of time to spare and sat there whisper-chatting. Brianna told me about her brother, about how she both detested him and worried about him constantly. "I mean, he got arrested two days ago, and I did something really big to help him and it's like he didn't even recognize the risk that—"

"Girls!" Mr. Mashariki said from his desk at the front of the class. "Less talk, more math."

I flushed. I probably would have been embarrassed at being chastised by a teacher on the first day of school (not my style), but I was too distracted by a coincidence so big that it didn't really seem like a coincidence. The bell rang.

Brianna and I had already determined that we had the next class together, too, and we swam through the crowds, rowdier now toward the end of the day, in the direction of our Physics classroom. Brianna dragged me along in her wake. I wanted to know more about her brother, and particularly about this arrest, but before I could form an intelligent question, I saw Tristan approaching the door from the opposite direction. Our eyes met again, but instead of birdsong and butterflies, it was a nervous frizzle. He half smiled at me and then put his head down and slunk inside the classroom. Not a word spoken. I felt sucker-punched.

How much did Brianna read from this scene? Impossible to know. She said only, "You know T?"

"I met him a couple days ago. He seemed, I don't know, nicer."

"Nice. Yeah, I guess. Kind of a weirdo, though." The crowd was starting to thin. She grabbed my elbow, leaned in conspiratorially. "He's like this super chess genius, right? And he beat this kid so bad on Sunday that the kid went psycho and pulled a knife and then everything blew up. And that's how my brother ended up in jail." Brianna shook her head and shrugged. "And it all comes back to quiet, nerdy little T. You wouldn't guess from looking at him, would you?"

I folded myself into a desk near the back of the classroom. The teacher, Mr. Hawkins, was goofy and fun, and he should have been my favorite teacher all day, but I was barely on the same plane of existence. I may have been missing some pieces, but the big ones were there. A chess-playing kid who pulled a knife and caused a scene? It wasn't hard to figure out who that was, sharing DNA with him the way I did. And Tristan was involved. And Brianna's brother. Tristan was sitting a few rows ahead of me, and I spent most of the period studying the back of his head, wondering how on earth the literal boy of my dreams had decided to have some kind of chess duel to the death with my twin brother.

I could tell you here about avoiding him after class, about slogging through French class, the last period of the day, but what's the point really? My heart and my pride were scraped up, and I was too disappointed to conjugate verbs, and even if you don't relate to anything else in this long, crazy story, I'd be willing to bet that you know what that feels like.

So this was my new life. I was left to face the first week at Carl Sagan by myself, to try to make friends, to obsess over the one person whose attention I craved but who had apparently become an enemy of the family before I even met him. Even with Brianna in several of my classes, I felt lonely. I'd never gone to school without Hull before.

Mom started driving him to therapy every day, and they'd come back in the evenings looking wrung out. My dad went to work as usual, since his new semester had started a couple weeks before, and he'd come home in the evenings looking preoccupied and vaguely angry. I sat through my classes, filling in the lines between Hull and Tristan, and I'd come home and not quite look my twin in the eye, thinking about who Hull had meant when he said *cretins*.

My parents have always been those let's-sit-down-and-have-dinner-as-a-family kind of parents, and never has that tendency been harder to swallow than it was that week. We were as strained and polite to one another as any unhappy family of Victorian Brits who made it onto Masterpiece Theatre. At first my dad tried to quiz Hull and my mom about what went down each day at the Columbia program, but Hull stonewalled him, and my mother would only say, "It's a long process." I made a brave sally or two into the fray, trying to tell amusing stories about something Brianna had said, but my parents looked distracted, smiling at me only as an afterthought.

I believed in doctors. I believed in the ones who were trying to help Hull every day. But during that time, I wanted more than anything to be one of those people who can fix everything through the power of their charisma and optimism. Once, I looked at Hull across the table, and his face was such a scary blank, and I tried to *will* the happiness and compassion into him, to shoot it into him like a laser beam. But I wasn't paying attention to where I put my arm while I was laser-beaming, and I knocked a spoon out of a bowl of tomato sauce, sending a messy red splatter across the tablecloth. Hull barely registered it. My father grimaced but said nothing. My mother said, "Oh, it's all right, Izzy." I'm still not sure what it was about the tomato sauce, but that was the closest I came to crying that whole long week.

THE KNIGHT

IN THE PARK ON THURSDAY NIGHT, I CONSIDER THROW-ing the game. I've played this kid before, and I could beat him with my hands tied behind my back, but I'm irritated with Marcus, with his posturing and his veiled threats and his running commentary about Izzy over the past couple days, and the only way I can think of striking back is by losing him a little cash that he's been counting on. But in the end, I panic, and winning kicks in like a reflex, like a bad habit, and I pull a flashy ending that involves sacrificing the queen, and my opponent groans when he realizes it's all over. Marcus crows in triumph and it's all worse than if I'd played it straight and won quickly. I can't do anything right.

Something right would have been to tell Marcus how I feel about Izzy when I saw him looking her up and down in the hallway yesterday. I know it wasn't much different from the way I look at her every opportunity I get. But it filled me with dread.

"So that's her, huh? She's not half bad, T," he said when he noticed me out of the corner of his eye, never breaking his gaze on Izzy. "Kinda plain, but a nice ass."

Why didn't I say something? Cowardice, certainly, but something else, too: There is simply no chance that Izzy wants me as badly as I want her. In fact, Izzy now shows every indication of despising me. I could see it in her face that first day of school, like someone had completely remolded it in the time between Lit class and Physics class; the pit of my stomach knew it before my brain did. She'd figured out my involvement in that bad scene with Hull. Her twin brother! Of course she had, because her obvious intelligence is one of the things that makes me want to lie down in front of a speeding truck for her.

"You got nasty up there at the end," Marcus says on the walk home from the park. "I know you think I can't follow what you're doing, but I've been watching you play for, what? Two years now? I'd probably be pretty good at the game myself since I've spent so many hours studying the master."

I shrug, still angry that I can never keep myself from doing exactly what Marcus wants me to do. "Maybe you should play the games yourself, then. Skip the middleman."

Marcus throws me a glance, and I inwardly flinch, worrying that maybe I overstepped, and hating myself for worrying about it, but he only laughs. "I wouldn't go that far, T."

We sidestep around a running club that is barreling toward us on the sidewalk like a pack of determined sled dogs. Marcus pauses to lean against a concrete pyramid that's been poured to support the base of a massive tree in danger of toppling over. Someone has painted a cheery pastoral scene on it: windmills and houses, nothing of Brooklyn in it. I could use something to take the edge off, but Marcus lights up one of those fruit-flavored cigarillos, the ones I can't stand. I snort like a horse, trying to force the blueberry smoke out of my nose. *Candy that will kill you*, he's called them in the past. It's a world full of things that will kill you.

"You think I'm not smart enough for this girl," he says.

It takes me half a second to understand that he's talking about Izzy. "Course you are," I say flatly.

"I know you think it's only about sticking it to White Boy," Marcus says, "and that gets to you somehow. But here's the thing, T. Maybe I'm not the dummy that everyone assumes I am."

"Nobody thinks you're a dummy, Marcus." The headache is starting, hastened by the smoke, and it kicks at the space between my eyes.

Marcus blows a perfect smoke ring, and we both watch it rise and disappear. "Maybe I want this girl because I deserve her."

Marcus slaps my shoulder, tells me again that it was a good game, and then his phone buzzes, and he ducks into a subway station without bothering to tell me where he's going. Normally, I wouldn't mind the opportunity to walk home alone, to unwind by myself. But today it's hard to turn off my brain. I'm not sure I believe Marcus that this has nothing to do with Hull. But telling him now that I've fallen for Izzy would imply that I'm the one who deserves the smart girl, not him.

The thing is, Marcus is smart. Not in the calm, deep way that Izzy is, but in a fast-thinking, quick-witted way. But he's also the most emotionally charged person I know, definitely not beyond doing some stupid, careless things. I've seen him shake people down for money they owe him, not because he needs the money but because their lack of respect offends him. There was also a night last summer when he came home with blood on his shirt. I was sitting on the stoop of his building, teaching his baby sister, Chantal, to play tic-tac-toe, and he told us to get inside, to stay there for the rest of the evening. Marcus, too, stayed in his apartment for the following few days, a rare occurrence, but then he'd reemerged and acted like none of it had happened. So he had either dabbled in some serious shit, or it was nothing and he got superstitious for a couple days, which would also be totally like Marcus. Now the difference between those two possibilities eats at me.

Walking home, I pass the Dominican restaurant with the yellow door. That girl from the park, Brianna, is clearing dishes from the outdoor tables, but she doesn't notice me. I've seen her around school a few times this week talking to Izzy, so I guess they're friends. After I've passed the place, I turn around and watch her, like a creeper, from the shadows of a doorway for a minute or two. Brianna's smart and pretty; why can't Marcus fall for her instead of Izzy? Why can't he fall for anyone instead of Izzy? Brianna goes back inside the restaurant, and I kick at the bricks of the nearest building, but they don't move, not even an inch.

———

Saturday will be our first scholastic chess meet of the year, a scrimmage with a tony boarding school in Manhattan, so I haul myself out of bed early on Friday for a chess club meeting.

Mr. Karapovsky, the coach of the high school chess club, is one of those ancient guys whose face seems to be shrinking under the weight of its own hair. Salt and pepper tangles sprout from each ear and each nostril, and with every passing month, it seems that his intense eyebrows come closer and closer to completely blocking his vision. He's old, really old, probably the oldest person still working at the school. In fact, he gave up his job teaching freshman Biology a few years ago, and now gets paid only a small stipend to run the chess club. He was close to quitting that, too, but then I came along.

"You get a brilliant student maybe once, maybe twice in this lifetime, Trees-tahn," he's said to me more than once while clapping me on the back and breathing his garlicky pickle breath on me. "For you, I stay." That's kind of a lot of pressure, since I get the feeling that if I don't make it to grand-master level before Mr. K dies, it's going to be one of the major disappointments of his life, which is really saying something since I'm pretty sure he hates his wife and lives in a terrible apartment and eats sardines for lunch every day. Reaching those higher echelons seemed like an inevitability near the end of last year. Our team took a surprise second place at the state tournament, and we only declined the invitation for nation-als because we were saving travel funds for this year, when our best players would all return and be even better. But while I've been soaring in the park, in the world of on-the-books tourna-ment chess, I've been hovering somewhere under a 2300 rating for a while now, unable to haul myself off that plateau, and I know that it makes Mr. K anxious.

Here's the way chess club usually works: We come in and have a little introductory puzzle with Mr. K and he explains the theme of the day, like working on our openings or using our knights to create forks or whatever, and then we'll break up into groups to work on that theme. Chess is pretty popular at Carl Sagan, and there are usually around thirty people in the room for the meetings, and the small groups correspond to three different skill levels. At least, there are technically three groups, but in actuality, there are four groups: Novice, Intermediate, and Advanced, and then me and Anaïs and Pankaj, who are so freakishly good that we basically exist out-side the usual categories.

I'm not bragging here. It's just a fact. And besides, freakish could easily apply to us, the trio of misfit nerds, the same way it applies to our level of chess skill, so it's not like we have to shoulder a heavy burden of envy on a daily basis. Pankaj has one of those faint, wispy mustaches that he never shaves, and even after years of crushing it at chess tournaments, he still gets so nervous that he often has to run to the restroom in the middle of a match with the timer running. Anaïs is an overweight, short-tempered blond girl who makes it clear that she'd rather be practicing her clarinet, and who exercises her natural talent at chess only to please her vaguely creepy dad, who shows up to the tournaments with flowers for her every single time. Anyway, I know I'm not exactly the king of cool myself, so I'm not trying to hate on poor Pankaj and Anaïs, who are very good chess players, good enough to be ranked at the state level for two years in a row, but I think it's safe to say that we're all pretty tired of one another's company at this point. Mr. K doesn't make us stick to the theme of the day if we don't feel like it, and he usually spends most of the hour going over famous games between grandmasters with us and pretty much ignoring whatever else goes on in the room.

On Friday, everyone is sleepy-eyed and cranky at having to come to an early morning meeting instead of our typical afternoon ones. Everyone, that is, except for Mr. K, who is nearly giddy with the idea of beating the boarding school, Westcroft, for the first time in years. They irk him, these expensive private schools with endless resources to pour into their chess teams. Mr. K loves an underdog, and since Anaïs and Pankaj and I are not the uniform-wearing preppies of Westcroft, we fit the bill well enough.

He sets everyone up with some work on how to bounce back from a material disadvantage and then comes over to strategize with us about the coming match. Instead of grandmasters, we talk about the strongest players on the Westcroft team: Dan Arshevsky, Ronald Santos, Isadora Desmains, Eamon Kennedy. The names sound familiar from last year, and I should be concentrating, trying to remember previous matches I've played against them. Instead, the only thing my mind will hold is the image of Izzy's face. When the first class bell rings and I'm called back to myself, Pankaj looks worried.

"You going to be this spacey tomorrow?" he says after we bid farewell to Mr. K, promising to get plenty of sleep before the meet.

"Pankaj, you could beat those fools while you're half in a coma," I say, and he gives me a wan smile. It's true, too. Winning at chess is easy; it's winning at love that I'm worried about. I square my shoulders and walk toward first period.

THE QUEEN

IT WAS FRIDAY BEFORE I TALKED TO TRISTAN AGAIN, and only because we were divided into randomly assigned discussion groups in AP Lit to talk about a Jonathan Edwards sermon. My heart plummeted as Mr. Berger read our names, one right after the other. We sank into adjacent desks, still not really making eye contact, along with an incredibly quiet girl named Mireille, and Alex, a tall kid with a dopey half smile, whose presence in an AP class seemed optimistic on somebody's part. I hate group discussions during the best of times, and this definitely wasn't the best of times. I kept my eyes on my notebook, like the secrets of the universe were written there. Alex stretched, arranged his gangly limbs.

"This early stuff is so boring," he said while surreptitiously playing a racing game on his phone. "The summer reading was at least a little bit hot. Why can't we skip ahead to the whale hunters and adultery and shit?"

"Language, Mr. Robinson," Mr. Berger said from his desk a few yards away, without even bothering to look up from the paper he was grading. "And stop with the texting before I confiscate that thing."

"Sorry," Alex mumbled. Then he lowered his voice and said, "This Edwards guy sounds like a real prick." Mireille tittered at this.

"I don't think he was trying to be harsh with all of that dangling-over-the-fires-of-hell stuff," Tristan said. "He sees it as being helpful. He's keeping everyone from making terrible mistakes."

"Yeah, but it's the usual patriarchal bullshit," I said, feeling my face start to burn. "He's so sure he has a monopoly on the truth, and he bullies everyone instead of letting people make their own decisions."

"Well, yeah, but you're taking it out of context," Tristan said, "The people who heard this all went to his church, so they agreed with his version of the truth."

"How do you know?" I asked.

"Well..."

"I mean, we don't know what they were thinking while they were sitting in the church listening to this."

"Ooh, she got you there, T," Alex said.

"Maybe they're just scared," I said. "They're scared because they're in this new land, trying to make a go of it, and they don't understand everything that's around them, but every day they're trying to do the best they can. And then this really powerful guy comes, wanting to reinforce his superiority, and just... he just..." My face was burning; I felt like I was fumbling forward into a fire myself.

"Acts like a dickhead," Mireille supplied.

"Thank you, Mireille," I said. "He acts like a dickhead."

"Language!" Mr. Berger interjected, giving me the stink eye over the rims of his glasses. I leaned back in my chair so that I was partially hidden behind Alex.

"You know only a man would say crap like this," Mireille said. "The world would be so much better if women ran it." I hadn't pegged Mireille for a feminist, but I was relieved that someone was backing me up.

"I mean, I guess we can sit here and talk about how unfair it is that white men have pretty much held the winning hand for all of modern history," Tristan said. "But is it really Edwards's fault that he lived in the time and place that he did?"

"What about Anne Bradstreet, then?" I asked, finally looking him squarely in the face. I was suddenly, senselessly enraged, and I wanted to punch him, wanted to shake that inscrutable expression right off his face. I wanted to kick him in his bad ankle until it hurt as badly as it had in that first

moment I saw him, and in doing so, erase all those embarrassing dreams I was still having about him.

"Well, what about her?' He sounded so calm, but he kept
licking his lips like his mouth was dry.

"She was religious. She was a product of the same age.
But you don't see her threatening people with hellfire. You
don't see her being a prick. She focused on her personal experience, and people loved her for it."

"Ooooh, snap," Alex said. "Who's Anne Bradstreet?"

"I think you're missing the point," Tristan said.

"And I think you and Jonathan Edwards are assholes
who deserve each other." Alex and Mireille were laughing,
giving each other a look like, *This girl is totally nuts.* Tristan's
mouth hung open a little as he stared at me.

"What's gotten into you guys today?" Mr. Berger sighed
as the bell rang. "All right, remember to read the section on
John Smith in preparation for Monday."

Tristan was gone, like a shot, out the door before the bell
stopped ringing. He wasn't even in Physics class that afternoon.
He had disappeared. I spent the whole period replaying the conversation. It might have still carried with it a hint of the original
indignation, but the overarching theme was embarrassment.

Don't bother telling me that the conversation wasn't
really about Jonathan Edwards. Trust me, I knew even while
it was happening that I was behaving like an arsonist holding
a match, eager and terrified to watch it all burn. That's what
made it so horrifying.

THE KNIGHT

SOMETIMES I IMAGINE THAT WHEN WE DIE, ON OUR way to whatever the next realm may be, we're forced to walk down a corridor of giant framed paintings of our most regrettable moments. That time in fifth grade when I told Benji that I'd sprouted pubic hair and this jerk named Curtis overheard and turned my words into a catchy jingle—that one's framed and hanging in a place of honor. The time that I promised our neighbor in Atlanta that I'd feed his fish while he was out of town and then I forgot and two of them died—that one's there, too.

But I'm definitely saving a nice frame for the time I thought it was a good idea to get in a pissing match with the girl of my dreams about something as stupid as early

American literature. There's something very wrong in me that needs to prove how right I am at every single moment. A part of me that needs to show everyone in the room how smart I am, even when the subject is as inconsequential as a Puritan with a bad attitude. Even when the person I'm arguing with is far more consequential than my idiotic desire to impress. Even when I know (of course I know) that what we're really talking about is me and her and the space between us. So there it goes, up on the wall in the cringe gallery.

The truth is, I can't shake the feeling that maybe Izzy would be better off if she'd never met me at all. So I've resolved to keep to the shadows. I can do it: admire her from afar or maybe even melt out of her life forever.

———————

Marcus, of course, has other ideas. When I sit down at the lunch table, he and the goons are grinning at me in a strange way, as though they stopped talking about me only when I was a few feet away. Frodo has a crust of something rimming one of his nostrils, and some valve deep inside me draws tight with disgust, but I nod a greeting to them. Pizza today, because it's Friday. Try to concentrate on that.

"Hey, T," Marcus says. "We were talking about R. J.'s party."

R. J.'s party is epic, so monumental that it has gone through multiple epochs, different geologic strata of party insanity, or so the lore goes. Its origins stretch back to the days when his older sisters, the most popular girls at our school at the time, started throwing ragers when their parents went on their yearly visit to an elderly grandmother in Jamaica and left their party-loving offspring home alone. That was over a decade ago, though, and ever since I arrived in Brooklyn, it's been R. J.'s party. Because he is the baby of the family and because he's a senior this year, this might be the final hurrah. No one would be stupid enough to miss it. And R. J. has already announced this year's theme: A Space Odyssey, complete with a dark room he is calling the Final Frontier, where surely dozens of my classmates are going to get lucky.

"Place is gonna be lit," K–Dawg says, half in his own world, as always.

I nod. "Cool." Pepperoni. Chewing. Think not of her.

"So tomorrow I need you to come over to Izzy's house with me," Marcus says. "Tell her about the party and get her to come with us. I can take care of it from there."

The briefest consideration of Marcus and Izzy in the Final Frontier together is enough to make me feel violently ill. Once he's embarked upon a plan, though, there's no diverting him. Besides, it's impossible to envision a world in which girls, or even one particular girl, would prefer me to Marcus. It's never happened before, and there's no reason to hope that Izzy will be any different, particularly after the scene this morning. And so I'm pinned. Time to walk away from the game.

"Marcus, I think you have the wrong idea. Izzy's not my

friend. She doesn't even like me." Frodo snickers, and I look over at him, but he doesn't say anything.

"Yeah, but you know her better than any of us, right?" Marcus says, thumping me once on the shoulder. The grease of the industrial pizza has coated my mouth in a terrible way, and I wish I could gag it all back up. Hanging out around Marcus might be the best weight-loss plan a person could find. I put the slice carefully back down on my tray as he goes on. "I think she might recognize my name from around school...."

"Course she will," Tyrone says too quickly. Faithful lap-dog. Marcus shoots him a look and he heels.

"As I was saying, I think she'll know who I am, but maybe you could put in a good word for me in advance. And I think I'll send her a little something tomorrow morning, just in case. Roses, maybe? You think she'll like roses?"

"All girls like roses," Tyrone supplies. "This one time I sent carnations to Roxanne on Valentine's Day and—"

"I want to know what T thinks," Marcus says, looking at me hard.

"Sure, roses," I say. Marcus nods and the table relaxes a little. K-Dawg starts to show us some stupid video of a dog dressed up as a spider, but then something occurs to me and I interrupt.

"You know, I have an idea. I heard her saying in AP Lit class that she likes Anne Bradstreet." Blank stares all around. Whatever. "I can help you find a book of her poems to give to Izzy instead of roses. It will be more meaningful." This is my attempt at a classic fork, a move with two different purposes. For one, it will convince Marcus that I'm trying to be truly helpful. But also, Izzy's too smart not to figure out who the book is really from, and even though I resolved two periods ago to leave her alone forever, you have to play the setup that's in front of you. Besides, I like the idea of giving her something to make up for this morning's argument. It's risky, and it could most certainly backfire, but it's the best thing I can come up with on the fly.

"All right, T," Marcus says, nodding thoughtfully. "We'll do what you think is best. We can get the book on the way to the park this afternoon. I set up a couple matches for you."

The bell rings, and they gather up their things. Frodo leans down to speak into my ear, his dirty nose a hairbreadth from my cheek. "Don't worry, man. Ain't nothing wrong with sloppy seconds."

I hate myself for not spitting on him for uttering such filth. I can't stand the idea of facing Izzy in Physics class, not today, so I decide to ditch the last two periods, something I've never done before, even though I'll have to come back here to meet up with Marcus at the park anyway. As I slip out the side door of the school, I pray to Anne Bradstreet or whoever is listening that Frodo should undergo a freak accident and slice his nose clean off his ugly face.

———

Competition chess, in direct opposition to a pickup game in a park, is not much of a spectator sport. There's a lot of sitting around, waiting for match pairings to be posted, while seventh-grade boys from the middle school division run around making fart jokes. The matches themselves are usually quiet except for the heavy breathing of the worried near-losers and the occasional frowned-upon exclamation. Unless it's an exhibition match, parents are shut out of the room to fret in the hallway. You're rarely aware of how your teammates are doing until it's all over, because you're too busy with your own game.

Patrice hates going to chess tournaments. She's never admitted this to my face, but she'll think up any possible reason to wriggle out of them. I can't blame her; I know that watching other people play a game you don't care about isn't anyone's definition of an exciting time. Even so, I usually get a dark twist of satisfaction whenever the otherwise play-by-the-rules Patrice comes up with a lame excuse, and I'm not surprised when I find a note on the kitchen counter Saturday morning explaining that she needs to winterize some of the beds in the Green Thumb garden around the corner. I grab one of the bran muffins she left for me (there's a little note on the Tupperware container that reads "Bra(i)n Food!"—which lets me know she's feeling plenty guilty for skipping the competition) and head for the subway.

Arriving at Westcroft feels less like entering a high school and more like going to church. It's not only the Gothic architecture or the hallowed history of the place as a parochial school; it's also the weightiness that falls upon you when you enter the house of geniuses. Rich geniuses. I've been here before, so I try to play it cool this time and breeze right past the middle schoolers from Sagan who are gaping at the soaring ceilings and stained glass windows. Money doesn't make you good at chess, I remind myself. It only makes you rich.

I find Mr. K in the dining hall, and he seems more than willing to forgive my distractedness yesterday if I'll present a couple easy wins to him today. He's wearing what Anaïs and I call his lucky sweater, which is a cardigan that has a little more blue in it than his everyday gray cardigans. Pankaj is already here, and so is a nervous-looking kid named Arthur who has been called upon to fill out our four-person varsity lineup today. He shakes my hand as though we've both been cast in the same film but I'm the headlining star. I sit down with them and put on my headphones while the rest of the team trickles in; it's an attempt to look like I'm listening to music to put me in the competitive zone, but really, it's only because I don't want to talk to anyone. I'd rather be alone and dwell upon that moment in the playground when I first met Izzy, when everything between us was new and perfect. I try to hold that feeling in my mind, even through Mr. K's disjointed pep talk.

We'll each play two matches this morning. First up for me is Isadora Desmains. Of course: Dorie. It's a sign of how preoccupied I was yesterday that I didn't recognize her full name. I haven't played her for almost two years, but she's notorious in our small circles. She wears fairy wings and fuzzy duck slippers and sparkly fingerless gloves as accents to the stuffy Westcroft uniform. She has a pet guinea pig named Mike Huckabee that she occasionally brings with her to tournaments. That's strictly forbidden, of course, but she got him registered as a service animal and lobbied the United States Chess Federation on his behalf, and they begrudgingly allow him to wait in his cage with the parents and other would-be spectators. She carries a thermos of Fruity Pebbles soaked in milk in her backpack and slugs it down like it's coffee throughout the day. She only weighs about a hundred pounds, but just when it starts to feel like there's a ten-year-old with Fruity Pebbles on her breath sitting across the table from you, she starts quoting Nietzsche. In short, Dorie's a fun weirdo, the kind you run into every once in a while in the chess world. She's not really my type, but I've known plenty of nerds with massive crushes on her, including Pankaj, who stares at our table longingly when I shake Dorie's hand.

"*Sacré bleu*," Dorie says to me. "Up against the great and mighty Tristan. I must be fortune's foe." She gives me a wink.

"Hey, Dorie," I say. "How's Mike Huckabee?"

"A touch of the scurvy, but he's convalescing in my room. Thanks for asking."

A moderator announces the start of game play, and we get down to it. Dorie's very good, and she plays creatively, not afraid to take risks and bend rules when it suits her. Even so, she gets in trouble with her rooks early and can never come back from the material disadvantage. I win without much trouble, and we wander out to the hall to pass time until the first round is over.

"What I don't get," Dorie says, "is why you're not playing for Westcroft yet. Ippolito is *salivating* to coach you. He'd probably commit hara-kiri in front of the administration if they refused to give you a tuition scholarship. So what gives?"

I shrug. Dorie's not that far off, to be honest. Westcroft tried to recruit me near the end of my freshman year, but that was when I was finally feeling like I fit in at Sagan. Living in Brooklyn with Patrice was still new then and a welcome change; moving out so quickly would have made me seem ungrateful. And even though Mr. K is old and a little depressing sometimes, he's a good coach. I didn't want to betray him. Today, though, I can't help but dwell on that unaccepted offer. I let myself imagine an alternative life for a moment: no more gauging Marcus's moods, no more taking up space in Patrice's apartment, no more fighting with the girl of my dreams about eighteenth-century poetry.

"Fine," Dorie says, blowing a strand of her pink bangs out of her eyes. "Leave me to languish with Eamon and his sophomoric observations. Seriously, though. You should think about it." She kisses me on the cheek, her lips sticky with gloss or Fruity Pebble glaze, and then dances off down the hallway to music that no one else can hear.

In the next round, I'm paired with Ronald Santos, the

star of the Westcroft team. He's tough, and I feel like we might end up with a draw, but I finally pull out a win with a sweet ending I remember from a famous Andersson versus Stean match. Anaïs, Pankaj, and Arthur all win their matches. It's a slaughter. Mr. K looks as happy as I've ever seen him, one whole side of his mouth drawn up into a smile.

THE ROOK

I GO OVER TO IZZY'S HOUSE ON SATURDAY AFTERNOON. We're supposed to be doing Physics homework, but mostly I'm here to read tarot for her. I know she doesn't believe in it, not yet, but when she sees how eerily accurate I am, she'll change her mind. Plus, her mom is one of those cool moms, and I'd rather not be around my parents and Hector right now, who have all been acting nervous and twitted up after the incident at the park, even though Hector was never formally charged with anything. Mai and Pai, they're old-school, and they never consider the possibility that the authorities might sometimes treat guys like my brother unfairly.

Izzy's house is the kind of nice that says serious money, which surprises me a little, since she's always so friendly and wearing those kind of boring clothes that she wears, and I feel shy while I stand there on the porch waiting. When she answers the door, I have to play it cool and not exclaim over every little thing, like the beautiful statues and vases and stuff that are sitting around on the bookshelves like someone just forgot them there, or the rack for vinyl records that looks like a piece of art itself, or the tapestries that her family probably brought back from far-flung vacations. It's so quiet inside that it feels like a tomb, though, and that helps me be a little less jealous of the sweet television in the living room.

"Where is everybody?" I ask.

"Um, my dad's at work, I guess," she says, doing a dramatic backward flop onto the overstuffed couch. "And my mom took my brother to an appointment."

"I didn't even know you had a brother."

"I do. A twin brother, actually."

"Whoa! That's so cool. Your star sign is Gemini and you're a real live twin? That has to be lucky."

Izzy snorts. "That's me. Lucky, lucky, lucky."

"Wait, so if you have a twin brother, why isn't he ever in school?"

Izzy curls herself into a ball, tucks herself into one corner of the couch. It looks like her big house is trying to swallow her. "It's complicated," she says. "He was supposed to be there, but now he has doctor appointments every day, so I'm not sure what's going to happen."

"He's sick?"

"Yeah," she says. "I guess he is."

She doesn't seem to want to talk about it, so I sit down cross-legged on the lush rug and pull a tarot deck out of my bag. It's my favorite, an old Rider-Waite deck that Hector found for me at a secondhand store for Christmas one year, soft and worn around the edges. "Maybe these will give you guidance about your brother."

Izzy plays along, mostly, though she gets up to get us some snacks while I'm laying out the cards on the living room carpet, so I can tell she's not concentrating all that hard on the questions she's supposed to be putting to the universe. The result is a chaotic mess of strong cards.

"Wow," I say. "There's a lot going on here. There are the Lovers, right next to the Wheel of Fortune, but there's also the Queen of Swords, which means sorrow and self-protection. And the Hanged Man, which is not always as bad as it sounds. I don't know, maybe that represents your brother? Lots of contradictions going on here. Way more powerful cards than in a typical layout. So, like, maybe you'll have to make some important decisions soon? And here's the Knight of Cups, but it's reversed, which can mean recklessness or trickery." I'm entirely absorbed in trying to sort through it all, so when Izzy speaks, it catches me off guard.

"Hey, Brianna," she says, "do you know anyone named Marcus?"

I snap to attention. Izzy still has that same sad, faraway

look, so I don't think she's messing with me. "I might know a Marcus. Why are you asking?"

"It was the weirdest thing," she says. She picks up a book lying on the coffee table and tosses it to me, and I'm trying to be calm about the whole thing, but when I see his name written inside the front cover, I run cold so fast that I almost get a brain freeze. It's definitely him. I recognize his handwriting. *Roses are red, violets are blue. You're so fine that I want to get to know you. From: Marcus*

"Where did you get this?" I ask, a little too sharp, because she looks at me funny before she answers.

"Someone slipped it through the mail slot this morning. But I've never even spoken to this Marcus guy."

"That's weird," I say.

"Is he nice?" Izzy asks.

"He's..." *Beautiful. Perfect. The love of my life, even if he doesn't know it yet*, my brain supplies in an unhelpful way. "He's cool. He's like one of those really cool guys at school who everyone knows. Or at least knows *about*."

"Huh," Izzy says. Her forehead is furrowed in concentration. I try to assess what Marcus would have seen in her to make this very un-Marcus-like gesture. She's pretty, in a low-key way: skinny, with lots of silky white-girl hair, and she smells nice, kind of powdery and flowery, like what I imagine the fairy godmother in *Cinderella* would smell like, but are those things that Marcus would go for? It's hard for me to believe.

"Marcus used to hang out with my brother a lot at school," I say cautiously. "Honestly, I'm not sure he's your type. I'll, um, point him out to you at school sometime."

"Huh," Izzy says again. "Why would he even know who I am? Maybe he's being nice to me because he knows I'm your friend."

I would like nothing more than for this to be true, but I can't fool myself into thinking it is. "Yeah, maybe so."

"Or maybe it wasn't even from him." She looks like she wants to say more, but then hesitates. "Do the cards say anything about it?" She nods at the spread of tarot on the carpet. The smile on the sphinx perched above the Wheel of Fortune suddenly looks like Marcus's grin, and I run my hands through the cards, scrambling them, then gathering them into a messy pile and sweeping them into my bag.

"The cards are confusing right now," I say. "Maybe we can try again later."

We work half-heartedly on the Physics homework for a while. Izzy's good at this stuff, I can tell, but she seems distracted, and I am, too, and the work stretches on for longer than it should, until finally she says that she promised to make dinner for her family and she needs to start cooking, and I decide to use the opportunity to exit.

"I'll walk you out," she says.

I go out the door first, so I'm the first one to see them. Marcus and T are on the sidewalk at the end of Izzy's short driveway. It seems as if they were standing there talking about something rather than simply walking past. They both look up at me. No, that's not right; they look past me. To Izzy.

"Tristan," Izzy says, coming out to stand beside me on the porch. It takes me a beat to realize that she's talking about T, because no one uses his real name. Then I remember that weird moment before Physics class a few days ago when she stared at him in the hallway.

Marcus shoves T's shoulder and, kind of like a puppet whose string has been jerked, T says, "Oh, hey, Izzy. We were... we were coming by to say hey." They walk toward us, and I sidle up to Izzy, the points of a quadrilateral drawing closer, four corners of the earth folding together. "Hi, Brianna," T adds as an afterthought.

"Hey, Caballito," Marcus says, but he's still staring at Izzy, seeming very pleased.

T looks as anxious and miserable about this situation as I feel. "Um, Izzy, I don't think you've met my cousin Marcus yet."

"Your cousin?" Izzy says.

"Yeah, me and T, we're almost like brothers, you know?" Marcus says, reaching out to shake Izzy's hand. "It's a pleasure to meet you."

"You sent me a book?" Izzy asks.

Marcus does a head-tipped-downward bashful thing. I've been watching him use that same gesture around girls since he was nine years old. He still hasn't let go of her hand, I notice. "Hey, you got it. T told me you might like it. But what we were talking about," he continues, "is that there's this party. You might not have heard about it yet, being new to the block and all. But you shouldn't miss this party, Izzy. She shouldn't miss it, right, T?"

"Right," T says.

"What kind of party?" Izzy asks, taking back her hand.

"Are you talking about R. J.'s party?" I ask.

"Yeah, see, Brianna knows what's up," Marcus says, smiling at me.

"We should all go together," I blurt out, almost before I know it's in my head. R. J.'s is a notorious hookup fest, and I can think of few things worse than watching Marcus put the moves on Izzy all night long, but maybe I can think of a way to put the whole thing on ice before next weekend.

"Yeah, sure," Marcus says smoothly. "We can all go together. How's that sound, T?" Marcus puts his fists up, shadowboxes T in a joking way, left-right, left-right.

"Sure, sounds good," T says, but he looks at Izzy as he does, not Marcus, and she looks back at him, and that's when I see the whole picture, a vision gift from the spirits. The sight line between their eyes is a fuse burning from both ends, and their bodies are giving off heat and light, two stars. The heat is so intense, in fact, that it inflates a helium balloon of relief in me, and I wonder how I possibly could have missed it before, but Marcus doesn't see it at all.

"It's settled, then," he says. "You ladies enjoy your beautiful Saturday, a'ight?" Then they turn around and head back toward the sidewalk, even though T looks like he might wither when he breaks eye contact with Izzy.

"Well, that was strange," I say when they're out of ear-shot, though it's obviously the understatement of the year.

"Yes," Izzy agrees. She hadn't bothered to put on shoes, and now she's shifting around on the concrete in her socked feet. The breeze ruffles her hair, and she looks like she came here from a different age, like she sailed in at the prow of a ship.

"You didn't tell me you had a crush on T." She doesn't say anything in response, but her face looks cracked open with embarrassment, maybe even fear. "It's okay," I say, sliding my arm around her waist and squeezing. "I have an idea."

THE QUEEN

THE PARTY: WE SAILED TOWARD IT ON THE SLOW-moving river of the week, peering at it through telescopes, trying to anticipate and map its contours, making plans long before we landed. If any of the others—Marcus, Tristan, Brianna—managed to think of anything besides the party that week, they were doing better than I was.

After Marcus invited us to the party, after I tried to read the truth about the book of poetry in Tristan's face, I dragged Brianna back inside the house and told her everything about my brother and Tristan. I even broached the subject that I'd been dreading, which is that I suspected Hull had been at least partially responsible for her brother crossing paths with the police. After muttering something about shoes that didn't make much sense, she told me I shouldn't worry about it. In fact, it seemed like a weight had been lifted from her own shoulders. "Guys in this neighborhood get in fights sometimes," she said, waving it off. "It's best to stay out of it and live your own life." Easier said than done, but I could see where she was coming from. Hull hadn't been thinking of me when he went to that chess match; why did I have to think of him, then, when I was deciding whom to be friends with?

The rest of what Brianna said sounded batshit crazy, to be honest, but my heart wanted it to be true when she told me that Tristan was avoiding me because he wouldn't move in on anything Marcus wanted for himself. Surely part of Brianna's conjecture had to be mistaken: The coolest guy at our high school was not obsessed with me. But if Tristan even *thought* this outlandish idea might be true, well . . . maybe that was why he had cooled toward me after those first blissful encounters. The mere suggestion that it was Marcus, a complete stranger, who was to blame for my troubles left me with a flicker of relief and hope.

"I have a plan," Brianna told me. "There's a way we can find out if he's into you without pissing off his cousin. And you won't have to deal with Marcus coming on to you at the party. It's all going to work out, lady. Trust me."

As Brianna talked through her plan, it didn't escape me that she pretty obviously had a thing for Marcus. But, so what? It was possible that this was the best way for everyone to get what he or she wanted. I turned her insane plot over in my mind while I chopped onions and garlic, and by the time the enchiladas were done and I heard Mom and Hull coming up the front walk, I'd decided that I would go along with it.

―――――――

In order to lay the groundwork for Brianna's plan, I gave up keeping my distance from Tristan. On Monday, when I sat behind him in AP Literature class, he seemed bewildered, understandably wary.

"Is this reserved for the Anne Bradstreet fan club?" I asked, smiling to cover my own nerves.

He paused, and I saw his face cycle rapidly through a dozen possible reactions—apologetic, distant, suspicious. But then it settled into that sweet, genuine smile that I came to crave.

"Yep," he said. "It is now."

Even now, I sometimes struggle to put my finger on what exactly it was about him that made me temporarily lose my mind. Normally, as someone comes into clearer focus, you're able to see all his imperfections, but with Tristan it was the opposite. The more I was around him, the more tiny perfections I could discern. The way he looked at me and listened, really listened, while I was saying something, rather than thinking about the next thing he was going to say. The way he shrugged bashfully when I asked him how he learned to play chess, though I knew even then that he must have been good to beat Hull. The way he could (provided I wasn't picking fights with him) flip the tenor of a conversation with such a gentle touch, turn everything to lightness again. That same day, after the bell rang, we walked into the hallway, and I was complaining about my mother, which is an easy fallback topic when you're the new kid. I was telling him that I had inherited my terrible singing voice from her but that at least I *knew* I had and didn't sing U2 songs so loudly in the shower that everyone in the kitchen below could hear every milk-curdling note, and every time I grumbled about it, she got a faraway look and talked about how she was certain that Bono had made eye contact with her during a concert in 1987.

"Tell me your mom does stuff like that," I pleaded. "Tell me I'm not alone here."

"My mom is dead," he said, as simply as if he'd said, "The sky is blue."

My mouth gaped open stupidly. I wanted to run to the fire alarm that was on the wall and pull it, just so I could escape. But Tristan said, "It's okay. It was a long time ago. As for whether my mother would have seduced Bono, I'm really not sure."

"Honestly, it's hard to imagine anyone besides my delusional mother attempting it."

"Don't be so hard on your mom. She raised you, so she's all right by me." Then he smiled, and we parted ways, and the thought of Tristan the Perfect made the knot of desire draw tight again, made me bite my lip so hard on the way to Government class that it started to bleed.

In short, I was more in love with him every day, but I worked to keep things friendly and polite, very controlled. A more truthful version of my feelings would be revealed at the party. Or I would chicken out and nothing at all would be revealed. By then, Brianna and I had a full and detailed plan, one that was bold and dizzyingly complicated and a tiny bit brilliant, and I wanted with every cell of my body for the whole thing to work, but every day I vacillated wildly between optimistic confidence and desperate fear of failure, and I was forever on the verge of calling the whole thing off.

As for Marcus, he couldn't have been nicer to me. I didn't have any classes with him, but every time I saw him in the hallway, he stopped whatever he was doing and smiled and hugged me, asked me how my day was going. I won't lie: It made my heart beat faster to be pressed against the hard, muscled planes of his chest, and it was a high unto itself to hear the whispers that rippled all around me as soon as Marcus began showering me with attention. I could easily understand why Brianna had fallen for him hard. And yet . . . the way he looked at me reminded me of the way that some of Mom's clients examined her jewelry before making a big purchase: appraising its value, searching carefully for a flaw.

Don't borrow trouble, I told myself. It would be like me to bask in the smile of the coolest kid in the school while secretly interpreting his actions as a harbinger of doom. "My little pragmatist," my mother used to call me.

All of this scheming and calculation distracted me from something I probably could have seen coming had I put any time into thinking about it. That Friday, my parents told me that after Hull finished his final upcoming week of the full-time therapy program, they would allow him to go back to Hope Springs Day School and finish out his remaining two years there. Not a huge surprise, but still, it bothered me. Never had my twin seemed so distant, so unreachable. He didn't even tell me himself; he was up in his room while my parents cooked dinner together and I did homework at the kitchen counter. Even though I knew this was the one thing Hull had wanted ever since my parents told us we were moving to Brooklyn, it seemed bizarre to me when my father made me the same offer, to return to Hope Springs. Sagan High was big, noisy, and sometimes overwhelming. There were a few tough, scary characters there, the food was terrible, and a lot of the facilities looked like they'd been built four decades ago, because they had been. And yet, I liked it. Hope Springs was like a fuzzy sweater, with its self-directed learning and familiar faces, but a sweater that I'd now outgrown. My schedule at Sagan was a workout, full as it was with AP classes, and I liked it that way. And there was Tristan, of course. It was odd to consider how little I cared about something that meant the world to Hull.

"No," I said. "I'm fine where I am."

"Thank God," Dad said, aggressively hacking into a head

of broccoli. "Because we can't afford it, anyway. But, you know, we had to ask."

<hr/>

I usually require a half hour to get ready to leave the house, and that includes showering. It's sort of a point of pride for me. But that Saturday, the day of the party, I took extra care. I borrowed a flowing, layered skirt from my mom's closet. It had a fuchsia-and-orange pattern that I'd always liked, and it looked like something Brianna might pick out, plus I knew my mom wouldn't miss it since her closet was the kind of exploding mess in which articles often got lost for two or three years. This I paired with a tight T-shirt that I would wear under a sweater on a typical day. I pinned my hair up into a bun, and put on more eyeliner than usual and berry-colored lipstick, which I normally don't even bother with since I have a bad habit of biting my lips when I'm concentrating on schoolwork. I was examining my work in the bathroom mirror, making sure it was exactly as Brianna and I had discussed, when Hull barged in without knocking.

"Um, hello? I could be naked in here. Learn some manners."

Instead of turning around and leaving me alone, Hull stood in the doorway and narrowed his eyes at me. "What are you up to? You look totally different."

"I don't know what you're talking about."

"Yes, you do. You look like a low-rent flamenco dancer."

I'd thought I looked nice, actually—at worst like a *talented* flamenco dancer—and the comment chafed. Besides, his hangdog skulking about the house was seeming more and more like a put-on, like a carefully calibrated performance of hardship rather than the thing itself.

"Well, you're looking more like your old self. Especially after manipulating Mom and Dad into giving you what you wanted."

"You don't know what you're—"

"Oh, save it, Hull," I said, shoving past him out of the bathroom.

"They're not your friends," he said, and the remark made me stop and look back at him.

"Who?"

"Whomever you're going to meet. They don't know the first thing about you. They're looking for ways to take advantage of you." What was twisting his face like that? Jealousy? Anger?

"Why do you always have to expect the worst of everyone?"

"Why do you always have to be so naive?" he asked, following me down the hall. "People haven't evolved to be cuddly teddy bears, and that goes for you, too, even though you like to pretend otherwise."

"You're so sad," I said, and shut my bedroom door like a period on the statement. I started gathering some things into my purse, pretending Hull couldn't get to me. But I felt shaky.

How well did I know Tristan, or even Brianna? Not very well. We'd known everyone at Hope Springs for most of our lives, and I experienced a moment of acute longing to be going to the movies with Philip or getting pizza with the girls from my old Girl Scout troop or, really, doing anything that didn't involve a party full of strangers. *But this is the new normal,* I thought while I put on some perfume that had been collecting dust on my bureau since we moved, *and I better learn to adapt to it.*

We had plans to meet on the corner of our block at 9:00 PM, but I was so nervous about being the first person there and having to stand by myself like a loser that I stalled for too long, and then all three of them were there waiting for me, watching me jog toward them on heels that were higher than I was used to. There was a moment, when I lurched to a stop, breathing hard, that I was certain they would laugh at me and tell me they were kidding, that I couldn't come with them after all. No room in the club.

"You look fantastic," Brianna said. *"Muy guapa, mami."* I could tell from the loosey-goosey nature of her movements that she'd already been drinking, which wasn't what we'd planned, but I was relieved that this was all real, that I was wanted. When she hugged me and breathed whiskey fumes into my face, I laughed out loud. No one at Hope Springs Day School was having a Saturday night like this one. I had a posse, unlikely as it was, and we would all live happily ever after. In that moment, I was sure of it.

"Yeah," Marcus said. "Brianna always knows what's up."

It was dark already, but his white teeth glowed as if illuminated from the inside. Tristan stole a couple indirect glances at me, and then dropped the end of a joint on the sidewalk and ground it out with the toe of his sneaker.

"Time to go," he said.

There was a twenty-minute walk ahead of us, but we'd barely started it when Brianna rummaged around in her purse and produced two innocuous-looking soda bottles, one dark, one clear.

"This one's got whiskey in it, so I brought it for T and Izzy to share," she said, thrusting the bottle into my hand. "I know you like gin better, so this one's for you," she said to Marcus, tossing the clear one up in the air for him to catch.

I tried to make eye contact with Brianna. We'd talked about not drinking too much so that we could pull off the switch. But she was singing a song in Spanish, accenting the beat with the clicks of her high-heeled sandals, and Marcus was smiling at her, taking long pulls from the bottle. The night was already taking on a nice bacchanalian blur, so I didn't hesitate too long before I dropped back to walk beside Tristan on the sidewalk and twisted off the cap. It didn't taste like whiskey. It tasted more like autumn leaves and ground mold and something else, the barest tang of hot metal. It made me cough and choke for a second. I offered the bottle to Tristan.

"I don't drink," he said, and I took it back, a little embarrassed. Brianna's head whipped around.

"Come on, Boy Genius. It's a *party*," she said.

Tristan shrugged, looking a little irritated with her, but he accepted the bottle from me and took a swig.

The drink itself was flat, but it felt as though it had carbonated my insides the second it hit my stomach, an effervescence that fizzed throughout my body, making my limbs feel light and loose, as though they might float away from me and rise up, up, up into the sky. I looked over at Tristan, who was taking another sip of the drink and who seemed more cheerful than he had moments before. He looked perfect, shiny, almost as if a corona of light surrounded him. Then he glanced over at me, and it was as if all the effervescent bubbles in me popped at once. It was the strangest feeling, like an internal tickle, and I couldn't help but start laughing, and Tristan started laughing, too. I'd only gotten tipsy a few times before, but whatever Brianna had put in this drink, I felt as if I could guzzle it and guzzle it. And Tristan, incandescent, laughing—I almost threw the whole plan out the window to grab him and kiss him right that second.

But that's when Marcus turned around and started walking backward so he could see us, so I stuffed my tingly hands deep in my pockets and commanded them to stay there. "What are you two giggling about back here?" he asked.

"Nothing," Tristan said, but for some reason that only made us laugh harder.

"How are you feeling?" Brianna said, and there was a note of real curiosity in her voice, so I gave the question the contemplation that I believed it was due.

"I feel," I said, "like a puppy with wings." And that made everyone laugh, and I linked arms with Marcus and Tristan like we were in *The Wizard of Oz* and skipped a little. If you had tried to tell me that we didn't all genuinely like each other, I wouldn't have believed you. Hull's words of caution had been released (hurled, maybe) to the evening breeze. I was in love, and the world was beautiful.

"You're crazy, girl," Marcus said, but he was laughing, too, and the laughter carried us all the way to the party, as swiftly and surely as if it were a magic carpet.

———

By the time we arrived, the party was in full swing. The house, a small split-level with peach siding, looked a little run-down, like most of the houses on the block, but maybe that was only because the front yard was already littered with beer cans. Kids from school, a few of whom I vaguely recognized, were scattered all over the concrete slab that served as a porch. Almost all of them said hey to Marcus, and he acknowledged them with a single nod before shouldering his way inside the front door.

The theme of the party was space, and someone had decorated the walls of the living room with hundreds of those little glow-in-the-dark star stickers, and the original *Star Wars* movie was playing soundlessly on the television. A song I didn't recognize made the walls buzz and vibrate. A girl a few feet to our left shrieked so loudly that everything stopped for a second, but then she went straight back to her conversation and everyone else did, too. We waded in, a snake of four bodies making its way through the crowd. Marcus in the lead, of course, and then Tristan, who reached behind and took my hand when he saw that Brianna and I were getting caught in the melee. Even though it was only a brief span of seconds, it was as if a circuit had been closed. A jolt of desire and a need for the plan to work shot through me.

A folding table had been set up against one wall, and a giant bowl of purple mystery punch sat atop it, tiny tremulous waves created by the music rolling across the surface of the liquid. A tented sheet of construction paper labeled the drink with the rather unfortunate moniker "Black Hole Juice." It didn't stop me from accepting a paper cupful when Marcus offered it. Brianna's drink had been ambrosia, but this tasted more like grape Kool-Aid.

A wiry, dark-skinned kid with short braids sticking out all over his head came over, clasped hands with Marcus and bumped shoulders with him. His lips were forming the word *welcome* over and over. So this was R. J., master of ceremonies. He was in my Government class, and I hadn't even realized he was the notorious party-thrower.

"You know T and Brianna," Marcus said, and his voice was so loud and commanding that I could hear it even in the middle of the party's cacophony. "And this is my date, Isabelle." So strange to be claimed, possessed by someone, and have that same person get your name wrong, all in the span of six words. I glanced at Tristan. He was leaning against the wall, staring down into a cup of the awful punch. He looked amazing.

I turned back to R. J. and leaned in. "Cool shirt!" I shouted. He was wearing a Neil deGrasse Tyson T-shirt, possibly home-made, with an image of the astrophysicist and the quote "Space exploration is a force of nature unto itself" emblazoned across the front.

"NDT is my *man!*" R. J. yelled, and then the music changed, and someone across the room screamed his name and he bounded happily away.

Marcus took my elbow and we walked toward the glow of the kitchen, Tristan and Brianna following behind. "You're so nice, Izzy," Marcus said, and he sounded surprised, as if he'd anticipated that he'd invited a world-class bitch to be his date to this party.

The kitchen was better lit and farther from the thumping speakers, but no less crowded. People were thronged around a table of snacks, bags of Cheetos and Fritos piled on top of each other and mostly ransacked. *Should have brought something to eat*, I thought; I'd been too distracted to behave like a polite guest. But people seemed thrilled to see Marcus, chips or no chips. Two of his friends, K-Dawg and Tyrone, whom Brianna had pointed out to me at school, hugged Marcus like a long-lost brother when we found them in the kitchen.

"Now the party's here," Tyrone said. He was lean and awkwardly put together, ears too low on his head, dry skin. He smirked in my general direction but didn't bother to introduce himself.

K-Dawg (whose real name was Kevin, Brianna had told me, but he had long ceased to respond even when teachers called him that) lifted a can of beer to his lips in a slow-motion arc. He had a baby face and heavy eyelids and a big Afro, which together made him look like a stuffed animal, maybe a sleepy lion. The beer can halted midway to his lips, which were dusted finely with snack food crumbs. "Hold on, hold on," he said, looking at me from below his long eyelashes. "Is this Izzy? She doesn't look anything like—"

He didn't finish his sentence, though, because Marcus reached out and shoved him a little and said, "Yeah, dumbass, this is Izzy."

"It's okay," I said. "Lots of people think it's weird that I don't look like my brother. We are twins, after all. But we're fraternal, so we can look as different as any other pair of siblings."

There aren't too many times in one's life when you get to bring a conversation to a screeching, record-stopping halt, and I would be lying to say I wasn't reveling in it. It was my chance to say, "Look, I know everything about your beef with my brother. And I'm so cool that it's all beneath me to care." I looked around at their faces. K-Dawg had forgotten to lower his beer can. Tyrone looked irritated, almost angry. Tristan looked nervous. And Marcus... if I had to guess, I'd say that he was looking at me with a little bit of admiration, like I had something in me that he hadn't anticipated. Anyway, even though the party kept swirling around us, there was nothing but cricket-filled silence in that one corner of the kitchen.

But then a pretty girl with a bright red scarf came over, kissed Tyrone on the jaw, leaped into the middle of our circle, and started to shimmy to the Drake song that had shuffled up on the speakers. The loaded silence broke the dam and time flowed forward again.

"Are you guys stoned?" the girl said. "Why are y'all so quiet?" Then she squealed and threw herself at Brianna. "Those earrings are so pretty that I could cut you for them, bitch."

Brianna laughed. "Roxanne, this is my friend Izzy!" she shouted over the clamor that had swept in once again.

"*Enchantée*," Roxanne shouted. If there was any discussion among the boys of my drop-the-mic moment I missed it, because I was busy talking with Brianna and Roxanne. What she was doing with Tyrone was a mystery, because she really was pretty cool, in that spotlight-hungry theater kid kind of way. Tristan greeted her with a fist bump and the four of us stood around for a few minutes, talking about movies, eating the dregs of a bag of sour cream and onion potato chips. Roxanne insisted that the best old-school Disney movie was *Cinderella*, but Tristan argued for *Beauty and the Beast*, which had always been my favorite, too.

"The Beast is so emotionally complicated. He walks the line between self-sacrificing and self-defeating," Tristan said, and I got a little echo of that bubbly feeling I had before.

"But if complicated is what you want, why not *The Lion King?*" Roxanne asked. "Simba as Hamlet, and all that."

"Yeah, but Hamlet doesn't get it on with Ophelia and live happily ever after in the original. They totally punked on the ending."

"I'd love to play Hamlet someday," Roxanne said. "The first black female Hamlet."

But before anyone had time to offer any thoughts on those aspirations, Marcus was pressing another cup of punch into my hand and asking if we wanted to check out the upstairs. "R. J. said the party continues all over the house," he said. "He said you've really got to check out all the rooms to appreciate the theme."

"Oh, sure," Roxanne said, rolling her eyes. "I'm sure the theme is really what you have on your mind, Marcus."

The riskiest moment of the plan was rushing toward us, so we had to look sharp. The four of us drifted out of the kitchen. Brianna and I linked arms on the staircase, but I was afraid to look her in the face in case my anxiety was contagious. We stayed that way, hips bumping, eyes determinedly forward, past R. J.'s bedroom, where a telescope was positioned next to the window (completely ignored while people sat cross-legged on the floor and passed a joint around). Past the bathroom, which had a big and remarkably detailed drawing of a space shuttle taped to the door, upon which someone had scrawled in Sharpie, "How do astronauts piss in space?" And finally, on toward another bedroom, R. J.'s sisters' or maybe his parents' room, a closed door with colorful signs posted all over it. **THE FINAL FRONTIER**, the signs read. PLEASE NO CELL PHONES OR ANY OTHER KIND OF LIGHT. ENTER QUIETLY AND AT YOUR OWN RISK.

The make-out room, of course. Brianna had told me that every one of R. J.'s parties had one. In fact, she'd said, she had let R. J. himself feel her up, bra off, at his baseball-themed party two years ago, in a room labeled UNDER THE BLEACHERS. I didn't tell Brianna that, two years on, I still hadn't allowed anyone to do that.

My chain of thoughts ran something like this: 1) Please let this work. 2) This will never work. 3) Please let this work.

Marcus reached toward the doorknob of the room and started to turn it. Brianna reached out and put her hand on his arm, making him pause.

"Wait," she said. "Ladies first."

THE ROOK

"WAIT," I SAY. "LADIES FIRST."

Marcus nods, performs a little bow, and gestures toward the door like a gentleman. I look over at T and give him a glance that I hope is smoldering and come-hither enough for Marcus to notice. Like I can't wait to get my hands on T inside that room. As if. T looks completely terrified, like he might bolt down the stairs at any moment. I'm not sure what Izzy sees in him, really. Ever since last weekend, when I saw him staring at her, I've been pretty sure that their feelings are mutual, but he's such an odd one, such a cold fish, that I took the added precaution of mixing up a love potion for the two of them to drink tonight. Mugwort and cinnamon bark and pomegranate seeds and a few other things, mashed together and allowed to marinate in the moonlight for two full nights, then mixed with a little whiskey for good measure and decanted carefully into a Coke bottle. Is it working? I think so, but the whole world feels tilted tonight so I can't be sure.

"Ladies first," Marcus repeats after me.

Izzy and I slip inside the room, almost drawing the door shut behind us, and move quickly away from the doorway into the pitch black. I'm worried that we'll bump into someone or something in the dark, feel or hear something that we'd rather not, but the room is quiet. The night is still young, after all. I can hear Izzy's nervous breathing beside me, and I almost whisper something reassuring to her, because I'm as calm as a runner before a race, but then the door pushes open, and there's no time, because even in this blackness, I can tell from the height and movements of the silhouette that it's Marcus. I reach out and wordlessly draw him toward me, pull him farther into the room, and I feel his strong hands, his strong arms, reaching back for me. Marcus is holding me, I can feel the hard metal of the necklace through the thin fabric of his shirt, and everything, Izzy and T and the entire world of the party, dissolves away.

What is there to say, really, about what happens in the dark emptiness of infinite space? There are moments like honey. There are moments like dancing. There are moments like we are both rushing toward something. Have you ever been running a great distance, and you see a landmark on the horizon, and at first it seems completely unchanging, as though you will never make it there? But as you get closer, near the end, it is speeding toward you so fast, and you realize you have been moving this quickly all along, hurtling toward this one determined point, sucked into the heart of a black hole. That is what it is like. It's like that.

THE KNIGHT

I WAIT FOR A FEW MOMENTS IN THE HALLWAY. I CAN-
not bear the thought of entering the room, because my heart
will stop if I am in the same space where Marcus is running
his hands over Izzy, tasting her skin. No, my heart will not
simply stop; it will explode, and they will find my dead body
on the second floor of R. J.'s house tomorrow morning, my
chest cavity blown out.

And yet.

I am not so self-absorbed that I cannot imagine how it
would feel to be Brianna, waiting in the dark for someone
who never comes. I remember her stopping in the park that
day, pulling me to my feet so that I could run from the cops.
She has always been decent to me, if not exactly my friend,

and God only knows why she wants to make out with me, but maybe it's as simple as loneliness, and because that's a topic I understand intimately, I can't abandon her to it. I will kiss her a few times and then we will get the hell out of here and go downstairs and, even though I can't stand hangovers because they give me migraines, we will drink beer until we are a little bit, blessedly, numbed. With this strategy clear in my mind, I go through the door.

She is there, immediately, one arm circling my neck, the other reaching around my waist, and I can't help it, I reflexively wince. But then her lips are next to my ear, so close that I can feel them brushing against the peach fuzz on my earlobe. *It's me.* The words are so soft, closer to a breath than a whisper, even, and I think that I've imagined them until they come again. *It's me.* I know, somehow, that it's Izzy, even though I can't really hear her voice and none of this makes any sense. But there it is, there *she* is, the truest thing in the world. Izzy. And as long as her body is pressed against mine, my brain doesn't care about explanations. I would float here for minutes, for hours, forever, in the limbo of the darkness, her arm around my neck the only certainty that matters.

She threads her fingers through mine, though, and we slip back out into the hallway. I can see her now, her eyes nervous and questioning, one finger over her lips. Downstairs, the party rages, but the upper level of the house has hit a moment of relative quiet. A few people waiting for the bathroom, a few going down the stairs. The pot smokers have vacated R. J.'s room and that's where I follow her. She glances quickly over her shoulder and pulls the door shut behind her.

"I'm sorry," she says. "I should have explained earlier, but I didn't know how. Marcus is your cousin, and I thought that maybe you thought that he thought..." She trails off.

I think again of that gallery of regretted moments, moments when I didn't know the right thing to do, a chain of them that form the story of my life. But even a fool can see when the universe is giving you a hint this big. I put my hand on her cheek and I lean toward her and I kiss her.

I'm not an expert or anything, but I'd be pretty comfortable betting that this is one of the top ten most perfect kisses in the history of human existence. Our lips fit together like they were made to do so, and the constant motion and noise in my head stops for a minute, and then I can taste the sweet warmth of her, and then our tongues are touching, not gross and slug-like as I've sometimes experienced, but a slice of soft quickness, perfectly timed to meet in the middle. I am filled with fizzing bubbles, and I can't feel where I end and she begins. It is so perfect that I'm afraid that my knees might give out under me, and I put my arm around her waist, ostensibly to embrace her, but really to steady myself. And that's wonderful, too, the warm, reassuring pressure of another body, two people holding each other up. The kiss ends, but she doesn't move her face away from mine. We are almost the same height. I notice a small freckle on the outer corner of her left eye, and the gentle curve of the bridge of her nose: the gift of tiny details.

"What are we going to do?" she says. "What are we going to do?"

"This," I say. "More of this."

Her worried expression relaxes, a silent laugh, and because I know she doesn't laugh easily, this, too, feels like a gift. The movement propels her into me again, a more forceful kiss this time, less gentle but more joyful. *You can laugh and kiss at the same time*, I think. *How amazing.*

Then her hands slide down onto my chest, and she pulls back. "We have to go back in there."

"In where?"

"In the...other room. I left Brianna with Marcus, and he can't know it's her." And then I see all of it, the whole mess of it, in a painful gulp. "No one can know about this," she says, and I think, *No shit, because Marcus will kill all three of us*, but that's not what I say.

"Everything will be okay," I say. "We'll talk later and figure everything out."

"Yes," she says, and kisses me a few more times, small, hasty kisses, still wonderful. We sneak back into the hallway, her hand gripped tightly in mine. As we duck back inside the Final Frontier, my eye catches on a dark shadow down the hall, and it makes me think that someone could be watching us, and anxiety twists in my gut. I'm not built for subterfuge. I tell myself that it is nothing.

We wait near the door, our arms twined around each other. It is too warm in here, and too dark. There are glow-in-the-dark star stickers but no other light, so I can't see any-one, but I can hear whispers and giggles and heavy breathing coming from some corner of the room. The whole scene feels so sleazy that I don't even want to kiss Izzy here, but I breathe in the scent of her skin and hold her tighter, and she squeezes back. It feels like an eternity that we wait there, when all I want to do is run far, far away with her.

There's a movement in the dark and her body tenses, pulls away from mine. She and Brianna must have worked out some kind of signal, because I hear her softly whisper, "Bri-anna?" Then they are out the door, pulling me with them. In the hallway, we stand there blinking at each other for a beat. It's hard to read their faces, and there's no time to think about the right thing to say, because Marcus comes into the hall-way, too. His expression is easier to discern: sleepy, satisfied, slightly smug.

"Izzy and I were just going to the bathroom," Brianna says in a rush, and drags Izzy with her down the hall. There's someone coming out of the bathroom at the moment they reach the door, and they dart into it, cutting in front of several people who were waiting in line.

"Oh, come on!" one person yells at them.

"Dykes!" yells another.

Downstairs, people are cheering for a song that's shuffled up on the playlist, and Marcus starts to nod along, but I can't feel it; my body is stuck in some quieter, more subtle rhythm, my heartbeat the bass line for the constantly replaying music video projected on the interior of my skull: what she looked like, what she felt like.

"It's the strangest thing," Marcus says.

"Huh?"

"When this whole thing started, I wanted to prove I could have her. You know that," Marcus says. I can see the dimple on the left side of his face, the one thing that can still make him look like a little kid. "But now . . . I don't know. She's so nice and kind of dorky-sweet. And full of surprises, if you know what I mean. Maybe it's fate that she moved to our block. I really like her, T. I might even love her."

THE QUEEN

BRIANNA WAS FUMBLING WITH THE DOOR LOCK, UN-leashing a stream of curse words at it, and when I reached past her to help, I saw that it was because her hands were shaky. I couldn't immediately think why. The plan had been her idea and, miraculously, it had worked, sailed by almost without a hitch. Honestly, in advance, I had been most concerned with how Tristan would react, wondering if I had been imagining that kernel of something between us. My mind was still reeling with the knowledge that it was true. Truer than true. A big, rapturous starry sky of true.

"Can you believe this actually worked?" I asked her.

Brianna didn't answer. She pulled a wad of toilet paper

from the roll and wiped at her face, which was sweaty, and then tossed it in the toilet. She leaned against the counter, and her breathing sounded funny. The room was claustrophobic, suddenly, and I could still taste the sugary tang of the punch at the back of my throat.

"Are you . . . sick?" I asked.

She gave me a withering gaze, a don't-be-so-fucking-stupid gaze. It does seem idiotic now, looking back on it, how much time I'd spent in the days leading up to the party contemplating the details of how to make the plan work and how little thought I'd given to what pulling it off would actually feel like. It didn't matter, in the end, whose idea it had been. The consequences were everyone's.

That night in the bathroom, though, I couldn't see all of that so clearly. Mostly, I was trying to think of a delicate way of asking how far things had gone between them, and also trying to wrap my head around what, exactly, Marcus had wanted to do with me. In fact, what he thought he *had* done with me. Me! And he didn't even know me.

"Are you all right?" I asked Brianna. She started to say something, then stopped, started again.

"Yeah," she said. "I'm fine. Let's get out of here, though, okay?"

"Sure." Oh, sure, it was all fine. Brianna was my one friend at Carl Sagan and I had already compromised that friendship in spectacular and innovative ways. I've never been one to stop grasping at straws, though, even when it was a little too late. "Brianna, I'm sorry. It's my fault. I should have thought this through more."

"It's not your fault," she said, sounding angrier by the second. "It's not like I'm a baby who can't think for myself. And besides, you have it all wrong. Making out with Marcus...I knew it was going to be great and it was great and I don't regret it. It's just...he didn't know that was me, you know? And he never will know that it was me. It's like I wasn't even there."

Comforting words melted on my tongue, never made it into the air. I couldn't urge her, like a real friend, to tell Marcus everything. I felt the full weight of the secret, even though I was relying upon other people to hold it for me.

Another *I'm sorry* rose into my mouth, but I swallowed it down like a hunk of unchewed food. "You look so beautiful tonight," I said instead.

The truth was, she looked so, so tired in that moment, and I could see what she was going to look like when she was fifty. But then she blew her nose on a piece of toilet paper and squared her shoulders like she was getting ready to step onto a stage. Someone was pounding on the door and yelling.

"Stop making out in there! I gotta pee!"

"Go fuck yourself!" Brianna shouted back, and then she turned to me and managed a thin smile. "Ready?" I nodded, and she looped her arm through mine, exactly as we had when we first came upstairs. It felt different now. "I'll pretend to be too drunk, all right? And you use that as an excuse to get us out of here."

We stumbled arm in arm out of the bathroom, where Brianna gave a drunken grin and the finger to the people waiting in line. I made some fast apologies to Marcus about needing to take Brianna home.

"Aw, Caballito's all right," Marcus said.

Brianna groaned pitiably, swayed on my arm like an unsecured sail. "I'm gonna throw uuuup."

"You already did, sweetie." I patted her shoulder, impressed with both of us.

Tristan said he'd walk us home. Marcus offered to leave, too, but I could tell he wanted to stay, and I vigorously urged him to do so. He grinned at me, and I tried not to read it as a leer.

"I'll stop over to see you tomorrow, baby," he said, and then, before I could think of a way of diverting it, he kissed me. If I needed any further evidence that what I had with Tristan was the real thing, then Marcus's sloppy kiss sufficed. It was like flat soda, warm and sticky without any sparkle, and it took all my concentration not to make a face afterward. I couldn't look at Tristan or Brianna.

"Okay," I said. "Let's get out of here."

Tristan and I looped our arms around Brianna's back, and she pretended to be loose-limbed and unsteady as we lurched our way downstairs and through the heart of the party. She was a better actress than Roxanne could ever be. The music had swerved toward old-school, stuff that was popular before we were born, and everyone was yelling

"Jump around!" and bouncing into us and off of us as we tried to make a break for the door. It was a relief to be out in open air, the concrete solid under our feet. We weren't even a block away when Brianna straightened up and shook us off. I glanced at Tristan and his face was one big question mark, but there was no way to explain then, and maybe there's still not.

Behind us, a police cruiser pulled up in front of R. J.'s house with lights circling and a few short bleats of siren to announce its arrival. Without discussing it, we picked up the pace, speedwalking until we put some distance between the party and us.

"What do you know, T?" Brianna said. "Running from the cops together again. It's getting to be a habit." And then she laughed, but it was a hard laugh.

Tristan didn't respond. From then on, it was a quiet walk, the only disturbance the music and chatter from a few bars that we passed. The moon wasn't quite full, but it had that curious orange hue of autumn; that night, the color looked almost fake, a garish splash of paint. I tried to remember why that happened, the scientific explanation for it, but I couldn't come up with anything, and I even considered putting the question to Brianna and Tristan, but it was as if a spell had fallen over them, all marching feet and downward gazes.

Brianna lived closer to the party than I had realized; she'd gone out of her way to meet up with us on our corner. Already, the walk to the party had receded in my mind; it belonged to an earlier era.

"Well," she said, in front of a shuttered café, "this is me. See you Monday." Brianna was usually a hugger, a fan of the big goodbye after every class, but that night she walked to the door without ceremony and started to let herself in.

"Brianna," I said, before considering that I had no way to follow it up. I settled for "thanks." She gave me a small smile, I think, though it was hard to tell in the dark, and then she disappeared into the building.

I took a breath, and it was only from its rattle that I noticed I was shivering. Tristan and I looked at each other, two castaways washed up on the other side of a storm. *Ship of fools.* The phrase came unbidden into my mind and anchored there, repeating in those long seconds. I thought that he was about to open his mouth and tell me that it would never work, that we should go home and pretend that the night, the party, the kiss had never happened. And if he had said that, I'm not sure I would have had the courage to disagree.

Instead, he said this: "I think I'm in love with you. I know it, actually. It's the only thing I've known for sure since I met you in the playground."

And then the distance between us had vanished, and we were kissing each other hard, urgently, as though we were trying to save something, and the effervescent feeling in my stomach was back, its reappearance so sudden it was almost painful, as if I had chugged a can of ice-cold soda in one long swallow. We stood there, melting together, for a couple of minutes, until I got a full-body shiver. I'm not sure if I saw something out of the corner of my eye, a movement in the second-story apartment window, or if it was the mere possibility that Brianna might be watching us, but at any rate, I whispered into his ear, "We should go somewhere."

It was hardly a moment of great eloquence on my part, but Tristan seemed to understand, and he nodded, his smooth cheek rubbing against mine, and so we started walking.

I thought, briefly, that he was going to say that I had to hop the fence, and I wouldn't have hesitated to try, though it was easily eight feet tall and scaling it would have been a noisy and possibly doomed endeavor. But to my surprise, Tristan fished his keys out of his pocket and selected one that fit the padlock on the gate.

"My aunt helps run it," he whispered in explanation. "She gave me a key so I could water it on my way to my summer job in the morning." We were standing outside of a Green Thumb garden, a series of small garden plots set up in an empty lot between two brownstones. We were very close to our own block. If I squinted through the dark to the next corner, I could see the playground where I first set eyes on him, and if I had crossed the street to get the right angle, I probably could have seen my own house. But home was the last thing I wanted to think about right now. Tristan slowly, soundlessly swung the gate open and I followed him inside.

A streetlight from the other side of the street provided

enough light to see where we were walking. A few of the plots were already cleaned out, the soil turned over in preparation for winter, but most of the garden was still in bloom, tomato plants and zucchini vines starting to turn brown and withered but still bending with the weight of big fruits. One ambitious person had taken up most of his plot with a single misshapen pumpkin. Fruit trees and geraniums in big pots flourished near the back of the lot, and some benches were set among them. Behind the benches, some kids had painted the brick wall with rainbows and fat birds, and as we sat down, I traced one edge of a bluebird's wing with my index finger. It was darker back here under the trees, beyond the reach of the streetlights, and the rest of the garden looked illuminated, enchanted.

"I didn't know you were a gardener," I said.

"I'm not. I just follow Aunt Patrice's instructions and try not to kill her plants." He picked up my hand and started to trace the lines in my palm.

"Izzy, the day that I hurt my ankle, the day I ran from the park..."

"You don't have to explain."

"I know, but let me say it." He moved as though to push up his glasses, even though he was wearing his contacts that night, and then he reached for my hands again. "I wish I could take it back," he said. "I wish I'd never played that game against Hull. Marcus can get some strange ideas in his head sometimes...." He trailed off.

"It doesn't matter."

"It does matter. I have to get tougher about standing up to Marcus. We'll find a way to tell him about us. *I'll* find a way to tell him about us. But you should know that I'm sorry about what happened."

I was sorry, too. I was sorry that Hull was so brash and intractable, sorry for whatever he'd done to attract Marcus's anger in the first place, sorry that our first kiss had to be akin to an act of espionage. But to say aloud that I was sorry would sound like I was apologizing for Hull's very existence, and that was something I wasn't ready to do.

Instead I said this: "You know what my grandma's last words to me were? She said, 'It's all water under the bridge, honey.' I think my dad took it badly, like she'd given up hope, but I still find it comforting, actually. There aren't all that many things that matter in the end, are there?" If you had asked me in that moment, there would only have been one item on the list. "So don't talk about Hull, not right now. Let's talk about something else."

"Let's talk about how you kissed me at the party."

I laughed. "I'm pretty sure you kissed me, actually."

"Are you sure?" He was leaning close to me now, and the tip of his nose was brushing mine, and I could feel the warmth of his breath. "Like this?" He was still tracing the patterns in my palm, and I wondered if he could read the future there, the way Brianna believed was possible.

Our kisses this time were deeper, more searching, as

if we could divine everything about the other by the way our bodies met. Brianna was the one who knew about alchemy, and I was the one stuck on scientific explanations, but that night, it seemed plausible that a magical change in our basic makeup had occurred. A mingling of our particles, maybe. Or transubstantiation. I kissed his neck, the outer edge of his ear, and tried to sink deeper.

In a mental flash, though, I saw Brianna in the bathroom, the age in the lines of her face, and I couldn't relax.

"I'm not sure," I said, my voice teetering on the edge of the sentence, uncertain about how to finish it. "I'm not sure I want to do anything more than this tonight."

Tristan put his arms around me, looked me in the eye. "You think I care? We could do just this for the rest of the night. We could do just this forever." And in one version of the story, the one I use to make myself fall asleep these days, that's exactly what happened.

PART 2

THE KNIGHT

IF IZZY IS THE BEST DRUG I'VE EVER TAKEN, AUNTIE Patrice is one terrible comedown. She doesn't even wait for me to fumble my way to the kitchen this time, instead barging into the room, her vocal cords already warmed up for yelling before I'm fully conscious. Izzy and I stayed in the garden until the wee hours of the morning, kissing and talking. I thought I had managed to slip back into the apartment undetected, though judging by the decibel level of Patrice's first sentence, now I'm not so sure.

"Twice in one month!" she's saying. "And before you tell me that you know absolutely nothing about this again, Cherry already told me you were at this same party, so I suggest you start explaining what happened."

I struggle to free my arms from the sheets, prop myself up on my elbows. I have a pounding headache from the punch I drank early in the evening, and maybe from the wallop of adrenaline that came after it. "What is twice in one month?"

Patrice exhales hard out of her nostrils, hands on her hips, before she answers me. "Your cousin getting arrested, that's what."

"What?" That wakes me up. I remember the cop cars pulling up, of course, but I'd been certain about Marcus's ability to slip out of something as banal as the cops breaking up a party. "Yeah, we were at a party, but I left early to walk home with a friend who was sick. And Marcus was doing what everybody else at the party was doing. He was when I left, at least."

"Which was what, exactly? Playing bridge?" Auntie Patrice lifts her arms in a gesture of disbelief. "Do I have to spell it out for you, Mr. Honor Roll, that underage drinking is against the law?"

She's right, of course, so I decide not to respond by saying that she must not remember high school very well if she thinks that no one drinks at parties. Plus, my only reasonable guess about what happened is that the cops arrested Marcus before all of the other people in that house because they recognized him from the fight in the park or possibly from something else Marcus has been up to, but I don't think Patrice is going to like that explanation very well, so I don't say anything at all.

"Tristan," she says, a little calmer now, "what has gotten into you?"

There's a tiny sliver of me that wants to tell her everything, wants to construct a model of the whole messy love triangle in front of her. She's always been good to me, after all, and I know she loved my mother, probably more than she'll ever be comfortable saying. But something holds me back. Maybe it's because I can't even begin to fathom Patrice's thoughts on love. Her single friends are always giggling about online dating when they come over, but that's clearly not Patrice's style. I know surprisingly little about her personal life, even after living with her for two years. So when I sit there in bed, trying to weigh the odds of Patrice understanding young love, I come down on the side of her thinking I'm foolish. I come down on the side of her not being too excited about the idea of Izzy or, more accurately, the idea of us together.

So I decide to try a different angle.

"Nothing," I say. "Nothing has gotten into me. And it's not Marcus's fault that the police are hassling him. I mean, you know how they are; they're never going to give Marcus the benefit of the doubt."

I can feel the angry pressure build inside her as if I've turned the burner higher under an already hot teakettle. Wrong move.

"I see. It's the cops' fault. Well, let's lessen the chances that you cross paths with any of these bad cops. School, chess club, and then straight back here. Until further notice. Is that clear?"

"But I had nothing to do with this! I told you, I'd already left."

"You seem to be under the impression that this is up for debate," she says coolly. "I'm serious, Tristan. If you're incapable of following some simple rules, we're going to have to rethink your living here." She doesn't exactly slam the door on her way out of the room, but it's something pretty close.

I fall back onto the bed, pull the sheets over my face. It's irony, I guess, that up to now I believed grounding to be a pretty stupid punishment, especially for an introvert like me. On any given day, I'd rather be by myself with my chess books and my laptop, anyway. But this isn't like any other day, and having Izzy down the block, barely out of reach, is going to be torturous.

I pick up my phone and see that she's already used the number I gave her last night to text me. *You are the sugar in my morning coffee. Thanks for last night.*

You're the sweet strawberry jam on my toast, I text back, wanting her to think I'm having the same sort of average, lazy Sunday that she seems to be having. I have to see her soon. I think for a few minutes and I text her again. *Do you play chess?*

On Monday, I race to the meeting room at the end of last period, hoping to land a conversation with Mr. K before anyone else shows up. There he is, scowling at a faulty timer that he's trying to fix. When he sees me, his face assumes an expression that is slightly less mournful than usual.

"Trees-tahn," he says, "there is a new Carlsen game that you are going to find verrrry interesting."

"That's great, Mr. K. But I was actually wondering if maybe I could help out with teaching the Novice group today." My angle here might seem a little obvious, but it isn't entirely out of the blue. Mr. K often gets the kids in the Advanced group to help the beginners. Even so, Mr. K looks at me like he smells a rat.

"You want to help the Novices?"

"Yeah, you know, I've been having trouble concentrating lately, so I thought it might help to explain moves to other people. Help me focus. You know." None of this is entirely untrue, I tell myself. It's not strictly true, either, but let's not split hairs.

"Yes, if this is what you want." Mr. K sighs. "We are needing to get ready for the first full tournament. This Yuri Zhubov at Stuyvesant is looking very good this year, you know this. But this week..." He scowls, and his eyebrows encroach farther down his face. "... is okay."

I grab a seat while the other chess club members file in and write their names on the sign-in sheet. When Izzy walks through the door, it's like the whole room is brighter, lighter. She's wearing a pale gray dress, and she's like the moon sailing across the sky as she crosses to Mr. K, tells him she's new and that she wants to join chess club. He gestures vaguely at the sign-in sheet, housekeeping details not being one of his strong suits. And then she turns and sees me, and everything else drains from my head.

"It's so good to see your face," she says as she slides into the desk in front of mine. "I almost forgot what it looked like since Physics class." I get the feeling that she says perfect things like this all the time.

The room is noisy enough to cover our conversation, and we conspire briefly about how much it sucked to see each other in class but not have an opportunity to talk. "The same way it sucks not to kiss you right now," she says, and it's so hard not to touch her, my whole body aching to do it, but we're trying to keep all this on the quiet until we figure out how to handle Marcus. I texted her yesterday about the trouble with Aunt Patrice, and she wrote back that it would all turn out okay, because that was all water and we were the bridge. But today she has some new problems to add to the mix.

"I feel like people have been staring at me all day," she says. "Marcus came up behind me while I was at my locker this morning and started kissing me on the neck. Everyone thinks I'm his new girlfriend, and suddenly I'm the hottest item of gossip in a hundred-mile radius."

Like an old projector getting warmed up, my mind shuffles through the frame-by-frame of Marcus leaning into Izzy like he owns her, breathing in her smell before he presses his lips to her neck. And when she turns to face him, is there a trace of excitement in her face, the pleasure of being flattered? It's hard to swallow.

"Whatever you're thinking right now, stop it," she says. "I know he's your cousin and all, but if he could vanish into thin air that would be ideal." She drops her quiet voice down another level. "There's only one person I want. That's the truth."

Mr. K shushes the room, starts talking about using the bishop during the endgame. I study the dark waves of Izzy's hair as his voice washes over me. I want to memorize every tiny part of her. I want to know her better than I know chess.

When we break into groups, Mr. K tells Pankaj and Anaïs that they'll be helping the Novice group, too. Pankaj looks relieved, and Anaïs gives a one-shoulder shrug. I tell them that Izzy is brand-new, so I can help get her up to speed if they want to oversee the matches between the more regular crowd of beginners. Anaïs purses her lips like she's on to me, but then she shrugs the other shoulder and sighs. "Whatever." She's wearing her favorite hoodie, the one that says CLARINET FOR LIFE over one breast.

"So, how much do you know about chess?" I say as I set up a board on the desk between Izzy and me.

"Mmm, the basics, I guess. My brother's pretty good, but I stopped playing with him a long time ago because it was boring to always lose. Tristan"—she lowers her voice to a whisper again—"why is everyone staring at you? Almost like they're afraid of you?"

"Eh," I say, not wanting to sound like a dick. It's hard to keep myself from smiling a tiny bit, though. "I guess because I'm pretty good."

"Just pretty good, huh?" There's a teasing note in her voice. She sees through my cool act. "Do we really have to play? I came to be around you, not to actually play chess."

"I mean we're here, right? Might as well."

"I know. It's just..." She shrugs and screws up her face into an expression of distaste, and I can't tell if she's teasing me again. "The way my brother was always studying those endless combinations of moves. So dull, like a race with no finish line."

"Oh, no, no, no, no, no. You're messing with me, right?"

She raises one eyebrow in response. It's sexy, I admit. The rest of the classroom, with its voices and rhythmic slamming of chess timers, has already faded away. "Look, you can't play chess like a computer, memorizing every move that's out there. That's when it really does get boring. You gotta feel the energy of the game. You gotta know the pieces like they're living, breathing human beings."

"But they're chess pieces. What can you know about them besides the way they move?"

"So much. Here, hold this one." I put a knight in her palm, close her fingers around it. "You feel it? It's not that he moves in an L shape. He's smart and wily and he's always looking around the next corner. He can dodge around the enemy like no other piece can. He's brave from the very beginning, charging out in front of the line of pawns, and even if he has to sacrifice himself eventually, he can do some serious damage to the enemy before that happens."

"Uh-huh," she says, sounding unconvinced. "Tell me more."

"Well, you've got your queen, of course," I say, balancing the black queen on the tips of my fingers. "She's the most powerful piece in the game."

"I thought that was the king."

"Nah. The king might be the most important, but only because everyone has decided he is. Like divine birthright. But the queen is powerful because of what she can *do*. She's more versatile and deadly than anyone else out there. But if she's in the right position, she can protect a lot of pieces, too. And if she's lost? It's like the center has fallen out of the game. It's like the rest of the pieces barely know what to do with themselves. They get desperate."

"I see. So it's like you're telling a story every time you play."

"Exactly. A story about life."

"What about this one?" she says, picking up the bishop.

We keep going like this for a while and then finally get around to playing a game. Izzy plays like someone who is inexperienced but very smart. I like watching her think about what to do next—the little crease that forms between her eyebrows, the way her fingers never stop moving, drumming on the table or hovering in the air like little hummingbirds. Occasionally,

Anaïs or Pankaj casts a curious look in my direction, but mostly they're busy putting the newbies through their paces, and they actually seem to be enjoying themselves. They're usually losing to me during chess practice, so I guess this is a little more entertaining. I'm pretty sure I even see Anaïs smiling at one of the freshmen at one point, which I hadn't previously thought possible.

I make empty moves in order to let Izzy keep playing, to let me keep watching her, but even so, the hour passes too quickly, and as the minute hand clicks forward, I'm filled with the dread of going back to my normal existence without her.

"This was nice," she says, leaning over the board in these final slipping moments. "Maybe I could be a chess enthusiast after all." And then, she does it again, she reads my mind and adds, "But I still think that we should sneak out some night this week. After your aunt is asleep. After my parents are." At the front of the room, Mr. K tells everyone to wrap things up and put the chess sets away in the big Rubbermaid containers that he lugs everywhere.

"Where would we go?" I say, and practically wince at how lame the words sound coming out of my mouth. Why would it even matter where we go? I should say yes, yes, and only yes. But she doesn't seem to mind.

"Wherever you want to take me," she says. "Someplace in Brooklyn that you think I should see."

As soon as she says this, I feel in my marrow where I will take her. It's almost like a memory of the future, it's so clear.

"Yeah, that's exactly what we should do. Let me say goodbye to Mr. K for a second and then we can walk back to the block together." She winks at me, those beautiful eyelashes brushing her cheek, and it's one of those moments when our shared secret seems more exciting than scary.

"I'll wait for you in the hallway," she says.

Everyone else is eager to get out, get away from the school, and the classroom is empty in a few moments. Mr. K is at the desk, looking absentmindedly at the attendance sheet, which he subsequently lets fall from his fingers into the trash.

"Thanks, Mr. K," I say. I'm afraid I'll startle him, but he doesn't look up. He knew I was there all along, I guess. "Today really helped with my concentration."

He leans against the desk, his big hairy hands spread out on its surface. "Yes, yes, good. Concentration is important." I make for the door, congratulating myself on how well this afternoon has gone. That's when he calls my name again, and I see when I look back at him that his jaw is clenched with something that looks an awful lot like worry. "But Trees-tahn. Love, it always leads to suffering. You know this, right?"

THE QUEEN

THE HUMAN EYE HAS ONLY THREE TYPES OF COLOR-sensing cells, but the eye of the mantis shrimp has sixteen kinds. Scientists speculate that, because of this, they can see a far wider spectrum of colors than we'll ever be able to see, like Dorothy in Oz compared to Dorothy in Kansas. I don't know what it's like to be a mantis shrimp, but I feel like the closest I'll ever come to finding out was during those first few days with Tristan, when the world around me seemed to crackle with hues I never knew existed. I looked at a blackberry the morning after the party, with its vibrant, perfect cluster of juice-filled spheres, its purples and reds and indigos, and was fairly certain I could sense the divine in it.

"Isn't it beautiful?" I asked, holding out the berry to my

mother, who was sketching a jewelry design at the kitchen counter, and she agreed, though not before looking at me with surprise. We both knew that it was the kind of thing she would say, not me.

Tristan told me he needed time, only a little time, to figure out how to tell Marcus, and since it was so important to him, I acquiesced and agreed to keep quiet. Temporarily, at least. I steered clear of Marcus—turning a cold cheek to his affectionate greetings at school, never picking up his phone calls—and when pressed, I mumbled vague statements about not wanting to be in a relationship. I remember thinking it was a little amusing, how bewildered Marcus looked by all of this. He wasn't accustomed to being rejected. If I'd paid attention, I might have seen that I was hurting his feelings.

But I probably wouldn't have cared, anyway. I sailed through those days not caring about anything with which I had previously been consumed—my brother or my parents or my grades or becoming a doctor or what anyone thought of me. One singular thing had replaced all of that. It was a certain brand of insanity, the kind that anyone who has ever fallen rapidly in love will recognize.

———

The first night we snuck out together, I was so nervous that every ordinary nighttime sound was a panic attack in miniature. The creak my foot made on one of the stairs, the louder-than-expected click of the door latch—agonies. We had agreed to meet by the playground at a little after midnight, and while I was walking there, a bird or a chipmunk rustled in a bush, startling me so much that I thought I might pee myself. But I was the first one there, and when my heart started to slow down, I realized it was nice to be out in the world when everyone else was tucked inside. It felt like the street, the whole neighborhood, belonged to me.

And then Tristan—I can see him now, the way he looked hurrying down the sidewalk toward me, with his strangely erect posture and his floppy Chuck Taylor sneakers and his face mostly hidden inside the hood of his sweatshirt. I folded myself into him, breathed in the fresh laundry scent of him. I stood there like that for a minute, holding him, and it was almost painful, not being able to experience, all at once, all the beautiful things we were going to do together. So much of life is waiting.

"You okay?" he whispered.

"Yeah."

"Then let's get out of here."

We walked to the nearest subway station, the C toward Manhattan. The station was nearly deserted so late at night, a homeless guy napping on the bench our only company. We walked to the other end of the platform and made out for a few minutes, the curves and crevices of his body becoming more and more familiar to me. It felt, sometimes, like we were growing together, becoming grafted like trees.

The train pulled up, and there was a smattering of people in the car, so we put the make-out session on pause and huddled together in one of the two-person seats at the end of the car, holding hands.

"Where are we going?" I asked.

"It's a surprise." When I made a face, he said, "Don't tell me you're one of those people who hates surprises."

"I don't hate them. But don't you think they're overrated? Isn't one of the key factors of enjoyment being able to look forward to something good?"

"But what about wondering? What about the endless possibilities?"

"Because I'd rather think about the one possibility that's about to become an actuality." It seemed like a perfectly reasonable request to me, but he mimed zipping his lips and throwing away the key. At the last stop in Brooklyn, we got off the train.

This was DUMBO, Down Under the Manhattan Bridge Overpass, the neighborhood of warehouses turned art galleries. I'd been here a few times with my mom while she sought out inspiration or met with a gallery owner, but I didn't know it well. To be honest, it had always struck me as one of those spots that was oppressively hip, all look-at-me clothes and snotty expressions, someplace I didn't fit in, so the surprise wasn't exactly blowing me away at this point, but I was keeping an open mind. Then Tristan seized my hand and started running, and we galloped down the sidewalk, laughing our heads off. Stupid *Sound of Music*–style stuff, but I still can't think of it without smiling.

I hesitated at the entrance to the park, knowing that all of the city-owned areas were officially closed at that hour. But Tristan squeezed my hand and tugged me forward and I wasn't about to say no. I knew of this park, one of the city's slow projects designed to make New York warmer and cuddlier. Take down the deserted warehouses, clean the place up, put in green spaces and beer gardens and basketball courts and jungle gyms to suit the already-gentrified neighborhood.

"I'm surprised you like this place," I whispered as we walk-ran up the path, past the volleyball courts. "Doesn't it make you sad somehow that they tore everything old down to put this stuff up?"

"Everything changes, Izzy," he said.

"Well, yeah, but..." I trailed off, my parents' complaints about the changes on the Lower East Side clanging in my memory.

"You really think you would have moved onto my block if it wasn't changing? If it looked like it did when my mom was a kid?"

He had a point, I knew he did, and I was the last one who could say anything about it, so I didn't. I kept my mouth shut and hurried to keep up with him. But it made me a little sad, anyway.

"Here," he said, and pulled me into a playground area

with all sorts of different swings. Baby swings and swings like seesaws and swings shaped like animals.

"This is where we're going?" I asked.

He put one finger in the air like an intellectual begging to differ. "Reserve judgment," he said. He walked into an area that had the standard sling-like, rubber-seated swings for older kids and pulled one under him. He nodded to the one next to him. "Go really high and then you'll see."

I hadn't done this since I was in elementary school, and I felt a little rusty, but when I saw how enthusiastically Tristan was pumping his legs, leaning forward on the backswing to gain more momentum, I followed suit. The drop, the weightlessness, the moment of suspension. Back and forth. It felt good, the widening arc of my body through space, my long skirt flapping against my legs, and I started laughing despite myself.

And then I saw it. At the highest point of the swing, above the newish line of trees, an explosion of light that was the Manhattan skyline. In those tiny bursts of vision, it looked almost unreal, an alien landscape dusted with stars. *No wonder everyone moves to Brooklyn*, I thought. *Even Manhattan looks better from here.*

"How did you find this place?" I asked, timing the question at the moment our swings flew past each other.

"Marcus comes here a lot in the summer to watch the evening games on the courts over that way. And I wander around." I looked behind me as the swing rushed back, and I could see the white smile of Tristan's teeth, as he grinned like a little kid.

Here are the things I was thinking right then: 1) We'll be young forever. 2) We're the only people on Earth. 3) My chest will burst with loving him so much.

As I neared the end of this list, I noticed Tristan working against the momentum of his swing, legs out on the backswing, bent as he came forward. I thought that he was stopping, and there was a little pang in my heart that the surprise, which had turned out to be so lovely, was over. But then I realized that he was only trying to slow down enough to match his swing to mine, and he held out his hand and I grabbed it and we flew in perfect synchronicity. We giggled, giddy in the face of our own power; the world, the beautiful entirety of it, was spread out before us.

I don't know how long we stayed like that, held in midair by physics and elation, before we saw a flashlight slicing through the darkness behind us. A police officer or a security guard. Someone who was already yelling muffled accusations at us. Before I could think of how to react, Tristan had let go of the swing and gone sailing through the air, grunting when he landed on his still-bruised ankle.

"Jump!" he yelled.

For a split second, I didn't think I could make my body obey. I held the chains so tightly on the backswing that I could feel them tattooing my palms. But as the swing came forward again, something dropped away from me and I let go, and the feeling of floating freely in space was exquisite.

I flubbed the landing, though, almost knocking Tristan over, and we got our feet tangled as we started to run. I could hear the staticky crackle of a walkie-talkie. The flashlight, bobbing up and down, was closer now, but not quite close enough, and we ducked back into the main expanse of the park, staying in the dark crevices where the orangey light from the halogen lamps didn't fall. A few minutes later, we were crouched in a line of trees, sucking wind and gazing at the river spread out below us and the skyline looming above. A police helicopter circled over the harbor, and for a heart-stopping instant, I thought that it was searching for us. It wasn't, obviously. Everything was quiet behind us, no hint of the security guard.

"Brianna was right. This is a habit with you," I said. "We should get out of here."

"Yeah," Tristan said. "Let me rest my ankle for a minute first, though." We sat in the grass, straw-like and prickly from a long, hot summer.

"It hurts?" I asked.

"Nah," he said. "Not really. It feels a little weak, still, is all."

I put my hand gently on the edge of his jeans and slid the fabric away from his ankle. Then I leaned down and kissed it.

I could hear the long release of his breath in the dark.

"You're a magician," he said. He reached for one of my feet and slipped off my shoe.

"No!" I said, mortified. "Don't! It will smell awful! We just ran across the park." I tried to pull away, but he had a firm grip on it, and then he drew his head close to my toes and I stopped struggling, afraid of kicking him in the face.

"I love your smelly feet," he said, planting a kiss on my sole. "I love every part of you."

And then, somehow, we were rolled up in each other, our lips pressed together, the roughness of the grass under my one bare foot and the rest of the world very far away.

THE ROOK

I KNEW, WHILE SCHEMING BEFORE THE PARTY, THAT Marcus wouldn't technically know it was me, of course he wouldn't, but I did think that it would somehow alter things, that some supernatural force would shrink the distance between us and he would be drawn to me without understanding why. It would realign the stars above our heads, change the navigational lines of our lives, set us on an inevitable collision course.

When I see him a few days after the party, leaning against a locker, texting someone on his phone, I draw close to him and try to make eye contact, try to let the electricity, so potent in that dark room, flow between us again.

"Marcus," I say, catching his elbow. "Do you think we could talk?"

He lets the phone drop out of his line of sight, but he doesn't quite meet my eye. "That's right," he says. "You were gonna tell me my future." Normally, I would be thrilled with him saying this, but it isn't quite what I was hoping for this time around.

"Sure," I say. "It takes time to do it right, though. Come over sometime."

"I'm a busy man, Caballito," he says, glancing at his phone again. I feel myself bristle, because come on, that sounds like something a sitcom dad might say to his annoying kids. But then he looks at me, really looks at me, and leans in so close that his forehead almost touches mine, and I can almost feel it again, that jolt of power between us. "Maybe you could read my palm or something right here. Give me a little taste."

And then his right hand is resting in the two of mine, wide and warm and strong, beautifully shaped, the lines crossing like a net that could lift me up and out of myself. I don't know much about palmistry. It doesn't matter.

"What do you want to know?" I ask.

"Where's my love line?" he asks, so low it's almost a whisper, and his eyes follow my fingertip as it traces across his skin.

"It's here. Deep, which is good, and unbroken." I want to take his hand, entwine it in mine, lay my head against his chest where it belongs. If he would only kiss me one more time, here in the light of day, he would know, he would recognize the touch of my lips, he would be alive to the possibilities between us.

"What's it say about me and Izzy? She's been acting weird ever since the party."

The first bell of the day rings; the walls of my heart cave in. Marcus promises to find me later, but I barely register his words. It doesn't matter how much it feels like the universe has altered since the party, because when it comes to Marcus and me, it's all just more of the stupid same.

Here is the real change: My spirit has a raw, raised edge, where before I was seamless. When I see the way Marcus's face rearranges itself as he notices Izzy in the hallway, when I see the looks that she and Tristan exchange in Physics class—these things rasp against this edge in me, snag on it, tear it open again. Out of it pours a rage that I know is unfair, unwarranted, but I can't help it: It's a scar that points straight at the worst part of myself.

———

For all of my previous plotting, the moment of my betrayal isn't premeditated. I'm at the café after hours, dawdling and watching my brother play dominoes with Carlo, the one everybody calls Frodo because he looks like a hairy little troll. He's been around a lot more than usual, Hector, that is, trying to get my parents off his ass, and I've been hanging with him more than usual, too, because he's around, I guess, and because it would never really occur to him to ask what's going on in my life, and it's nice to not have to explain yourself all the time. Anyway, Frodo has started to show up more and more, and if Hector tells my parents that he's hanging out downstairs, they leave him alone, even though the real reason Frodo comes by at all is because my brother is overgenerous, if you ask me, in rolling joints for them to share.

Tonight Frodo is determined to talk about Marcus, even though it's a subject that Hector doesn't like to discuss after that close call with the police. He's not mad at Marcus, but he's keeping his distance until things blow over. Whatever: It would surprise me if Frodo has ever taken a hint in his entire life.

"He's, like, totally psycho over this girl, man. You really got to see it to believe it. I never knew that Marcus had a taste for weird *chocha*, man."

"Weird how?"

"White, for one. And not like hot supermodel white, neither. I asked him the other day if her *cuca* was paved with diamonds or some shit. . . ."

"Come on, man, my sister's standing right there."

"And he was like, 'I don't kiss and tell.' Do you believe that shit? Like he's some kind of Boy Scout or something? I don't know, man. It's crazy."

"Strange," my brother says, but I can tell he's totally checked out of the conversation.

"Whatever she's got, T wants a piece, too," I say. That's all it takes. Frodo literally jerks to attention, like he is a dog that has caught sight of a squirrel.

"What do you mean?" he asks, talking directly to me for the first time tonight or maybe ever. Boys will treat you like wallpaper whenever they can.

"Exactly what I said. I mean, Izzy's nice, but both of them?" Saying these words is like picking a scab, and I feel a tiny bit better for a few seconds before it starts bleeding.

"You think T's creeping with this girl?" Frodo says. "Because Marcus is definitely under the impression that he and this girl, this Izzy, are, like, together."

I shrug.

"Huh," Frodo says, and he narrows his little troll eyes, and then Hector changes the course of the conversation, complaining about the Jets coaching staff. The whole thing takes less than a minute, maybe, and if I was better at forgetting things, I might toss it out of my memory immediately, one little sentence about something that people were bound to notice sooner or later anyway.

I'm not so good at forgetting, though. When I read the cards tonight, I can tell that something bad is on its way. Reversed sword cards popping up like I'm stacking the deck. It's coming, the cards say to me. And when it does, I'll know who to blame.

THE KNIGHT

LIFE IS NO LONGER LIVED IN THE BRIGHT TRANSPAR-
ency of the day. It's lived in times and places owned by shadow,
in the dark spaces where skin can press against skin. At night,
we dive beneath ground, trace the train lines like water drop-
lets in the city's root system, resurface to bask in the sodium
glow of the streetlights. We prowl the nighttime versions of
Williamsburg, SoHo, Astoria, the Upper West Side. The dark
is full of strange visions: the woman in an evening gown playing the accordion on the empty F train platform; the panhan-
dler with elaborate swirling tattoos covering his face and a
pet goldfish in a bowl; the man sitting on a park bench under
a streetlamp, smoothing a surgical drape over his lap before
eating a lox bagel with rubber-gloved hands.

One night we walk past the blanket cocoons of the home-less men in Tompkins Square Park and sit on the front steps of Izzy's old building. We make out urgently there, both of us, I think, catching a trace of all the past what-ifs, all the possi-ble scenarios in which we never would have met. But then, as always, we migrate back toward home, dreading the inevita-ble rise of the sun and the struggle through the daylight hours.

She comes to chess club religiously now, so there's at least one part of the day to look forward to, but because I'm still grounded and because Marcus is still in the dark about us, it becomes a different kind of torture, strolling politely home from practice with empty air between us. Sometimes, as we walk, she tells me all the ways she would like to be kissing or touching me right then, all the things she will do to me the next time we manage to creep out of our houses in the middle of the night. She means it playfully, of course, a lighthearted flirt, but it verges on cruel. The endless longing for her is too much like pain.

We are careful. Usually. In Physics class one day, there is a lab about the diffusion of light, an experiment in which our entire lab group, me, Izzy, and two others, must squeeze into the dark supply closet to collect data. I try to concentrate on the task at hand, on the pencil marks we are supposed to be making on the wall to be measured later, charting the path of a tiny pinprick of light. I try to focus on the equation that Tricia and Deshawn are talking about. It's the dark that gets to me, even more than the sweetly familiar sound of Izzy's breathing.

The bliss of finding ourselves in our natural habitat in the middle of the long day. I find her shoulder, slide my hand over it, bite it gently. And then my fingers dip below the neckline of her dress, into the warm shelter of her bra, and I hold the perfect weight of her breast. Deshawn is sitting maybe a foot to my left, so close that I can hear when he shoves his eyeglasses higher up on the bridge of his nose. I try not to let there be any change in my breathing when Izzy reaches into my lap, feels me through my jeans.

"I don't get it," Tricia is saying, and I can hear the sound of her pencil against the wall again. "The numbers aren't going to come out right."

"It's because you're not accounting for dust particles in the air," I say, but my voice is unnaturally high and strained, almost as if I've taken a hit of helium, and Izzy laughs. I clear my throat.

Tricia pauses. "I'm going to turn the lights on," she says, and my hands, Izzy's hands, instantaneously retract, creatures scurrying back inside their shells. How ruffled do we look when the lights flicker on? It's hard to say, but Deshawn is grinning, amused. Tricia is red-faced, eyes down, scribbling in her notebook. She mutters something that might be "Jesus, you guys," or might be something about physics. I can't look at Izzy.

It's no big deal, of course. We're nothing but faces in the crowd to Deshawn and Tricia, and to them it's only a slightly funny or annoying blip in their existence. I can't help but worry, though, about what will happen when Marcus learns to see in the dark.

On our walk home from chess club, Izzy lets me know that she'd rather illuminate Marcus immediately. I know she's right. But every time I ready myself to do so, the anticipation of conflict stops me short. It's not only fear of his anger, though that's part of it. It will also hurt him when he realizes that he's lost her, when he realizes that she was never his at all. For maybe the first time in my life, I wouldn't want to switch places with Marcus.

"But we have to tell him sometime, right? Plus, he invited me to a haunted house thing this weekend and swore he wouldn't take no for an answer," Izzy says glumly, shifting her heavy backpack higher on her shoulders. I'd like to carry it for her, but even this seems like too public of an act when we're so close to home.

"Yeah, that makes sense," I say. "He loves that stuff."

Halloween is Marcus's favorite holiday, and every year, he finds new ways of embracing it with a manic glee. Not many high school students still get dressed up for Halloween; they're too afraid it will make them look like dweeby trick-or-treaters. But Marcus always wears a costume and, of course, because it's Marcus, it never seems anything but cool. Every year I've been in Brooklyn, he has dragged me and a few others to one of those expensive haunted houses in

Manhattan, practically knocking down the door as soon as the place opens for the season, bribing some manager dude he knows to get us all in for free. He hasn't mentioned it to me this year, though. In fact, Marcus hasn't said a lot of anything to me over the past couple weeks. Last weekend passed without a single chess match. Entire lunch periods have slipped past listening to K-Dawg drone on about obscure hip-hop, playing tracks no one else cares about on his phone, with barely a word exchanged between me and Marcus. I wonder if he's pining for Izzy or if it's merely my guilty paranoia at work.

"I hate Halloween," Izzy says, the closest to whining I've heard from her. "Aren't there enough real-world horrors without creating more? And I don't want Marcus groping me in some haunted house."

"You'll think of a way to shut him down. You're brilliant at thinking of excuses."

She laughs, but there's an edge of annoyance in it. "People are good at all sorts of things. It doesn't mean they necessarily want to do them."

"I know. It isn't fair. We'll think of some way to tell him about us. But...you know. Delicately."

"But why? What's he going to do?"

I think of that time Marcus showed up with a bloody shirt and a secret to keep, imagine that blood as my own. "Nothing. Probably nothing."

"So what am I supposed to do? About the haunted house?"

"There's always a group of people who go with him. It will be more like a party than a date. I'll figure out a way to come, too." This will be no small feat, since I'm technically grounded, but I can tell that Izzy needs a promise right now.

Izzy makes a face, obviously displeased.

"Don't worry. We'll figure it out."

"*We* will?" She cuts her eyes sideways at me.

"You're mad. I get it." I take her hand and squeeze, and though the thought of someone witnessing this makes me sweat, the gesture seems to relax her. "Besides, you can't stay mad at me for long. I'm too cute."

"Maybe I'll stand you up tonight," she says, but I can tell by her half smile that she's joking.

"You wouldn't," I say. "It would kill me."

————

Marcus has been keeping scarce around the apartment lately, and though I'm pretty paranoid where he's concerned, even I know that the most likely explanation for this is that he's steering clear of Auntie Patrice. Usually, he's able to divine better than anyone when she's acting prickly; it's as if there are special sensors installed in his brain. And though I've caught the edge of her anger this time around (see my de facto house arrest), I know the real reason she's up in arms is that she's worried to death about Marcus. Patrice never got into the kind of trouble that Marcus flirts with every day. She kept her nose clean, got good grades. Brooklyn was different then, and it's one more sign of Auntie Patrice's resolve of pure steel that she became who she is. Almost superhumanly, she seemed to elevate big portions of the neighborhood right along with her. But Marcus is made of gold, not steel.

Anyway, it's a little surprising when I wave goodbye to Izzy and go home to find Marcus sitting at the kitchen table with Patrice. She hasn't even changed out of her work clothes yet, but she and Marcus are drinking big glasses of maubey and laughing. None of the quiet brooding I've seen at lunch. There's an electrical kick in my blood as I take this in, like I've consumed too much caffeine.

"T, my man," Marcus says. "The person I've been looking for."

"Really?" I say. "What's up?"

"I've been telling Auntie about Izzy."

My brain splinters into all the different things that this could mean. I look to Patrice's face for clues, but it's a closed book. She leans back in her seat and folds her arms like she's in a business meeting, trying to make a tough decision.

"Izzy, down-the-block Izzy?" I say stupidly. "What about her?"

"Yeah, of course that Izzy, the one you're friends with, bro. I see you guys walking home together," he says. I wonder for a moment if it is beyond Marcus to command an army of spy drones. Then he adds: "It's all good, though. I like that you guys get along. You're both smart. That's why I want her to come over to dinner and meet Auntie Patrice, too, since she's the smartest person in our family."

This feels like a trap. I stand there dumbly, my thoughts a hundred hamsters on a hundred different wheels, until Patrice smiles at me and says: "What do you think, Tristan? You think I will like this girl?"

If I were the person Izzy wants me to be, this is when I'd say it: It doesn't matter if you'll like her. She's mine. She wants me. You can't have her, either of you.

Instead, I swallow hard and say: "Of course you will. Everybody likes Izzy."

Patrice sighs. "Marcus swears that this girl is a good influence on him. That she is what has been keeping him out of trouble these past few weeks. So I certainly want to meet her."

"T is right. You'll love her." He pushes back from the table as though it's all settled. "Let's do it this Saturday."

"What about the haunted house?" I ask. It's the wrong thing to say. Something passes over Marcus's face; he hates the idea of anyone discussing him behind his back.

"What about it?"

"Izzy asked me about it today. She said you and a bunch of people are going next weekend, but you haven't said anything about it to me."

"You're jealous, my man?" Marcus laughs. "I thought you didn't even like the scary stuff. But okay. We'll have dinner here and then go into the city afterward."

"Tristan hasn't been going out these days," Patrice says.

"Can we make an exception?" I ask.

"Come on, Auntie. Spring him from his jail cell," Marcus says. "He's not the one who got in trouble, anyway."

"I'll think about it," Patrice says. Then she stands up and walks toward the hallway, touching Marcus on the shoulder as she goes.

Marcus doesn't say anything after she's left the room, so I go to the sink and get a glass of water. My hand is shaking. It's not fear, exactly, but a sense of things rushing toward some point that I can't quite see. In chess, this is called *zugzwang*: the setup in which a move, any move, is a bad one.

"There's some talk out there, T, about you and Izzy." I don't turn around when he speaks. The air feels thick, viscous, and the words hang there like scum floating in a pond.

"Who's doing the talking?"

"What does it matter if they're only talking shit?"

I steady my hand, turn around, and drain half the glass of water, trying to read Marcus while I'm swallowing, but he looks like his usual calm, cool self.

"She's right for me, T. I know it. Thing is, she doesn't seem to know it yet. Maybe the family dinner will convince her I'm serious about her."

I set the glass down on the counter but keep my fingers wrapped around it, as though it's a rock that can steady me. "Izzy's great," I say. "But there's a lot of shit going on with her family. I think she's too on edge to be into the idea of dating someone right now." Nothing I'm saying is a lie. What Izzy and I are doing isn't dating. It can't even be compared to dating. It's swimming, flying, devouring, living.

"She tell you that?"

"Nah, man. But I can tell from the stuff she does say, you know? Plus, I still feel like an asshole every time she mentions her brother."

I can't tell if this is helping or merely digging me further into a hole. Marcus stands up, his muscles noticeable even under his loose clothing. "But she talks to you anyway, T. She likes you. That's why she'll listen to you when you tell her what a good guy I am." Marcus walks over to put his glass in the sink. He's wearing basketball shorts even though it's chilly today, and he smells of sweat.

"What did you tell them?" I ask.

"Huh?"

"These shit-talkers. What did you tell them when they started spreading rumors about me and Izzy?"

"I said you were family," Marcus says, crossing to the front door. "End of story." I stand there for a long time after he's gone, wondering about that word, *family*, and whether it still applies to anyone in my life. It's a word that has been sapped of its power.

THE QUEEN

WHEN I THINK BACK ON THAT TIME, I STILL HAVE SO
many questions: 1) How did we get by on so little sleep? 2)
How did my parents or brother never hear me sneak out? 3)
What did we talk about for all those hours? There are no sat-
isfactory answers to the first two questions. We didn't go out
every night, so there were some nights of rest, but even so, I
remember functioning in a twilight state, a confusion of waking and dreaming. But such petty concerns don't matter when
one is so young, so in love. And as for my family, I suspect that
maybe they did hear me once or twice. The old house creaked;
no door latch is perfectly silent. Hull could have been keeping
a detailed log of my comings and goings to use against me in
some later argument, for all I know. And my parents...maybe

they thought I was going on a walk because I couldn't sleep. Or maybe it was the least of their worries.

But I do know the answer to the third question, because I still strive to recall every detail: the way his face looked when he first told me about his parents and his childhood, the words he used to describe Marcus, the tone of his voice when he remembered certain chess matches and what it had felt like to play them. Sometimes I truly believe I can recall every word he breathed in my presence. We talked until our throats went dry and scratchy, and then snuck into a park or the garden and kissed until our lips were raw.

For as vivid as these memories are, they've all become interchangeable pearls on a single winding strand; I can no longer remember which night was which, or in what order the conversations happened. The exception was the night he invited me to have dinner at his aunt's house, a request that flooded me with both anxiety and self-importance as I imagined him claiming me as his girlfriend in front of Patrice. Then he clarified that Marcus would be there, too. I could hear the apology in his voice for this, and it irritated me, as it likewise irritated me that he'd been sitting on this piece of news all night, only breaking it out as we rounded the corner onto our block. But that's not why the night in question sticks in my mind.

As we passed the playground, Tristan seized my wrist so suddenly and squeezed it with such pressure that I almost cried out. Then I saw what he was looking at and bit my lip.

People standing near the monkey bars where Tristan and I had first met, three of them, only about twenty yards from us. Tristan pulled me down into the shadows cast by a bike rack. I recognized his voice first, the same that accosted me in the hallways of Carl Sagan—Marcus. The other two were unfamiliar, but they looked tall, big, not at all like Marcus's ragtag band of usual followers. My breath sounded too loud in my ears, and I tried to hold it, tried to catch the muffled words. No luck. My calf cramped, and I gritted my teeth so hard my jaw ached, trying to stay perfectly still and quiet.

In the darkness, I thought I saw a glint as something passed from the hand of one of the men and into Marcus's. And then they drifted away, Marcus down our block, the two men up the street past the community garden. We didn't move a muscle until they were out of sight.

"Tristan," I whispered, my heart trembling like a panicked Chihuahua. "Was that a gun?"

"A gun? Nah, I didn't see a gun."

I ran a replay in my mind, trying to assess how sure I was about it. "Something scared you, though."

"Those guys," Tristan said. "I think I recognized them. I thought Marcus stopped hanging out with them a long time ago."

"Why would he stop hanging out with them?"

"I don't know, exactly. Look, let's go home. We can get a couple of hours of sleep." We crept forward, feeling shaken, feeling watched, and gave each other a perfunctory kiss good-bye in front of my house.

Nothing terrible had happened. I kept reminding myself of that as I snuck up to my room, but even after I'd crawled beneath the warm comforter on my bed, there was still a deep metallic chill in my bones.

THE KNIGHT

WHEN I GET HOME, I LIE DOWN ON THE BED, BUT SLEEP won't even flirt with me. I count sheep, mentally run through one of my favorite matches, Kasparov versus Topalov in 1999. I flip the pillow over to feel the cooler side. I grope in the darkness for my phone in order to check the time: 4:38 AM. Since the phone is already in my hand, I call my father's number to hear his voice on his voice mail, but to my surprise, he picks up.

"Hey, Dad."

"Tristan?" he says, as though anyone else would greet him in this way. There are voices in the background and spurts of laughter; he's probably hanging out with musicians or bar owners after hours. "How's Brooklyn, son?" It's so perfectly my father to not even bother to ask why I might be calling him at this strange hour.

"Brooklyn is..." My tired brain searches for the right description. "Brooklyn is changing."

"Huh," my dad says, possibly distracted by someone else in the room. "You doin' all right, kid? You're not getting in any trouble, are you?"

"No," I say, though I'm not sure which of his two questions I'm answering. "Can I ask you something?"

"Sure, sure," Dad says, and I can hear a squeak like a door opening and then quiet in the background. It's not much, but I feel good that he's making space for this strange call from out of the blue. "What's up?"

I haven't really considered how to ask this question until my mouth starts moving. "When you think back to the days when you and mom were first together, is there anything you regret?" I can feel the intensity of his listening on the other end, and then there's a long sigh, and he takes his time before he starts talking.

"I guess," he says, "that I regret any of those little things that got in the way of me spending more time with her while she was still on this earth. I wish we had argued less, slept less, worried less about what people were saying about us. When I think about that time, it's so obvious that your mom was the only thing that mattered, and I wish I had acted like that was the truth, every day, all the time." He coughs, audibly inhales, and I wonder if he's smoking again. "Does that answer your question?"

"I think so."

"Okay," he says, and then sighs again. "I'd ask who she is, but I expect you'll tell me when you're ready."

"I will." He's given me the answers I knew he would, the ones I'd probably been fishing for when I dialed his number.

We say our goodbyes and when I hang up, I pick up the photo that's been lying facedown on the bedside table. From what I know of my mother, she wasn't the type to regret much of anything. "But what about Marcus?" I say to her smiling, newlywed face. "What's he doing out this late?" She refuses to give away any secrets before I fall asleep.

———————

To say that Izzy is not particularly pleased about the family gathering would be an understatement. This is when we were supposed to be coming clean to Marcus, but instead I'm asking her to turn our lies into dinner theater. Even so, Izzy is curious about Patrice. "What should I talk to her about?" she's been asking, and "Which dress of mine do you think she'd like better: the navy blue one or the green one?" Izzy knows almost everything about me, but I've probably soft-pedaled the fact that Patrice is pretty hard for me to figure out myself. I'm not sure how smooth I can make this meeting.

"Also, have I mentioned that I hate haunted houses?"

"You've mentioned it a few times," I say to her, the day before the dinner. We're lugging plastic bins full of chess sets to Mr. K's car, helping out in service of getting a few minutes alone. I had to practice one-on-one with Mr. K in advance of a big district tournament coming up, even though my head wasn't really in it. Izzy spent the period slumped across from a freshman with adenoid problems, looking miserable. "I'll be there, though. It'll be all right." I set the bin down on the asphalt in order to wrestle with the tricky lock on the back of Mr. K's ancient dark blue hatchback. It is true that I'll be there, Patrice having been convinced to officially relax her imposed rules for the evening. I'm less certain about the latter part of my statement, since I'm dreading the outing myself.

"Sure," Izzy says, heaving her box into the back of the car. "What could go wrong?" She smiles wryly at me, and I kiss her impulsively, out in the light of day, just once.

———

Izzy has chosen the green dress, I notice when Patrice answers the door on Saturday night, and she looks even more beautiful than she usually does: a flush to her cheeks, her hair pinned back from her face. She's carrying a big bouquet of orange daylilies.

"How lovely," Auntie Patrice says, accepting them. "It's been ages since I've bought cut flowers. They live for such a short time." I can see something crumble a little in Izzy's expression, but she's careful to keep her smile in place.

"It was so nice of you to invite me over," Izzy says, her eyes straying nervously to mine.

"Marcus wouldn't take no for an answer."

"Oh, yes, sure," Izzy says. "I've noticed he's quite good at that."

They both laugh uneasily. "That boy," Patrice says. "And now he's not even here yet."

"Come in and sit down, Izzy. I'm sure Marcus will get here soon." I try to make my voice calm, to cool the sizzle of nerves we're all feeling, and Izzy looks as though I've tossed her a life jacket. When she answers, her voice sounds almost normal.

"Thanks, Tristan."

"You call him Tristan?" Patrice asks as we walk into the kitchen. "I thought I was the only one who used his full name."

"Oh, well. It's a nice name. I like names that are unusual. He's the only Tristan I know, and now you're the only Patrice I know." I know that Izzy means this sweetly, but I see Aunt Patrice bristle a little, since all the kids on the block, and even some of the former kids who are long since grown up, call her Ms. White. She goes to stir something that's bubbling on the stove, and that thing happens when I see, really see, the apartment for the first time in a long time, see it as though I'm Izzy looking at it with fresh eyes. The walls have decades' worth of paint layers on them, and the refrigerator is old and shabby. For the first time, I consider how strange it is that Izzy has never been here, and I've never been beyond the doorway of her house. From what I glimpsed, their refrigerator probably isn't shabby in the slightest.

"Smells delicious," Izzy says, though it sounds a little like she's trying to convince herself that it's true. I can tell from the smell of cumin and ginger that Patrice is making something Caribbean, and I wonder if she cooked this up as some sort of test.

"So, how are you liking the neighborhood?" Patrice asks nonchalantly, though I know it's a question with a million land mines attached.

"I like it a lot," Izzy says. "Tristan... Tristan and Marcus said that you've lived here a long time. You must have seen a lot of changes come and go." I internally applaud this admirable evasion, really the best one she could have managed under the circumstances.

"Not so many until these past few years," Patrice answers breezily, her back turned, but then the front door swings open and Marcus's voice fills the apartment.

"Knock, knock!"

"You made it," Patrice says as Marcus swings around the doorframe into the kitchen.

"Of course," Marcus says. He goes in to kiss Izzy on the cheek first, and she stiffens, causing his lips to land somewhere near her right ear. He draws back, a little stung, but then walks over to kiss Patrice, who is pretending to still be absorbed in her cooking. He doesn't glance in my direction. It's like I'm a ghost in this scene, no one even seeing me aside from Izzy, who stares at me, her uneasiness contagious.

"Let's eat," Marcus says, rubbing his hands together cartoonishly. It's strange that he hasn't greeted me, but I chalk it up to his moodiness, and things start off smoothly enough. Patrice has gone all out on dinner, with roti and stewed goat and her famous macaroni and cheese, and even though I know that Izzy is largely vegetarian, she tastes everything anyway and praises it enthusiastically. Marcus talks about how smart Izzy is ("Maybe even smarter than T," he says, finally looking me in the eye, and I respond with "Gee, thanks for saying so, Marcus"), and Patrice likes that, and they talk for a little while about her plans to be a doctor. I let myself relax a tiny bit, like a belt that is loosened one notch after all that mac and cheese.

"You see how Izzy is always thinking ahead?" Patrice says to Marcus. "I keep telling you that that is what you need to do."

"How do you know I don't think ahead?" Marcus says. "I got all sorts of plans."

"Phoo. This one and his plans," Patrice says, rolling her eyes heavenward. "I'd like to know what you were planning when you decided to have your run-in with the police."

Izzy pretends to be overly invested in her plate, not wanting to get in the middle of this one. I'm with her.

"Aw, come on, Auntie," Marcus says. "There's no planning around that. They say that only three things are certain in life: death, taxes, and the fuzz." I laugh at this, but Patrice's smile is tight. She turns her gaze to Izzy.

"Izzy," she says, "I see why Marcus has been talking

about you so much. But what is such a nice girl doing with a troublemaker?"

She means it lightly, I think, more a product of her constant teasing of Marcus than an attempt to catch Izzy out, but I watch as Izzy's face passes quickly through a palette of colors, landing on a mottled pink.

"I been wondering that myself," Marcus says, smiling sweetly at her. He reaches toward her, and Izzy lets him cover her hand with his giant one.

"I..." she says, faltering, then stops and tries again. "Even though I'm sort of a nerd..." She stops again, clears her throat. "Marcus and Tristan were both so nice to me, before they even knew who I was, really. And that must mean that they're..." She pauses to swallow, and then finishes in a small voice. "That they're pure of heart. Both of them. Maybe more than I am."

There's a quiet beat in which all three of us take in what she's said. "That's very sweet, Izzy," Patrice says finally. "You're a very sweet girl, I can tell." Patrice is smiling now, but it's as opaque as the dining room table. My eyes flick over to Marcus and I realize he's been studying me while Izzy has been talking. What does he see there? The thought cartwheels through my brain: He knows. I don't know how, but he knows.

"Tristan," Patrice says, turning to me, "why don't you help me clear this and get the dessert?"

I comply, though I don't really want to leave Izzy alone at

the table with Marcus. He's speaking in a low murmur to her, only a few paces away in the little dining area, but I can't make out their words over the clink of dishes in the sink. I start to cut the sweet potato pie, still straining my ears, while Patrice pulls out forks and plates.

"Boy, you're making a mess of this," Patrice whisper-hisses at me, and I think she's talking about the pie at first, but she lays a hand on my wrist and I see her expression is serious. "Why didn't you tell me Izzy was sweet on you? You're going to mess around and get that girl hurt, Tristan."

"How did you . . . ?" I ask dumbly, as if it matters.

"I'm not a blind person is how." She aggressively stabs some crumbs with her thumb and flicks them into the sink. "You've got to tell Marcus right away. You know how he can be."

My face feels too hot and the sight of the pie, quivering and glistening, makes me feel queasy. I close my eyes. "I know. I'll figure it out."

"And what about you? You have feelings for her?"

I can't look at her. There's too much I could say in response, so I don't say any of it.

I hear her release of breath, an extended whistling exhale through her teeth, which says more clearly than words that I'm a fool to have gotten myself into this situation, but when I open my eyes, she's already gone, walking back to the table with the two slices of pie I cut. I hurry up with the other two and slink back to the scene.

"I can't understand how being scared feels good," Izzy is

saying. She's smiling in a good-natured way, though I know she could fill a book with the things she'd rather do than go to the haunted house.

"Gets your blood pumping," Marcus says, bumping a fist against his broad chest. "Makes you feel alive."

"If you say so."

"Maybe I should come, too," Aunt Patrice says. "You wouldn't want me to miss all that fun, would you?" She might be teasing Marcus. Or she might be thinking that he's less likely to kill me if she's present, which I find oddly heart-warming. They gaze at each other across the table until Marcus laughs.

"You're too live already, Auntie. Eat up, guys, we have to get going." He tucks into the pie with enthusiasm, and Izzy sets about emptying her plate one polite bite at a time. It's one of Patrice's specialties, but the filling turns to paste in my mouth, so I mostly push it around my plate. It's a brilliant orange, the color of Halloween.

THE ROOK

She's surprised and happy to see me outside the Delancey Street subway station, and I smile and wave, feeling the whole time like the worst kind of snitch. Marcus and T are on either side of her, and for a second, I have a hot rush of blood to the head that tells me to grab her hand and run.

"Caballito," Marcus says, before I have time to make good on my impulse, before Izzy has a chance to say a word. His voice still makes my heart pound faster, even though I'm beginning to wish it didn't. "I didn't realize you were coming tonight."

That's because I wasn't invited, not really. I happened to be cleaning up in the back of the restaurant when Hector's phone, lying nearby, buzzed with a text message from Marcus. *Chateau Fright, tonight at 9.* Then, a few beats later, *Something might be poppin off. You should be there.* I heard Hector coming back from the bathroom seconds before the phone buzzed for a third time, so I never got to see what that one said. I went back to unscrewing and filling salt and pepper shakers without saying a word, but I was dying to know if it had anything to do with Frodo. Later, I asked Hector, trying to play it cool, whether he was going to this haunted house thing I'd heard some people talking about. "Nah," he said, almost under his breath. "Too much goin' on without any more of Marcus's shit." Then he looked at me and poked a threatening big brother finger at my nose. "You shouldn't be there, either. Not if you're smart."

Smart was never my strong suit. I can't say that Marcus looks pleased to see me, but he doesn't bother to dwell on it. As for me, I don't have a plan (the last one worked out so well), but I couldn't sit at home, wondering what was happening, so instead I link my arm through Izzy's and drop a little behind the boys as we walk to our destination.

She tells me that they're coming from a dinner with Tristan and Marcus's aunt, which must have been a big helping of awkward. "The whole thing was such a bad idea," Izzy whispers to me. "Like we're supposed to be one big happy family now?"

"A seriously dysfunctional one," I say.

"Sorry," she says, squeezing my arm tighter. "I didn't ask how you were."

I start to mumble something, but then someone leaps, shrieking, into our path. It's just stupid fucking Tyrone, but my nerves are shredded and I make a noise like a frightened pig. Izzy jumps, too. It's the usual assholes, cackling and bumping shoulders with Marcus: Tyrone, Frodo, K-Dawg, plus a couple trashy-looking girls I don't recognize. No Roxanne; maybe she's wised up and broken up with Tyrone again. They don't even bother to acknowledge me or Izzy. I see Frodo lean in and whisper something in Marcus's ear. Izzy's arm feels very small and thin wrapped through mine.

We move in a herd down the street, and the boys are loud, getting in everyone's way on the sidewalk. An older white lady coming from the opposite direction grits her teeth, shoots us a look. *Stupid kids*, she's probably thinking, or maybe something much worse.

The haunted house is really a dingy-looking office building with some cheesy fake hotel signs out front. I never come to these things because they're too expensive, but Marcus knows someone who works here, of course, and we get waved in without tickets. In the waiting room, made up like a hotel reception area full of cobwebs and already half-full of tourists clutching bags from souvenir shops, the boys are noisy, teasing one another, reminding K-Dawg how loud he screamed last year when someone put a bag over his head. Frodo is trying to impress the unknown girls with a tattoo he got a few days ago. I can't work out what it's supposed to be at first, and then I realize that it's the outline of Brooklyn with BK in the middle, red and puffy and totally butt-ugly, but the dumb girls make appreciative noises like it's so smart and novel. Only T is silent, watchful.

A guy comes out in a tuxedo and a stringy wig, made up to look like a zombie innkeeper. He gives us his spiel about people checking into this "hotel" and never checking out again, about how it's not the fault of the Chateau Fright if we all die of heart attacks, etc., etc. Then he tells us that only a certain number of people can go through at a time. He starts to herd the tourists that were there ahead of us into a little roped-off area.

"Seven more," the innkeeper drones, and Marcus throws his hand in the air like a little kid.

"Come on, T," he says, dragging his cousin into the line with him. The three stooges fall into step, and the two girls shuffle in to take the last two spots, leaving Izzy and me for the next group. Fine by me. "Aw, no," Marcus says when he sees the shape of things. "I gotta go through with my girl." Maybe it's the casual ownership in his tone, or maybe it's some protective impulse, but I step right up to him.

"What, you think we're not tough enough to handle it on our own?" I snap, throwing my arm around Izzy. It's a tone I never take with Marcus, and it feels good. "Go on."

The boys hoot at my rudeness, and the tourists look sort of scared, but Marcus does a little bow.

"Sure. If you say so, Caballito." But he's smiling as if he planned it this way all along.

Then the innkeeper grumbles at them to hurry up, and they're gone, disappearing through the door in a puff of dry ice, and I feel like I can relax a little. I don't have time to say a word to Izzy, though, because another employee comes in to wrangle the next group and stops short when he sees her. He's done up like a bellboy with boils and decaying skin, seriously gruesome, so it's weird when he announces flamboyantly, "Izzy! You've come back to us!"

Izzy laughs, something I haven't seen her do much of lately, and hugs the bellhop. "I do still remember how to get to Manhattan," she says.

"Well, you wouldn't know it, missy, from how often you visit," he fake-scolds her. "Careful, don't get my makeup on your shirt." I feel out of place and start to recede toward a wall, but Izzy reaches over and tugs on my wrist.

"This is my friend Brianna," she says, and the kid makes a funny little noise, maybe a coo of curiosity about me, and extends his hand, palm down. I shake it awkwardly.

"Philip," he says to me, and then, before I can respond, he heaves a sigh. "I can't be breaking character like this. I'll totally get fired, and it's the closest thing to a paid acting job I've ever had."

"Congratulations?" I offer.

"It's a start," Philip says. He smiles at me for seemingly no reason, and for the first time, I can tell that he's probably pretty cute under the hideous makeup. "Well, one twin has made a surprise return," he says to Izzy. "When are you going to do the same?"

Izzy shrugs, instantly uncomfortable. "It's complicated."

Philip laughs. "Hull has a way of making things complicated. But we love him anyway. Can you hang out later?"

"I can't. I'm with a big group of people who are ahead of us. I'll visit soon, though. I promise."

"Promises, promises. Call me, why don't you?" Philip says, but he's limping away already, gasping and croaking, harassing the new bunch of visitors that has started to fill up the waiting room.

"Would you believe that he was the first person I ever kissed?" Izzy whispers in my ear, and then laughs at whatever face I make in response. "We were in sixth grade. I had no idea he was gay. I was...maybe a little naive. He's always been a good friend, even if I don't see him much anymore." She smiles, remembering something maybe, but then goes quiet. Philip shepherds us toward the dark doorway, beyond which can be heard yawps and screeches and maybe even the faraway buzz of a chainsaw, and the group snakes its way into the building's shadowy interior.

The haunted house is a pretty decent one: people in bloody makeup jumping out from dark corners, some cool special effects that make it look like there are ghosts drifting out of the paintings on the wall, a guy who really does look a lot like Jack Nicholson in *The Shining* chasing us through the last part. Izzy has a serious startle reflex, and she spends most of the time gripping my left arm so tightly that it's asleep by the time we reach the end. I'm distracted, though, thinking of Izzy and how she smiled when she saw Philip and how her life must have been pretty nice before she met all of us. It makes me feel jealous. It also makes me feel sharply all the ways I've messed up since becoming her friend. Philip wouldn't have ratted on her and Tristan, I'm pretty sure, especially to someone as dumb as Frodo.

The room where everyone is dumped at the end of the tour is brightly lit and disorienting, not to mention crowded with people buying stupid T-shirts and mugs, and maybe it's the fluorescent lights or maybe she really was scared, but Izzy looks a little green.

"Where's Tristan?" she asks. "Where's Marcus?"

I look around, see nothing but strangers, and I realize she's right; it's strange they haven't waited for us here.

"Bathroom?" I wonder hopefully, but Izzy shakes her head.

"I have a bad feeling," she says, and then she makes for an exit, not the main glass ones where people are pouring out onto Delancey, but a fire door, marked with an exit sign but painted the same color as the pinkish-brown walls. And maybe she's a little clairvoyant, Izzy, because no alarms go off and I can hear Frodo's high-pitched little whine as we push our way outside.

We're in a narrow side alley, rare enough in New York,

but here we are. It smells like a homeless person or two sleeps here on the regular. That's not the most important revelation I have, though, in those first few seconds after we step outside. That prize goes to the fact that Tyrone has T up against a wall, shaking him so hard that his head knocks against the bricks like a door knocker. Even K–Dawg is bouncing on his toes like he's ready to fight. The skanky girls have fled, probably at the first sign of trouble. Marcus looks grim; he's holding a phone out toward T, thrusting it close to his face, and Frodo is spitting words excitedly.

"This is the first good photo I've been able to get, sure, but it's not like this hasn't been going on for weeks. Shit, my man, you know it's true."

Marcus drops the phone (Frodo's, I guess) and punches T in the face, the kind of clean, hard punch that makes a terrible crunching sound on impact. And at the same time, or so quickly afterward that it feels like the same time, Izzy lets out a shriek so loud that it raises the hair on my arms and probably halts traffic for a block in all directions: "Stop!"

Marcus pays no attention to her, lands another punch. Izzy's on him immediately, trying to pull him back. "What is this about? What are you doing?" she's demanding. She looks tiny compared to him, he could break her in an instant, and a jab of real fear stabs me: We shouldn't be here.

I scoop the phone up from where it's landed a couple feet from me and look at the screen. It's an image of Izzy and T, standing next to some beater of a car, their faces close to each other. It doesn't look good, but it's probably not as damning as it could be. Frodo is just as shit at being a spy as he is at everything else. I glance at T, but it's impossible to read his face since his nose is a fountain of blood and he's thrashing around, trying to break free from Tyrone.

"I don't care what Frodo says!" Izzy is shouting. "Since when do you care more about what that asshole says than your own cousin?"

Marcus flexes the hand that he used to punch T. "Thing is, my cousin hasn't said much of anything to defend himself."

Izzy's face is flushed now; it's the thing that shows up best in this shadowy alley. She's still hanging on Marcus's elbow, staring straight up into his face. I can hear that her breaths are ragged, but when she speaks, her voice is low and even and that makes me feel strangely proud of her. "Well, then listen to me instead."

Marcus takes the hand he's been flexing, rests it on Izzy's collarbone. As recently as a few days ago, the sight of Marcus touching Izzy would have flooded me with envy, but now I look at that hand, at the raw knuckles, and thinking about being in her place makes me feel a little sick. "You're saying you haven't been creeping with T?"

Everything has become suspended; even T has stopped struggling. Everyone's eyes are on her, waiting.

"Yeah, right," she says. "I'm such a slut. I've made out with your cousin. Just like I've made out with that leper back there in the haunted house." She reaches up and flicks his hand off of her. "Enough, Marcus. Enough."

It's some quick thinking. It's a pretty good try, given the circumstances, but when I look at Marcus's face, I know it hasn't quite worked. He looks wounded, like something inside him has worked itself loose. It's a face that I've known so well, one that I've dreamed about, loved, but I can't help what springs to my mind when I see it, a moment later, twist with rage: *He'll kill them both.*

"Izzy . . ." he says.

No one finds out what he means to say, though, because a mountainous security guard comes crashing around the corner at that moment, followed by one of the missing girls, and I can see now that she's younger than I first thought. Not trashy, just a scared fourteen-year-old wearing too much makeup.

"Can't have y'all makin' trouble out here," the guard growls in a bass voice, and he rolls his bulk right up to Marcus, sensing somehow that he's in charge here. "Get outta here." Tyrone lets go of T, and T kind of slides down the wall, but Marcus looks anything but scared and gives the guard a disdainful thousand-yard stare. The guard is unarmed. There's not even real menace in his voice.

"This here, is this your property?" Marcus says. He runs his hand over his head like he's contemplating something. "Nope. I can't see how any of this is your business."

The guard looks taken aback for a second, and then he

looks pretty pissed off. "You got some nerve, kid. I *said*, get outta here." He takes a walkie-talkie out of his belt. "You don't want to get tangled up with the police."

Slow, like a cobra backing down, Marcus takes a step away from the guard, puts his hands up in false apology, and then he turns to Izzy.

"Let me guess," he says. "You're staying with T?"

She doesn't answer. With a tiny head movement to signal his lackeys, Marcus ambles toward the street.

"See you later, cuz," he says over his shoulder, grinning broadly, and his friends laugh and whistle as they follow him.

THE QUEEN

HE WAS A PRINCE, REALLY, THE SECURITY GUARD. HE let us follow him into his tiny office, where he gave tissues to Tristan for his nose and to Tina, Frodo's would-be friend, for her running mascara. Then he let us watch on the security monitors as Marcus and company lingered in front of the haunted house, waiting for us, then got bored and wandered off.

"You leave and go straight home," the guard told us. "But not the route you'd normally take." He walked us to the door. "Y'all are good kids, I can tell. You don't need to go getting mixed up in that." This made Tina burst into a fresh round of tears, and she ran off, disappearing down Essex Street. I wondered, much later, if she remembered any of our names, if she heard about anything that happened after.

Every time we passed beneath a streetlight, I could tell that Tristan's face looked terrible, already puffy and misshapen. He told us that Tyrone had gotten a couple of punches in before we'd shown up, but it had been the first one from Marcus that might have broken his nose. Brianna told him it didn't look broken. I thought it did, but I kept my mouth shut. Other than that, we didn't say much, just walked down Delancey, hands shoved in our pockets and our eyes darting around for any sign of Marcus and the others. Luck was on our side; we never saw them.

It felt like a small victory when we got to the bridge, as though we'd made it, we'd gotten away. And then a second later, the thought rushed at me that we were never going to get away, because we were going back to the neighborhood, where Marcus was always half a block away. But my feet kept moving, because where else was there to go? We joined the flow of people, Hasidic Jews and hipster twentysomethings, walking up and over the bridge on their way back to Brooklyn. In front of us, a girl with an elaborate floral neck tattoo leaped onto the back of her boyfriend. Cheerful Technicolor graffiti decorated the concrete. It was Saturday night, and I felt like we were the undertakers who had shown up at a birthday party.

The one good moment was when Brianna stopped walking and pulled something out of her pocket. "Frodo's phone," she said. "He forgot to take it back." I started to reach for it, wanting to see for myself how bad the photos were, but before I could, Brianna took a slow, major league–style windup and sent the phone flying over the high fence railing and into the East River. We were far too high to see the splash it made, but it was satisfying all the same. Tristan laughed, even though the movement caused him to wince and finger his tender jaw.

When we arrived on the Brooklyn side, Brianna hopped on a bus toward her parents' restaurant, but Tristan and I kept walking, partially out of habit and partially because we were in no hurry to get home.

"Marcus will calm down," I said. I knew that this was wishful thinking at its finest, but I let myself keep saying the things I wanted to hear. "That's what people do. He was angry, but now he's cooling down somewhere."

"Or he's stewing in it, getting angrier."

"But he's your family. He'd never do anything to truly hurt you."

"Right. He feels betrayed by his family. No one ever does anything irrational when they feel that way."

South Williamsburg was eerily quiet, a world away from the bars and restaurants that lay to the north. We had the sidewalks mostly to ourselves except for a few men in their big fur hats running errands as Shabbat came to an end. I thought about their families waiting for them. I thought about ours waiting for us.

We came to a larger cross street and ducked inside a

bodega to buy a cup of ice to hold against Tristan's nose. On a wire rack by the door were a bunch of cheap Halloween costumes, polyester fabric tucked into cellophane packages.

"Wait," I said. "Are any of these big enough to fit us?"

I didn't have to explain. We bought two of the white *Scream*-style masks that came attached to black cloaks. They were designed for people much shorter than us, but even so, they covered us down to the waist. It would have to do. When we were a few blocks north of home, we put on the masks and parted, Tristan circling around to the end of the block closer to his building, me heading straight for the corner where my parents' Brooklyn dream house stood.

My blood echoed unpleasantly in my ears, the throb of nervous fear, but I reached my porch without seeing Marcus or Frodo or anyone else, and I quickly switched to feeling silly for thinking the disguises necessary. I pulled the mask off and peered down the block where I thought I could see Tristan's door open just long enough for a ghost to slip inside.

Home. I leaned against the inside of the door, my eyes closed, and allowed myself a moment of thinking about our old apartment, the smell of the foyer, the twenty-six steps (a flight of twelve, then seven, then seven) up to our floor, the wobbly table next to the front door that held my parents' keys and umbrellas and whatnot and that must have been left behind during the move. That building had felt like home. For a second I felt sorry for myself, for having been uprooted and transported away from that safe haven. For half a second, I felt sorry for my brother.

"You've been out trick-or-treating, I presume?"

I jumped, startled, and lowered the Halloween mask from where I'd been clutching it to my chest. Hull was coming from the direction of the kitchen, holding a steaming mug. It smelled like the dandelion tea that I'd thought only my mother could stomach.

"Something like that," I said. "Where are Mom and Dad?"

"Reviving date night." The way he leaned casually against the newel post, newspaper tucked under his arm, made him look like he was about forty. "Reclaiming their identity as a couple, I think they said."

"They're such love children sometimes. I bet Dad wore that cologne that makes everyone gag. Sandalwood Sunset."

"Everyone except for Mom. Turns her on."

"Ew," I said. "Don't be gross."

"Come upstairs," he said, in a voice that was quiet, almost shy. "Keep me company."

And so I followed him into his room. I hadn't set foot in there for weeks, and it was reassuring to find that it actually resembled a bedroom now, though it was missing some of the things that had been hallmarks of his room in Manhattan. The poster listing all the Supreme Court justices in order of appointment, the carefully arranged collection of presidential biographies, the bust of Winston Churchill that he kept on his desk—all gone. I had to toss aside a book called *The Drama of the Gifted Child* and a biography of Elon Musk before I could drop into his creased leather desk chair.

"So, honestly: Where were you tonight?" he said, folding himself cross-legged onto the bed, carefully, so as not to spill the tea. His feigned nonchalance made my skin prickle with irritation.

"Long story," I said. "Plus, definitely none of your business."

"Okay, whatever. But you didn't look very happy when you came in."

"We both know you're an expert on happiness."

He shrugged.

"Why didn't you ever tell me about the day in the park?" I said. "About Tristan?"

"Who's Tristan?" he asked, honestly bewildered. I shut my eyes, counting the seconds it took him to figure it out, marveling at how little we now knew about each other. I got to a full seven before he said, "Oh, the chess player?" Another short pause. "Wait, are you involved in ... *une affaire de coeur* with that guy?" I reopened my eyes in time to see his mouth drop open with the realization. Seven seconds to figure it out. Not bad, really. We were twins, after all.

"I guess you could say that."

He cleared his throat with a careful little cough. "Wonders never cease. But isn't he the patsy of that thug down the block?"

I wanted to snap that Marcus wasn't a thug, but after the events of the evening, I wasn't sure anymore. "Way to always bring nuance to your judgments, Hull."

"That guy has an arrest record a mile long."

"How do you know that?"

Hull sighed. "The internet exists, Izzy."

"Yeah, but he's a minor and . . . you know what, don't tell me. Surely you have better ways of spending your time than digging for dirt on Marcus." Of course, I was itching to know what he had found, because the memory of Marcus that night in the playground, that flash of metal in his palm, was looming large in my memory, but I didn't want to give Hull the satisfaction.

"Look, I know you're going to say that I have no right to interfere, but you shouldn't mess with them. You should cut this off and run in the opposite direction. You should trust me on this one."

"Sorry, but you don't seem to be a trusted authority figure on how to deal with our neighbors. And besides, what do you know about Tristan? You didn't even remember his name."

"They don't care about you, Izzy," Hull said. "They're not who you want them to be." His voice was soft, breaking it to me gently.

"Who's *they*?" I asked, daring him to say something truly racist, so I could dismiss everything he was saying, so that his warning would lose all of its credence. But he was too smart for that.

"The world, I guess."

"So that's it? We go through life not trusting the world? Never trusting anyone but ourselves?"

We studied each other for a few seconds. He looked small to me, sitting cross-legged on the bed, sort of fragile, like a kid at story time. It occurred to me then that he might be right, that maybe I'd spent too long being told that I was special and that I could achieve anything, when in fact the world was out to break me. "I think that's right," he said, finally. "Sad but true."

"And you still think I'm naive if I disagree?"

He didn't answer, merely stared down into his tea.

For years, talking to Hull had almost always made me feel better, but that night, I felt exhausted and panicky. We were receding from each other's grasp, and maybe we'd already reached a point at which the changes were irreversible. I pushed myself out of the chair, but before I left, I summoned up the energy for a moment of courtesy.

"You know, I haven't been so good these past couple months at paying attention to what's going on with you. I assume you're class president again?"

Hull smiled. "Nah. I missed the election while I was

in the program. But it's all good. I'm a new man now, Izzy."
Something about the way he said it was both sad and kind of
admirable, and I improvised a little salute in his direction.
Hull was doing his best to look out for himself in a world he
believed to be cruel, and I couldn't blame him for that, not
really.

I heard him quietly say our twin word as I was walking
out the door, but I was too heartbroken to say it back.

THE KNIGHT

SUNDAY IS SUPPOSED TO BE FOR LAZY UNWINDING, FOR recharging before the week starts again, but I awaken this morning with a ballooned face, a dagger-in-the-eye headache, and a sinking acknowledgment that I have a chess tournament at some school out near Coney Island that I've neglected to prepare for. I also can't manage to scrape up much enthusiasm for showing my face, either to Auntie Patrice or to whomever is sitting outside my building right now, ready to beat the living crap out of me at the first word from Marcus.

I need Patrice to drive me so I don't get jumped by Marcus or one of his henchmen on the walk to the train. No one will touch me if I'm with her; they're not that stupid. After sitting in bed for a few minutes with my head in my hands, marinating in my own dread, I pull on some clothes and prepare to bite the bullet.

The joke is on me this morning, though, because there's already a note from Patrice saying she has some Green Thumb event in Queens, and she's already been gone for half an hour. With heavy fingers, I dial Mr. K's number. It's out of his way, but I already know that he'll say yes and I already know that I'll feel guilty about it.

After twenty minutes, I hear his Ford Escort wheeze around the corner before I see it. It rolls up in front of the building and slumps against the curb. Taking the stairs, I feel like one of those lab rats that learn to be fearful, anticipating a static electricity shock from the floor of their maze. Even familiar territory feels dangerous.

This is not simple paranoia. The car is right in front, only a few steps from the door, but that gives me enough time to notice that Tyrone is sitting on a stoop across the street, watching me. He grins, slides one index finger across his throat as I dive into the passenger seat.

"So we are ready, yes?" Mr. K says, with as cheerful a tone as his voice ever has, which is to say, not very.

"Sure," I say. "Let's go. I'm pretty sure I've made us late already." I'm careful not to look through the driver's side window toward Tyrone.

Mr. K puts the car in gear and glances at me sideways as I wipe the sweat off my forehead. He makes a tiny harrumph as he realizes I've been punched in the face, and I'm worried he's going to put it in park again. But instead he sighs, eases the groaning Escort toward Franklin Avenue.

"I am not liking what I am seeing," Mr. K mutters. "This is not good. This is because of the girl, yes?" I don't have a good response, because it is about Izzy, but about much more than her, too. So I stay quiet and close my eyes, listen to Mr. K cluck wordlessly like a mother hen in the driver's seat all the way to Coney Island.

———

A few times, looking down at the chessboard, I've thought about what it actually represents, what a battle must have looked like back in the ancient days when the game was invented. The spears, the clubs, the battle-axes, the maces. The mangled limbs and cleaved skulls. How close the participants had to be, face-to-face, as one drove a blade into the other's flesh. That's what we're really talking about every time I take a piece.

I'm consumed by thoughts like these during the tournament, my nose throbbing in sympathy with the gore streaming through my imagination. I win two matches, though one is on a prayer and a stupid misstep on the part of the Korean girl I'm playing, whose eyes fill with frustrated tears before the match is even called. On a normal day, I'd feel bad for her, but I'm reduced to a more primitive state of mind. Maybe she was distracted by my pulverized mug: good. The third match twists out of my control, though with a desperate, last-ditch effort, I manage to achieve a draw. Out of the corner of my eye, I can see Mr. K take all of this in, his hands stuffed deep in his armpits, his eyebrows drooping. I know he's disappointed in me.

I'm not matched against anyone from Westcroft, but I run into Dorie between the second and third rounds. She's wearing a silver raincoat, even though it isn't raining today, and she has Mike Huckabee cradled in one arm; he squeaks as she plays with the fur on his head.

"Damn," she says. "Who did that to your face?"

It's refreshing, I guess, that someone is willing to say it instead of carefully avoiding my face with their eyes, like all of my teammates did, but that doesn't mean I'm going to answer the question.

"Well," she says, dangling the guinea pig in front of my face, "Governor Huckabee would like to remind you that you're always welcome at Westcroft." Her white gloves smell strange, as if she's worn them for days without washing them. The guinea pig bicycles his rear legs furiously in protest, and I feel for him in his helplessness. Dorie whisks him back into her arms and gives me a wave. "Later, gator."

I watch her go, letting myself imagine what it would be like to go to Westcroft. In my mind, the school has morphed into a fortress that Tyrone and Frodo and even Marcus would never be able to breach. Maybe thick walls aren't a good enough reason to transplant my life again, but I can't keep myself from being tempted by the possibility.

Marcus has been battering his way into my thoughts all day. I imagine him in lots of different escalating scenarios, wondering where, if at all, a line would be drawn. Would he hurt me? Clearly, yes. Would he tell Tyrone or, God help me, Brianna's brother to do whatever they wanted to me? Absolutely. Would he throttle me, stab me, gouge my eyes out? Would he run me over with a car? Would he slip a draught of poison in my drink, lance me with a medieval spear? If Izzy was right and he was buying a gun the night we saw him in the playground, would he ever press the muzzle to my temple?

This is a team competition, at least, and since Pankaj and Anaïs and some sophomore whose name I forget are all playing well, we easily secure first place. I talk Anaïs and her dad into giving me a lift home so that I don't have to endure dismal warnings or, worse, silent disapproval from Mr. K. Anaïs and I sit in the back seat like little kids on a playdate, the flowers her father brought her lying on the middle seat between us. She's had a good day, won all three of her matches, chatters about them happily in the car, not even bringing up the clarinet. It's only when we're nearing my block that she turns her attention to my split lip and swollen nose.

"So what happened to you, anyway?"

"Long story," I say, scanning the shadows outside the car window for any sign of Marcus. My heart is starting to race, and I think again of swords skewering flesh.

"Boys will be boys, Anaïs," her father chimes in from the front seat, as if he really has any clue what he's talking about.

"Well, see you at practice this week," she sighs while I nervously flirt with the door handle, readying myself to make a frantic dash to the door. "You're welcome. For the ride."

"Yeah, thanks, really nice of you guys." I say the empty words, but my body is already in flight. I scurry, unprotected, a crab without a shell. I would almost welcome the relief of someone sliding obliquely forward to put me out of my misery. But no one does.

Upstairs, the apartment is dark. Patrice has gone out again. I don't even bother turning on the light. I lean against the inside of the door, slide down to the floor, waiting for my lungs to unclench. This isn't a person I recognize, this victim of my own terror, but I can't help that every time I close my eyes, Marcus is there, blood on his shirt, battle-ax in hand. Instead, I dig my phone out of my pocket.

Come away with me, I text to Izzy.

Where would we go? she responds a minute later.

"Anywhere," I say to the empty apartment. "Anywhere."

THE QUEEN

THERE'S ALWAYS THE OPTION TO SAY NO TO THE WORLD. You can wear masks to hide from it, you can shut yourself away from it, you can put all your energy into trying to protect yourself from it. That was Hull's choice, I think; he saw himself as a lone warrior, doing battle against everyone on the outside. But that's not me. It's never been me, and it certainly wasn't me after I fell in love with Tristan, after a part of the outside found its way in, after it wended itself inside me and took root there. That's the kind of thing that can only happen when you choose to say yes instead of no, and even now, I can't bring myself to believe that it's a bad thing.

I was thinking about all of this when I got Tristan's text message on Sunday night, and a few hours later, unable to sleep, I was standing outside Tristan's apartment building, shivering and staring up at the small square of glass that was his bedroom window, still lit when almost all of the other windows in the building had gone dark. There was a narrow, weedy space between his building and the next, the same side as his window. Here are the things that occurred to me: 1) There was a fire escape, and even though Tristan's window wasn't directly accessible from it, I thought if I could lean out a little bit over the railing, I could reach far enough to knock on the window, and 2) Saying yes to the world should be proclaimed loudly, with a grand gesture, not with a quick text message.

From the ground, I could barely touch the bottom of the fire escape ladder with my fingertips. I had to scramble, the toes of my sneakers scrabbling for purchase against the brick wall, and pull myself up until I managed to hook my legs through the bottom rung, and then I had to swing myself upright. It took a few tries, since I hadn't done anything remotely like that since I was about seven years old on the monkey bars, but it felt exhilarating when I managed it. My arms already felt gelatinous and my palms were scraped up from the rough metal, but I thought, *Say yes*, and started climbing, trying to be as quiet as possible, lest someone on one of the lower floors hear me and spot me creeping past their windows.

Four stories feels a lot more significant when you're not inside a building but rather perched on the outside of it on a flimsy Erector Set of rust. The lights were on in his aunt's kitchen, and for a second my breath froze in my chest at the sight of the same table I'd sat at little more than twenty-four hours before. But no one was there.

The bedroom window was farther from the fire escape than it had appeared from the ground, and I would have to sling at least one leg over the railing in order to reach it. Also, I was pretty sure that it wasn't only my fear that made the railing seem wobbly and ready to fall off. I took one last look down at the ground, but it was too dark to see much of anything. I gripped the loose railing in my hands, afraid to think about the physics of it for too long, and heaved my right leg over it.

I wasn't brave enough to pull my left leg over as well and lean out over open space, so I could only reach far enough to give a feeble knock on the window frame. His face appeared immediately anyway. He fumbled to put on his glasses, and his lower lip dropped, forming a fishlike gape. Maybe it was the goofiness of his expression or maybe it was the sudden realization that there was absolutely no way I was going to be able to pull myself over to and through the window anyway, but I started laughing with more than a tinge of hysteria. Tristan was now sticking his head over the sill.

"Have you completely lost your mind?" he hissed. "Get back onto the fire escape. I'll come around to the kitchen." I was still laughing as I swung my leg back over and waited for him, and my muscles were shaky and weak both from strain and my giggling fit. Tristan wasn't laughing, though, as he struggled to heft open the stubborn kitchen window enough for me to crawl through.

"Are you trying to get yourself killed? Resorting to unusual methods to make our situation worse?" he whispered.

"Of course not," I said. "I was saying yes."

"Yes to . . . ?"

"To running away with you."

And so we did.

THE ROOK

I GO BY IZZY'S HOUSE EARLY ON MONDAY MORNING, because ever since I left them on Saturday night, I've felt an ugly tremor in the cosmos, a hideous foreboding. I called her multiple times yesterday, in the few seconds when I managed to slip away from bussing tables at Sunday brunch service, but by the time the dinner shift ended, she still hadn't called me back. Maybe it was guilt that made me mix up an anti–love potion late last night—a rush job, to be sure, but the best I could do on short notice—but it felt like more than that. It felt like a last-ditch effort to push the future back up onto its fulcrum, to keep it from crushing us all.

And so I tuck it in my bag, the bottle of murky amber liquid, and I pedal in a fever to her massive house, ring the bell even though it's barely past seven. It's her dad who opens the door, his hair still sticking up in the back like a child waking up from a nap. Is there suspicion in his face when he looks me over? There's certainly confusion; he has no idea who I am, though we've been introduced once or twice.

"Um, hi. Sorry to bother you so early, but Izzy and I had plans to go to practice for the, um, for the chess team this morning, so…"

He's already nodding, acting like he knows about this fictional practice. "Oh, sure, sure, hold on a minute." He turns back into the house and calls "Izzy!" up the stairs, and then his rich-person politeness kicks in and he motions for me to come inside. "Do you need juice or coffee or anything?"

"I'm fine."

"Izzeeee! Your friend's here!"

There's motion at the top of the stairs, but it's not Izzy. It's her brother.

"She's not in her room," he says.

"Well, where is she?" her dad asks. "Did she leave for school already?"

Hull shrugs. I can't tell if it's a trick of the light, but his face looks like it holds complicated secrets, and my heart plummets. He disappears into the shadows of the second story.

Her dad is turning back to me, offering apologies, saying that she probably forgot, that I probably missed her by a hair. But somehow or other I already know that I'm too late.

THE KNIGHT

Izzy wants to go straight to Port Authority, buy bus tickets to Atlanta, and deal with the consequences later. I can see that she is absolutely serious about this plan, and it scares me a little, the degree to which she is committed. Maybe she's right; I can't tell anymore if a southbound Greyhound is what I meant when I sent her that text message. Still, I imagine my father's surprised and not-exactly-pleased face when I show up in Atlanta, imagine Izzy's impotent rage when they force her, a minor, to return to her parents in New York without me. I need to think. I need time to think.

We creep beneath the city like rodents seeking shelter in a familiar burrow, and we ride the trains endlessly, talking about what Marcus would or wouldn't do. We are capable of convincing ourselves of all sorts of things that probably aren't true but might be, and eventually we become sick of it and stop talking and fall asleep against each other, her mittened hands clutching mine, my chin hooked over the top of her head.

I wake up with a gasp of breath, as though someone who was choking me in my sleep has suddenly released me. It's rush hour, and the car is a crush of neckties and school uniforms heading downtown. People in business suits are shooting us little poisoned glances, irritated that in the sprawl of sleep we've taken up too much space. We're on the B train somehow, even though I don't remember transferring to it. I shake Izzy awake.

"This is Ninety-Sixth Street," the recorded subway voice announces, and without discussion, we pull on our backpacks and scramble onto the platform.

Ascending into the open air, it becomes easier to breathe. Even during the morning rush, it's relatively quiet up here, in the borderlands of Central Park. I can sense Izzy's displeasure at our lack of direction, though, like an insistent thrum barely under the audible range.

"Let's walk in the park for a while," I say. "We can figure this out." I don't say that this is a chess strategy more than a life strategy: Sometimes you have to play for a while and buy yourself time before the endgame becomes clear to you. But she nods and adds that we should eat something, so we walk over to a deli on Columbus Avenue to buy egg and cheese on rolls, New York's greasy and blessedly cheap solution to breakfast. It's not until we're about to enter the park, paper bags in hands, that a cop steps in front of us.

"A little young not to be in school right now."

He's smiling, but not in a particularly friendly way. His radio crackles, and I can see the butt of his gun out of the corner of my eye, daring me to look at it directly.

"We're students at Juilliard," Izzy says smoothly. "No classes this morning."

"Huh," the cop says. "College kids? You some kind of baby geniuses or something?" He laughs, a phlegmy heh-heh-heh, like it's the funniest thing he's heard for a while.

"It's hard being this smart," I say, attempting a polite smile. It pulls at the scabby seam of my split lip.

The cop stops laughing. "Must be a burden," he says. His badge says DEATS, a stupid name. If he asks us for ID, this adventure is over. "Whatcha studying over there? Acting, I bet." He smirks.

"Nope," Izzy says, a cool arch in her voice. "The actors are morons. I play piano, and he's a cellist."

"Real shiner you got there," he says, ignoring Izzy. His eyes crawl over my face. "How'd you come by that?"

"Just in the wrong place at the wrong time, I guess." My voice sounds tight, unnatural. I can't help it.

"I'd say." Officer Deats studies me for another uncomfortable beat, then flicks his bulgy little eyes in Izzy's direction. "And you're all right, miss?"

She nods, slips her hand into mine.

"All right," he says, stepping aside a few inches. "Get out of here, then." We have to step off the dirt path to avoid brushing the hard dome of his belly. We're only a few steps away when he says, "Hey," and as I turn back to face him, a wave of irrational fear crests inside me. We look at each other, Officer Deats and I, and every stupid little infraction of the law that I've ever committed goes pinwheeling through my brain.

"Don't do anything to make me regret letting you go," he says. "You understand?"

I nod, because yes, I do understand.

"What bullshit," Izzy says when we're barely out of earshot. "It's a crime now for me to walk into the park with a black guy?" I hear anger and defiance in Izzy's voice, but none of the panic that's still thundering through my chest.

"A black guy who looks like he gets into fights. I'm guessing that, in his mind, you're not the one who's committing the crime, Izzy."

She looks, for a moment, like she has more that she wants to add, but instead, she clamps her mouth shut. We haven't said much about race to each other, and that's fine with me; most of the time, it makes me feel like the love between us trumps everything else. But it throws me off-balance, how surprised Izzy is by the cop's words, how indignant. Didn't she ever consider that this would be part of dating me? Her face goes impassive, takes on a blank glassiness, something I've only seen happen on the occasions when talk of her brother starts to get too emotional, so I drop the subject, even though part of my brain snags on Officer Deats and trails like a thread behind me.

We find a bench and sit to eat our sandwiches. The ground is lower in this section of the park, like we're down at the bottom of a bowl, and the buildings rise around the rim on all sides, watchful. Two middle-aged men on the tennis courts swat at a ball, but they keep hitting it out of bounds, and their feet drag, joyless, along the pavement as they walk to the fence to retrieve it. The sound of an ambulance spirals up out of the unseen Upper West Side, rising in tone like a bomb siren. The bites of roll stick in my throat. I don't want to be sitting here.

"Come on," I say. "It's cold. Let's eat while we walk." It's true; it's unseasonably cold today, and we both should have chosen warmer clothes. But, really, it's not the chill I want to walk away from; it's the strange loneliness that has set in. Izzy's still far away, lost in thoughts that she's not sharing, but she follows.

The cold air nips at us as we circle the reservoir. In the distance, the reservoir's fountain shoots into the air, the powerful gush of it shattering on the wind as it falls. It's early enough that there are still dogged runners doing their laps around the water, and I get the abrupt urge to join them. I swallow my last bit of sandwich and take Izzy's elbow, pull her into a trot with me. She's reluctant at first, dragging me back to a walk, but I smile at her, coaxing without words, and she relents. We break into a slow jog. We go on like this, for a minute maybe, our backpacks thumping against our hips, our breath coming harder. The fountain shifts shape as we round the curve of the reservoir. It is a feather, a mountain, an icy staircase, an arched doorway. Then Izzy speeds up, and then I speed up, and we run faster and faster, until we are passing people and our panting turns into laughter and everything but her face is a blur. We are leaving the world behind us. It is the two of us again, alone, and it is beautiful.

———————

"What if we told the school about what Marcus did to you? Would they expel him?" she asks. We're heading south, pretending we have a destination.

"Maybe," I say. I don't want to add fuel to the fire that is Marcus. I want him to leave me alone, alone with Izzy, and getting him expelled isn't the way to achieve that. But Izzy and I promised, after we reached the southern end of the reservoir and slowed to a walk and caught our breath and leaned into each other, that we would discuss any option we could think of, so I don't tell her that getting the school officials involved is a terrible idea.

"I still think we should tell your dad what's going on. What if he can come up with some other relative you can stay with, even if it's only temporary?"

"There's a reason I live with Patrice, Izzy. She's the only viable option."

"What if I agree to be Marcus's girlfriend for a while? So he can see that I'm not that much of a prize."

"You're kidding, right?"

Izzy sighs, exasperated. "Of course I'm kidding. But we're both supposed to be coming up with ideas."

I do have an idea, one that looms larger and larger as the only real choice, but I'm not ready to say it aloud yet. I need to sit with it.

"I get my best ideas when I'm asleep," I say. "Do you think we could find a place to rest for a while?"

Izzy thinks the Shakespeare Garden might work, so we walk past the theater and search for a comfortable bench. I don't see what's very Shakespearean about this place, aside from some little plaques with quotes. There's a massive holly bush, more like a tree, with some words from *As You Like It* at its base. MOST FRIENDSHIP IS FEIGNING, MOST LOVING MERE FOLLY. Neither of us says the words, but I can see Izzy's eyes scan over the line, take in the meaning.

"Maybe the Ramble instead," she says.

I don't know it until I'm there, but the Ramble is exactly where I've wanted to be ever since Marcus punched me. The trees are crowded close together, and the pathways form a twisted labyrinth, snaking up and down small slopes. I lose my sense of direction almost immediately, and the lattice of branches provides the illusion of being far from New York City.

"Maybe we could stay here," I say. "Live in Central Park forever."

"Maybe," Izzy says. Her eyes have dark circles under

them. It has only been a couple hours since we woke on the train, but it is as though all the sleepless nights from the past few weeks have descended upon us at once. She droops, and I can feel the weight of our situation on my own eyelids.

Approaching the far end of the Ramble, we find a bench. The voices of birders and tourists float up from the edge of the lake, no more than a few dozen yards away, but if I softly recite the opening lines to "Verses Upon the Burning of Our House" into Izzy's ear, I can't even hear them. "In silent night when rest I took, for sorrow near I did not look..." We are asleep in seconds.

In my dream, I spiral upward, above our sleeping forms. I see us there on the bench, hunched protectively around our bags, barely touching. We are Hansel and Gretel in the wood, beleaguered siblings instead of lovers. From a bird's-eye perspective, I watch Marcus walk up the path toward us, but then I drop back down into my body as he approaches. He stands over us, as if he is weighing a decision, and I am paralyzed as he does, unable to turn my head to look at Izzy, unable to move a fraction of an inch. In the distance, I can hear a dog howling, so mournful that I am certain it has lost its way home. Marcus bends toward me, his face looming larger and larger, his lips slightly parted, but I am unsure whether he is about to kiss me on the forehead or bite me like a vampire. I wake before he can do either, my limbs jerking wildly.

Izzy is already awake. "I'm tired of being outside," she says. "It's cold." She might be talking to me, or she might be talking to the squirrel, made brazen and fat with human handouts, who sits almost on her shoe, staring up at her. "Shoo," she says, and he reluctantly scampers away.

"It's probably warmer in the sun," I say. "Let's walk."

After the comfortable closeness of the Ramble, the wide-open expanse of the Sheep Meadow feels exposed and ugly, but we trudge toward the far side, searching for something that neither of us can name. We are not planning to end up at the Chess and Checkers House, but here we are, as though it has dragged me slowly across the park, a metal filing to a faraway magnet. I've been here a few times, especially in those first heady days in New York, when it felt like a miracle that such a place existed. The central enclosed room isn't open on Mondays, but a few games are in process on the circular porch, mostly old guys who have suckered tourists into playing with them. Izzy and I slide into seats on opposite sides of one of the tables, even though we don't have any pieces with us. To our left, a guy with a gold tooth is explaining the game to a pig-tailed blond girl, whose father hovers over her shoulder.

"Look at this one!" Gold Tooth says. "It's a knight!"

"Horse!" the girl says. "Neigh!"

"That's right, that's right. It moves like an L. You know L?"

It's cute, this mismatched pair, and part of my brain knows it. But there's a cynical voice inside me that wonders how large of a tip the dad, in his polo shirt and tennis shoes, is going to kick this hustler at the end of the lesson.

"I think we need to tell your aunt," Izzy is saying. "Are you even listening to me?"

"I know," I tell her. "I know I need to tell Patrice. But I'm trying to make up my mind about some things first. Because I don't want Patrice to make up my mind for me."

"What things?" Izzy asks, narrowing her eyes. I hate when she does that. It makes her look like a different person, not my gentle, wide-eyed Izzy.

"I think I can get a scholarship to go to a different school. One of the fancy schools in Manhattan that stakes a lot on their chess team. They asked before, and I turned them down without ever telling Patrice. But they can win state this year, maybe nationals, if they have me on their team, and that's why I think they'll let me transfer. Why they'll go out of their way to let me transfer."

"What school?" Izzy asks. Sometimes I forget that she's been a New Yorker for far longer than I have.

"Westcroft."

"Ohhh." She nods, but I can see something draw tight behind her calm mask. "The sweater and necktie set. My brother would die to have an offer like that." She clears her throat. "You should do it. You should accept it. I can't believe you didn't tell me this was an option until now."

"I don't want to go."

"Why not?" she asks. "Westcroft is a great school. Everyone says so." There's the tiniest tremor in her voice.

"You know."

Izzy shakes her head, not meeting my eye.

"You," I say. "Of course. You."

I don't know how much she needs that answer until I've already said it, until she puts her forehead down on the chessboard so I can't see her choking down tears. There are other reasons: Mr. K and his belief in me, not being able to live with Aunt Patrice, having to be the new kid again, a lingering loyalty to Brooklyn and Sagan High School and, yes, Marcus, too. But I don't say any of this. I lean down and kiss the part in Izzy's hair.

"I can't be the reason you don't go," Izzy says, her voice muffled.

"I haven't decided yet," I whisper. "Besides, we have to talk about what you're going to do. You could come with me to Westcroft."

"Fat chance. I'm not a chess prodigy, Tristan. And my parents don't have the money for that school."

"You could go back to your old school."

"Maybe," she says. "Maybe." She takes a deep breath, raises her head. Her face is dry, but the skin around her eyes is raw and pink. "Could we get out of here? I have an old friend who lives near here. It's just...I don't want to make an important decision while I'm cold and miserable and tired. You know?"

"I know."

I'd rather go back to the Ramble, but we leave the chess tables and walk toward the perimeter of the park as Izzy texts her friend. The sun dips lower behind us, the shadows lengthening into late afternoon, as we abandon our urban wilderness for the Upper East Side.

THE QUEEN

I STEERED US INTO A SLEEK APARTMENT BUILDING ON Madison Avenue. The lobby was a cave of white marble, and there was a glass sculpture hanging from the ceiling that looked like an enormous purple sea anemone preparing to descend and feed. We approached the curved white reception desk and the doorman stared at Tristan's black eye, made a face like he had caught the scent of something rotten.

"Stetman," I told him. "In 21A." He looked at me for the first time. "He's expecting us."

The doorman gave a reluctant nod.

In the elevator, I could hear Tristan steady his breath, but before I could say something about the doorman, the doors opened and we were in front of apartment 21A. The doorman must have called up, because the door burst open without either of us knocking.

"Two Izzy sightings in a single week?" Philip proclaimed as he pulled me in for a hug. "Nothing less than an unparalleled delight."

The moment Philip squeezed me in that easy, uncomplicated hug, I felt a burden lifted. We had met when we were five years old. We had witnessed each other's most awkward haircuts. We had been star mathletes together in fifth grade (a fact I had sworn never to reveal should he become a famous actor). And he knew my family—liked them, even. I didn't have to pretend to be anyone around him.

He drew Tristan and me into the apartment as if he'd been waiting for us all day. The apartment was exactly as I remembered it: big, full of light and bookcases and graceful modern furniture, the kind of place that most New Yorkers only dream about. When we were kids, he would have birthday parties here and invite our entire elementary school class. The final one, when we were in sixth grade, had been when Philip was obsessed with *The Great Gatsby*, and his mom had served us virgin cocktails in fancy glassware. I couldn't help but smile when I glimpsed the big living room where Kaleo Perkins and Hull had taught everyone how to do the Charleston, which they had learned specifically for the occasion. I caught Tristan looking at me out of the corner of his eye, his expression apprehensive, so I wiped the stupid grin off my face and introduced the two of them properly.

Philip gave us glasses of water at the long marble counter in the kitchen and nudged a bowl of fruit toward us. "Look, I know we just met, Tristan, but... are you guys all right? Those bruises look painful. And Izzy, honey, don't take this the wrong way, but I've seen you look better."

Something tightened in my chest. Tristan was looking down at his hands, and I hoped that he didn't hear anything accusatory in Philip's question. I knew that his worry came from a decent place.

"To be totally honest, I'm not sure if we're okay or not," I said. "I know I shouldn't have shown up here without asking you, but we needed someplace to... think things through, I guess."

Philip nodded. "Well, this is a someplace. I have to go to work at Chateau Fright in a half hour, but you can hang out here, of course. No one will bother you."

"Won't your parents mind?" Tristan asked.

"My father's in Argentina on business," Philip said. He rolled his eyes. "Izzy knows how often he's around. And my mom is at a fund-raiser for..." He walked over to a wall calendar hanging near the door, completely full of small, neat handwriting. "What is it tonight? Sudanese orphans, looks like. So she won't be back until late, but she won't care if you want to spend the night. She'd be happy to see Izzy again."

In response, Tristan gulped down his water in one go and asked if he could use the bathroom. Philip directed him around the corner and after he left the room, Philip leaned over to me and punched me in the arm.

"Well, look at you. I never thought that I'd see Izzy Steinbach in love."

I squirmed, not used to admitting that fact. "How'd you know?"

"Because you're so *worried* about him. You've always been unflappable, even when we were little kids. And now... you are *flapped*, girl."

"I guess I am. But, Philip, if you have something critical to say, keep it to yourself, okay? I can't take it right now."

Philip frowned, hurt. "Hardly. I gotta ask, though: Did he get punched in the face because of you? Do you have men fighting over you?" I cringed, and Philip burst into laughter. "Livin' the dream," he said, and I laughed a little, too, and it felt good to see the situation with something other than utter gravity. Then Tristan came back into the kitchen, and I picked up an apple and bit into it to hide my smile.

"Come on," Philip said. "I'll show you the guest bedroom."

———

Philip made small talk about his coworkers at the haunted house until it was time for him to go. ("Would you believe there was a fight there the other night?" Philip said. "In the alley, like something out of *West Side Story*." But Tristan and I both played dumb, and he didn't make the connection to

Tristan's fat lip.) As he chatted to us easily, I thought I could sense Tristan relaxing a little, becoming more comfortable. The instant the door was closed behind my friend, though, he turned to me and shook his head.

"I don't want to stay here, Izzy. I don't know these people."

"But I know them."

"Do you have any idea how much that chess set costs?" He pointed to a crystal set that was displayed decoratively on a pedestal in the entryway, something I'd never noticed before. "I'm afraid to even be in the same room. There's no dust on it, either. You think Philip's dusting it every day?"

"So they're terrible people because they have a house-keeper?"

"I don't know. Maybe."

His words stung, mostly because I knew they weren't only about Philip. My family wasn't wealthy the way that Philip's parents were, but Tristan probably saw Hull as a spoiled brat. Maybe he saw me as one, too. "Philip gave you the benefit of the doubt. Would it kill you to do the same?"

Tristan shrugged, barely, with only one shoulder.

"Look, I'm exhausted. And we're alone for now. Couldn't we lie down for a few minutes and think about what to do next?" I walked over to him, put my arms around him, rested my head on his shoulder. He didn't hug me back, but I could feel when he nodded in agreement.

The guest bedroom boasted a giant cloud of a bed, so comfortable-looking that it was hard to believe it was real. We gazed at it for a moment in the pink evening light and then folded ourselves, fully clothed, between the sheets. I fitted myself against Tristan's tense body, breathing in the perfume of the fabric softener on the pillowcases.

"Sorry," he said. "Philip seems like a nice guy, and if you like him, he probably is."

"Okay," I said.

"I can't go to Westcroft. Everyone is going to be coming from places like this."

"Not everyone."

"Almost everyone, then. I'm not going to fit in, not in a million years."

"But people there will love you. Of course they'll love you."

"Izzy," he said, turning his head on the pillow to look me in the eye. "Fitting in, that's about how I feel, not how other people feel about me. Is there any way you can understand that?"

I did understand it, or at least understood that the world was designed to let one of us fit in at Westcroft more easily than the other, but when I tried to tell him so, I couldn't find the right words. Instead I brought my head close to his on the pillow and kissed him gently. His swollen lip felt strange against mine, and I could sense his loneliness as though it were a real, physical presence in the room with us. Everything I wanted for him surged up in me. I could fight off the loneliness for him. I could fill up the space where it had been. I knew I could.

"You deserve to fit in," I said. "You deserve to feel that way."

I kissed him again, fiercely this time, and I felt that burst of effervescence, that frenzied need of him. I reached down to feel for the hem of his shirt and then struggled to pull it over his head.

"Izzy," he breathed, and I thought he might be trying to stop me, but I needed to keep going, and so I did, and then he was kissing me back. Outside, the last of twilight had faded from the sky. I folded his glasses and put them on the bedside table and reached up to turn on the lamp.

"We're always in the dark. I want to see you." I kissed the smooth skin along his collarbone, ran my tongue over one of his nipples and felt a shiver go through him. I hesitated for a second before I pulled my shirt over my head, because I couldn't remember what underwear I'd put on the evening before, already an eternity ago. I stole a quick glance down. It was one of my newer bras, at least, even if it was just plain black. Tristan traced the line of the strap, slipped his finger beneath the fabric. We had gone further than that before, pawing each other in dark parks, but I got a shiver when I threw my jeans on the floor.

"It's not possible," he said, and I froze, thinking he was going to say something about wanting to leave the apartment, but instead, he pulled me close, so close our noses were almost touching. "It's not possible for you to be this beautiful."

I delicately licked at his damaged lip, kissed his swollen eye socket. "Not as beautiful as you," I whispered.

What can I say about the riptide current that was carrying us along? There was the teenage carnality of it, I guess, the hormonal fever pitch. And there was the wonderful novelty of it all; the luxurious sheets and the soft, velvety brush of our torsos against each other, unencumbered by the clothes that we had to wear or partially struggle out of during our nighttime excursions—the sensations were overwhelming, revelatory. But it was more than that. I wanted so badly in that moment to have decided something important, to no longer exist in the purgatory of youth, to have the die irrevocably cast. And it did feel like that, when we grappled closer and closer, mutually burrowing into each other until there was no longer a clear border between us.

"You're sure?" he asked.

And I said yes, to him, to all of it.

When I think now of all the things it is possible to regret about those few months, that moment, with our sweat mingling, the unfamiliar ache between my legs, the raw openness of his face—that one never makes the list.

THE KNIGHT

IZZY FALLS ASLEEP AFTERWARD, HER SOFT, ROUND cheeks glowing in the warm light of the lamp, but my heart is racing and I can't imagine closing my eyes.

Now, lying in this strange bed, our love feels more real, more solid than ever before. When I put my forehead against Izzy's, I can feel my mind clicking into sync with hers, the way our bodies did a few minutes before, and if I let myself, I could drift off and collide with her in some single shared dream. But the other side of that golden coin is that the fear of losing her is more real, too. If Izzy and I share everything, I have to solve my problems before they become her problems. I waited too long to tell Marcus the truth, stalled too long in making that decision, and it landed us here. I can't afford to make the same mistake twice. That's why I slip out of bed, find my cell phone, and call Aunt Patrice (who must know something is wrong, because she's left me four voice mails over the course of the day, something she never does), and ask her to drive into Manhattan and pick us up. She agrees without questioning it; she must somehow sense the gravity of the situation.

After I hang up, I wrap my arms around Izzy for a few more stolen minutes, holding her close enough to feel the calm, even breaths move through her body. I float there, on the swell of air that sustains her, that ties her to life, that ties her to me. And then I wake her up and tell her that I've decided to go to Westcroft.

———————

We leave the apartment before Philip or his mother comes home, and when we get to the lobby, there's a new security guard on duty. This one doesn't give me a second glance, and this small sign confirms my belief that my decision has the power to remake the world. Even Patrice seems changed. When she pulls up to the curb and we climb into the back seat of her reliable Volvo, her face looks worried, genuinely worried, more like a real parent instead of a reluctant guardian.

"Tristan, your face." She sighs. "It's worse than I thought. And Marcus did this to you."

"How'd you know?"

"Chantal, of all people," Patrice says as she puts the car in gear and merges into the chain of headlights making its slow way downtown. "That girl is such a chatterbox, and only eight years old, too. I almost scolded her for lying when I remembered that I never saw you on Sunday, not since dinner on Saturday. And then I can't reach you or Marcus on the phone all day, and I'm going crazy with worry, and then you don't come home after school. Do you have any idea how scared I was?"

"Sorry," I mumble.

"I could kill you if I wasn't so worried about Marcus doing the job for me." I know that this is the way Patrice talks, that she doesn't mean it literally, but that statement produces a chilly space in the conversation when it lands. Izzy flicks her eyes in my direction but stays quiet, waiting for me to take the lead. When I rush into an explanation of my plan to get a scholarship to Westcroft, it's half to chase the silence out of the car, half because I know if I don't say the words now, I'll chicken out. I try to describe to Patrice how good Westcroft is for chess, how this is a great opportunity, infusing the words with more enthusiasm than I feel.

Patrice, predictably, is less than thrilled.

"Something like this, it's not up to you alone," she says. "This was never the plan when you came to live with me. Not to mention that Marcus is family. You have to confront problems when they confront you."

"It's not only about Marcus." It's about solving my own problems without waiting for Patrice to bully Marcus into submission for me, but I don't say this out loud.

"We'll see what your father has to say about all this,"

Patrice says. But I already know, and maybe she does, too, that I can talk my father into going along with my wishes. For better or worse, he's always treated me more like an adult than a child.

"And what about Izzy?" Patrice says. "Is she planning to go to the fancy boarding school as well?" Patrice is squeezing the steering wheel so tightly that her knuckles look pale and bloodless under the streetlights. We are sailing over the Manhattan Bridge, racing toward the neighborhood faster than I'd like. I wish she wouldn't talk about Izzy in the third person.

"I'm staying at Sagan," Izzy says quickly.

"You could go back to Hope Springs," I say.

"No."

"You're not afraid of Marcus, then," Patrice says. It's not a question, the way she phrases it, but Izzy ponders it as though it is.

"Sometimes," she says.

Even in the dim light, I can see that there is grim resolve in Patrice's face, and maybe some respect for Izzy, too. "Believe me, Marcus won't give you any trouble. I will see to that."

Izzy doesn't respond to this, simply stares out the window at the dark glitter of the East River. I reach for her hand, wanting to close the space between us, and I find it already reaching for mine.

THE ROOK

As I anticipated when I showed up at her house, Izzy is missing from school after the fight. No one can tell me where she is, which isn't a huge surprise since she hasn't bothered making many friends here other than me and T. I go to school on Monday, since Mai has ceased to be fooled by the many illnesses I've been claiming lately, and since I can't exactly pull out my tarot deck and do a full reading in the middle of class, I start seeing signs everywhere I look. The lunch line features apple crisp, Izzy's favorite, even though it isn't a Friday; does it mean something? Ms. Rathscott slips and calls me by Izzy's name in Government class; is she channeling something out of alignment? I test the universe, making up my own signs. If the library door stays shut until I've walked past, she is safe (it does). If my notoriously crappy locker opens on the first try, she isn't mad at me (it doesn't). It's a day of endless small agonies, death by a thousand superstitions.

And then, she comes back the very next day, as if nothing has happened. She sits right next to me in Trigonometry, and I try to ask her about T, about how badly he's hurt, but I keep getting the evil eye from Mr. Mashariki, and Izzy only nods in the direction of the teacher and shrugs and goes back to doing the assigned problems. The whole day I get all kinds of negative energy swirling around her. She isn't giving me the cold shoulder, not exactly, but it's like she is occupying a different mental plane than me.

At lunch, I figure I'll get the whole story, and I do, sort of. She says that T is gone for good, that he's transferring to another school, effective immediately, and though they are still together, they'll see each other much less.

"You know, I'm sorry I got you messed up in this," I say, needing to apologize for something, even if I can't bear the thought of telling her about Frodo. "Really. I wish I'd been smart enough to keep all of this from happening."

"There's nothing you could have done. All those astrology books and tarot cards—don't you believe in fate, Brianna?"

I used to think that no one understood fate more than I did. Fate was a map of a place called the future, a land that already existed, and all you had to do was learn to read that map and connect the dots. Now I'm not so sure. I think that fate might be more like a very intricately choreographed dance; it's set up in advance, but it's up to you to hit the right moves, and I've been missing so many of the steps lately.

THE QUEEN

BECAUSE I KNEW TRISTAN WOULD NEVER LEAVE IF I didn't, I put on a brave show about Marcus. Patrice would follow through, I told Tristan; she would insist that Marcus needed to stay away from me. Besides, if he was going to lash out in anger again, Tristan would be the likely target. Brianna agreed with this prediction, though she said that maybe I should keep my distance until Venus moved out of Scorpio. I was perfectly happy following her advice, because in actual fact, I was scared of everything I didn't know about Marcus and some of what I did.

But for a few days, it seemed like this détente might actually hold. Tristan had already enrolled at Westcroft. Marcus had been conspicuously missing from school. I had run into several of his friends, but they did little more than shoot me dirty looks. One of them, probably Frodo, started a rumor on Snapchat that I was pregnant with Tristan's baby and that was why he was sent away, but bookish little me was of limited interest to the high school gossip mill and the story burned out almost immediately.

Then, one evening, I rounded a corner on my way to the public library, and there was Marcus, leaning against the fence, talking to a kid I'd never seen before. He made eye contact with me, murmured something to his companion, and the kid disappeared in an instant. I tried to turn down the volume on my thoughts when they shrieked that Marcus was clearing the scene of possible witnesses. I'm pretty sure that my knees actually knocked together in fear, something I thought was only a saying until that moment.

"Izzy," he said.

"Marcus." At least, I think I said that. I was having a hard time making my voice work properly. We eyed each other, waiting to see who would speak next. He wasn't wearing a winter coat, only a sweatshirt, and I considered asking him if he was cold, even though that was the least of our concerns.

"You want to walk somewhere?" he asked.

I wasn't going to go wandering through the night with Marcus when no one knew where I was. "I'm heading to the library," I told him, nodding at the building. "You could come in with me."

"You mean you haven't already read every book in there?" He gave me that trademark smile. No wonder everyone was charmed by him. When I didn't smile back, he swept his arm toward the door and said, "After you."

The mind will play all sorts of tricks on you if you let it, and for a nauseating second, I was certain he was going to actually stab me in the back. But then I gained control of myself and walked into the library and Marcus followed me, no knife thrusts involved.

I picked up the books I'd reserved from the hold shelf and pointed to a line of small tables at the back of the nonfiction section. My brain was churning, trying to figure out what I should say, but Marcus beat me to it, speaking up almost before we fully slid onto the scarred wooden chairs.

"You know, Izzy, some people might call me soft after what happened. Some people might think that if a guy's cousin is sneaking with his girl, he should do a lot more than what I did to T."

I could feel heat flickering in my cheeks, and it took me a moment to realize that it was anger rushing in to mix with my fear. It warmed up my vocal cords, loosened my tongue. "Some people? Like the people who follow you around telling you what you want to hear?"

"A lot of people, I'd bet."

"Interesting. Of course, it doesn't really apply here. I was never your girl."

Marcus looked startled by this. Maybe he was accustomed to hearing a softened version of the truth from all the people who were afraid of him.

"Damn. That's cold, Izzy."

"At what point did I do anything to indicate that I was your girlfriend, Marcus?" As the words slipped past my lips, I remembered the party, the Final Frontier, Brianna's face in the bathroom. I remembered how eager I'd been in the alley to say anything that would keep Tristan safe. I swallowed, wishing my mouth wasn't so dry and sticky.

"It's like that, then?" Marcus shook his head. "It still doesn't explain why T had to lie to my face about it."

Why had we lied about it for so long? It was hard to remember. It all seemed so silly when I was looking across the table at Marcus, trying to justify everything that had happened for the past few weeks. Love is madness, they say, and I had to admit we'd been acting madly. But we weren't the only ones. I thought of my conversation with Tristan over Skype earlier that day, thought of how his lip hadn't fully healed, how the bruises around his eye had turned a sick green.

"You're not an easy person to talk to," I said, "and you like it that way. If you act like people should be afraid to tell you something, they're not going to tell you."

"Hold on. You're going to act like this is my fault?"

"It's your fault that you're a bully. It's your fault that people are afraid to cross you."

"No." Marcus shoved his chair back from the table,

crossed his arms. "If people are afraid, that's on them, not me. I can't be responsible for the way every crazy person feels."

"The thing is, Marcus, people aren't crazy to be afraid of you. You beat him up! You beat up your own cousin."

"You think I've never taken a punch? And I didn't run away to some rich-kid school."

I could see two of the librarians shooting perturbed glances our way on account of our raised voices. I leaned across the table, prepared to quietly lay down the winning card. "Tristan and I saw you that night in the playground. Buying... something."

Marcus leaned in close again. I was having a hard time reading his expression. "What are you talking about?" he whispered.

"A gun. Let's just say it. You were buying a gun."

"What?" He made a strange noise, a sort of choking snort. With a start, I recognized the emotion playing over his face. He was scared. "You gotta be kidding me. Keep your voice down when you're spreading lies like that."

"So what was it, then?"

"What was what? You're not even talking sense."

I felt thrown off-balance, as though my foot had missed the bottom stair, and I flailed to regain my certainty. "You were in the playground. It was you. You were with two older guys, and Tristan saw them, too." I saw some connection snap together behind Marcus's eyes and felt a moment of relief. "Who were they?"

"It's your business?"

"After everything that's happened, yeah, maybe it's my business."

"It's like this: Somebody asked if I could find them the new iPhone on the cheap. And those were the only guys who could get it for me." Marcus gripped the sides of the table as if he were on a ride that was making him dizzy. I couldn't tell anymore if he was scared because I'd gotten too close to the truth or had landed so very far from it. "Shit, Izzy."

I closed my eyes, trying to remember. The metallic glint I'd seen. It couldn't have been from a phone. Or maybe it could have? "You mean it was stolen."

"I think even you know there's a difference between a hot cell phone and an unlicensed weapon. Who do you think I am?"

It was a good question, actually. I'd gotten used to thinking of Marcus as some hybrid between criminal mastermind and supernatural bogeyman. Now I wasn't so sure.

"You know what, don't answer that," he said. "I think I know the answer."

He slipped away from the table and out of the library so quickly that I had to question whether he'd ever been there in the first place.

When I walked out of the doors after him, I was so distracted that I forgot to check out the books that had been on hold and set off the alarm at the door, further annoying the librarians. I clawed through my bag to find them and mumbled an apology, but my mind was still with Marcus. He was arrogant, hotheaded, threatening. He acted like the neighborhood belonged to him. He had hurt Tristan, physically and emotionally, and had maybe considered hurting him worse. All of that was still true.

But what about me? Marcus and Tristan had been getting along pretty well until I barged into their lives. At the most basic level, I was the reason they were no longer speaking. I had also lied to my parents, jeopardized my friendship with Brianna, grown estranged from my twin brother, and discounted the fact that Marcus might have had real human emotions. Even the best thing in my life, the love between Tristan and me, I had finagled into existence with an act of spectacular deception and, some might say, destruction.

The thing is, we get used to spinning a narrative in which we're the heroes. If we do something good, it's because we're good; if we do something bad, it's an excusable offense, and we expect allowances to be made. But that doesn't change the fact that sometimes we do good and sometimes we do bad. That none of us is blameless.

That's what I thought about on the walk home, shouldering the guilt along with my library books. But it wasn't until later, when I was lying in bed alone, that dread began to press down on me. If you'd asked me at the time, I wouldn't have been able to describe clearly what was causing that suffocating feeling. With the gift of hindsight, though, I can guess: It was the first small recognition that fate was far more complicated than my love for Tristan and bigger than our troubles with Marcus. That the seeds of pain are sown into our fate before we realize, and none of us, in the end, survives it.

THE ROOK

I GET DRESSED IN MY OLD-FASHIONED FORTUNE-teller's costume: a full skirt that belongs to my mother, a frilled long-sleeved shirt, big hoop earrings, and a scarf pulled over my hair and knotted at the nape of my neck. A crystal ball, even though it's not a real one. It's Halloween, All Hallows' Eve, the night when the spirits are up and walking. An important day, even if I've been too busy to give it much thought this year.

"If it isn't Miss Cleo herself," Hector says to me when I walk downstairs. He's setting up the tables in the café, even though it's early still and we don't open until lunch. Playing the good son, I guess, trying to get Mai and Pai off his back.

"Who's Miss Cleo?" I ask, and Hector shakes his head, says something about kids these days and offers to give me a ride to school. Playing the good brother, too, though I don't know why. I am running late, though, so I accept, and we listen to "Thriller" twice in a row on the way there, and I remember when Hector and I found the video online when we were younger and played it over and over again and learned the whole dance from start to finish, and my mood actually starts to lift a little.

It plummets again when we pull up in front of the school and I see Marcus standing there, clearly waiting for us. It was Marcus, probably, that inspired this ride, not brotherly love, and (at the risk of sounding like my parents) I don't like the idea of Hector and Marcus doing business so close to the school, where charges would be much worse if they ever got caught. Hector rolls up and Marcus leans his elbows on the door, face framed in the open window.

"You're probably not going to like this," Hector says. "That's why I came down here to tell you in person." Marcus makes a sour face, and my mind spins, wondering what Hector is up to here. "I'm getting out of the game, man. I've been doing this shit too long."

This is news to me, and it must be news to Marcus, too, because he stands up straight for a moment, and all I can see through the window is his arms held slack at his sides. Then his face reappears inside the car, but it's not angry; in fact, he looks sort of downcast, like Hector told him he didn't want to be his friend anymore.

"What do you have going instead?" he asks.

"I've had this idea cooking for a while. My own store. I've got some saved up and my pops is helping me get a business loan. I can tell you more when I've got the details locked down."

"You sure about this?"

"Yeah, man. Something I gotta do."

Marcus nods, exhales slowly through puffed-out cheeks. "A'ight. Anything changes, you know where to find me."

"No doubt," Hector says, then turns to me. "Brianna, you gonna get out of the damn car already or what?"

I do, and Hector barely waits for me to shut the door before he hits the gas and takes off down the street. It's quiet in front of the school, so it's pretty obvious that Marcus and I are late and I should be running to get to class, but neither of us moves in that direction.

"Shit," Marcus says, maybe to me or maybe to himself. "Ain't nothing around here stays the same, is there?"

I tuck the crystal ball into my armpit so I can untangle my hair from one of my earrings. "You didn't dress up for Halloween. That doesn't seem like you."

He glances at me for maybe the first time this morning, takes in my costume. "I am dressed up," he says. "I'm a monster." He smiles at me, but it looks leached of its usual charm. "What kind of store is your brother talking about?"

"A liquor store. A fancy one to match some of the changes around here." I've heard him discuss it plenty of times with my father, though I had no idea it was so close to being a reality.

A recession-proof industry, my father calls it. What Hector hasn't told Pai is that he thinks having a storefront in place will set him up to make mad cash if recreational weed is ever legalized in New York.

"Should have thought of that myself. T's gone, now Hector, too. I'm losing my edge, Caballito." Marcus puts his hands on top of his head. He's breathing funny, like the air in front of him has turned liquid, and I know it's stupid, but the thought of seeing him cry, of seeing him laid so low, makes me feel like the world is breaking apart, and I'm sure I won't be able to take it.

"Hey. Let's go somewhere. I'll finally read your cards properly." I try not to let any pity creep into my voice, and when he looks at me . . . I won't say there's gratitude in his face, exactly, but there is relief.

"You talked to T since the haunted house?" I ask as we wander toward Eastern Parkway, not too far from the park where Marcus used to set up games for T. I try to steer us in a different direction, but Marcus seems drawn there, and I feel its pull, too.

"Nah," he says. "I don't know. Sometimes I want to tell him I'm sorry about how things went down, because I miss him, for real. And then I think of all the lies, and my brain gets hot, and I want to hunt him down at that fancy new school and hurt him worse."

"Yeah," I say. "His face is sort of punchable." Because that's just the truth.

Marcus smiles at that, a real smile this time, but it starts to fade almost immediately. "It doesn't matter. Auntie Patrice is all over me, worse than a prison guard, and she's got my mom riled up, too. They swear they'll turn me in for dealing if I step out of line, some sort of 'scared straight' thing. Now my supply dried up, so joke's on them, I guess. Still... I don't know, Brianna. I'm tired of the way they look at me, like I'm a dog that pisses on the carpet all the time."

Marcus has never said this many words to me at once. I'd like to bask in that fact for a few minutes, but there's also something nagging at me, and the next question jumps to my tongue.

"What about Izzy?" I ask as we enter the south end of the park.

"What about her?" he says, anger suddenly brightening his voice. Then he shrugs, shakes his head. "Aw, shit. The stuff she said to me, it doesn't seem right. And what, I'm supposed to just let it all go?" We reach the statue of a long-dead astronaut, the one the park is named for, and stop walking. Marcus slides down onto the concrete base, and I sit down next to him, pull the scarf off my head to spread out between us. When I look at him, he's fiddling with his necklace.

"Where'd you get it? The house pendant?"

"It's stupid," he says, but I hold his gaze, shake my head, try to let him know that even now, nothing he could say would be stupid to me, and maybe it works because he sighs and keeps going. "I bought it off one of those tables by Union

Square years ago. It's cheap, fake, nothing special. But the guy who sold it to me, this guy with dreads and no teeth, said, 'I see you. You're headed for greatness.' And so greatness became... I don't know, a real place to me. A place I was going to reach, a place I was going to live in, like it was a house. And this necklace represented that." Marcus closes his eyes, lets the chain go slack. "But now, shit. That's all over."

"It's not."

"I think you're wrong, Caballito. But go on." He nods at the tarot deck. "Tell me what to do."

"Hold the cards and think of a question," I tell him. "Concentrate on it." He closes his eyes, and when he does, he looks less like a tough neighborhood kingpin and more like what he really is: a barely-adult trying to figure out what comes next. I take the deck from him and lay them out in a star guide formation: only six cards, so simple, but good at getting to an answer.

The Tower, the Two of Pentacles. At first glance, the cards give me the shivers.

"I see a lot of change. Loss, too. I'm not going to lie. There's some scary stuff here, and there might be more conflict before things are resolved. But there's the Star, which can mean healing and transformation. And in the final position, there's the Five of Cups, which can represent some sort of forgiveness."

"More conflict and then forgiveness?" The look that

Marcus gives me is raw and searching. "Like maybe this is about Izzy and T? Come on, Brianna. Are you just messing with me here?"

"No," I say. "I'm only telling you what I see. Not what I want to see."

And for once, it's true.

THE KNIGHT

HERE'S A STRANGE TURN OF EVENTS: I'M COOL NOW. Me, nerd among nerds! It makes me laugh out loud whenever I think about it. The other day, my roommate, Patrick, a scrawny computer science genius with a minor lisp and a deep and abiding affection for early-nineties hip-hop, actually said it out loud: "I'm glad I ended up with a cool roommate." At Sagan, even as the new kid, I was immediately a known entity: Marcus's cousin. But here, I'm a man of mystery. I showed up with a murky background, a distant girlfriend, and a still-busted lip. And I'm black. Everyone wants to be my friend.

Don't get me wrong—there was still a little bit of culture shock when I rolled onto the scene. My fears about feeling different weren't completely unfounded, and I'd never been around so many kids who acted almost like adults, who had as a presupposition their own eventual success. But in other ways, it was as easy as slipping into a warm bath. High school is such a closed system, such a biodome, that if you stay in one place, you can get it in your head that you and the people around you are inventing the world. But that's not the case. When I got to Westcroft, most everyone already looked so *familiar*, like I could see their whole stories before I met them. Some of them seemed like people from my old school, only inhabiting different bodies: Oh, you're the quirky kid who digs space and sci-fi, just like R. J. Oh, you're the girl who commands the drama club and dreams of being on Broadway, just like Roxanne.

Even the chess club meetings are peppered with moments of déjà vu. Eamon is a classical musician like Anaïs, though he plays the upright bass instead of the clarinet. Dan is a quiet white dude with dreads who always has a paperback book called something like *The Dissident's Guidebook* sticking out of his back pocket, but sometimes he gets rattled at matches, and his nerves remind me of Pankaj.

And there's Dorie, of course. Living at the same school as Dorie is far more intense than seeing her once in a while at a chess tournament. Beneath the sparkles there are some dark shadows that I'm careful not to mess with. One time when I was sitting next to her in class, she was absentmind-edly scratching at the long cuff of one of her gloves, and I saw what looked like scars under there. I don't ask questions, and

I don't have any desire to go toe-to-toe with her in terms of traumatic histories. But I can't deny that the girl is magnetic. All of the popular kids, the charmers and the athletes, hang out with her because she confuses them and so it's easiest to label her as cool. I hang out with her, not because she reminds me of people at my old school, but because she reminds me of no one.

Aside from chess practice, which is every day at Westcroft, what Dorie and I do together is go to political events around the city, at least several times a month. She's an ace at getting permission to go off campus; she knows when the administration will buy an event as an "invaluable learning experience" or when it's better to dream up a cover story or leave the details fuzzy. If it's the kind of thing that sounds interesting, then she can usually get a small crowd of people to come along. If not, if it's a demonstration for the rights of oysters or a rally to save a statue she's never seen before, then it's typically me and Dan. Dorie goes because she loves to yell and "finds it cathartic to do it for a good cause"; Dan goes because he's a true believer; I go because I like wandering the city, even if it can't be with Izzy at the moment.

So I guess you'd call the two of them my best friends, here in this strange, alternative life that I'm living. They come close to filling the space that Marcus left behind, but it's an awkward fit, gaps in the corners and bulges at the sides. I refused to see Marcus before I came here, despite Auntie Patrice wanting me to do so, and when I speak to her now on the phone, we avoid the subject of Marcus, though it's always right there, bubbling under the surface of our words. Sometimes I think of those last words he said to me, right after he punched me in the face, *See you later, cuz*, and I tell myself that I will see him later, that this is only a pause. Even so, it's hard not to feel like the best solution I could come up with, uprooting my life and moving it to Westcroft, wasn't enough. I've picked up the phone, scrolled down to his name, toyed with the idea of touching that one green button that will connect us again. But then I put the phone down, thinking *later, later*, without wanting to consider how much later that might be.

Here at school, I never talk about Marcus, and I don't say much about Izzy, either. It's not because anything illicit is going on between me and Dorie, any more than there is between me and Dan, though people around here tease me about her all the time. All the same, I'm not sure that Izzy and Dorie would like each other very much. One's a strawberry jelly doughnut, and the other's a perfectly ripe strawberry. One's a tinsel-covered Christmas tree, and the other's a bonsai. One is Isadora and the other's *Izzy*.

THE QUEEN

ALL OF THAT LATE FALL AND EARLY WINTER, TRISTAN got even better at chess. Mr. K still loomed as the seminal and formative teacher of Tristan's chess career, and they still talked on the phone sometimes, but his new school had resources to spare: several coaches, a perennially strong team, the money to travel to tournaments, some of them far-flung. Tristan soaked it all up like a sponge. He had broken free of his plateau and was closing in on grandmaster level. For the first time, he wasn't viewed as merely a promising contender for the adult tournaments that would take place in the spring; he was among the handful of favorites. I still didn't understand chess much better than I ever had. On the few occasions when I watched Tristan in competition, however, I didn't need to know much of the game; it was almost as though I could sense him getting better and better, more sharply focused. More ruthless, in a way.

"I thought that kid from Stuyvesant was supposed to be good," I said to him one Sunday over Skype. "You ate him for breakfast yesterday."

It was hard to tell on the laptop screen, but I'm pretty sure he was blushing with pleasure. "Tasted like scrambled eggs," he said. We spoke over Skype constantly, and we met up whenever we could, but more often than not, we ended up studying side by side in a coffee shop rather than staring into each other's eyes. No more sneaking out, because Tristan couldn't afford to get in trouble. But the distance didn't weaken our emotions. When my feelings no longer had an easy outlet, they collected inside of me; my love for him gathered and pooled, grew deeper and deeper.

"When we make it to Yale . . ." I told him.

"Or Stanford, maybe."

"Right. My point is, you have to try not to intimidate everyone too badly with your chess skills. We'll want some friends."

"What's wrong with putting a little fear in people? We'll be notorious. The first celebrity couple made up of a surgeon and a chess expert: Dr. Izzy and Grandmaster T."

Confidence looked so good on him. I wanted to bask in his happiness and achievement, enjoy it with him, and yet I couldn't prevent my mind from churning out a chain of other thoughts: 1) Putting fear into people sounds more like something Marcus would say. 2) Maybe I don't know anything about what Marcus would say. 3) Those perfect future versions of ourselves: How did they manage to fix everything that was broken about the past?

———————

With all of the distractions of my first few weeks at Carl Sagan, I had ground to make up. So I hit the books. I aced all of my classes that semester, including the APs. I joined the Spanish club. I helped build sets for the school play. I wrote some preparatory drafts of college application essays in which I tried to capture some of the dark, slippery feelings that appeared after my discussion with Marcus in the library.

I did eventually tell my parents a version of what had been going on, leaving out the dicier bits, and they looked alarmed, possibly disconcerted by how much had escaped their notice. When they took Tristan and me out to dinner for the first time, they seemed unable to get over their surprise that I had a serious boyfriend, even though they swore to me later that night and ever after that they liked him.

Hull, the new Hull, started to seem sturdier, less like a floating apparition, but he was getting more eccentric as well. After one of his friends showed him a documentary about David Lynch, he got really into transcendental meditation. My mom thought it was a good thing and paid for him to take a class. Maybe it was. But he also decided to switch his focus from politics to business, reading massive biographies of Steve Jobs and Warren Buffett. He started a young investors club at Hope Springs. Philip wrote me an email about a presentation Hull had done, idolizing the bankers who made tons of money on the 2008 housing crash, and though Philip meant it to be a funny story, an isn't-Hull-so-wacky kind of story, it made me deeply uncomfortable. It was pretty easy to imagine Hull as a CEO out in Silicon Valley, the kind who wears sandals and an unnervingly calm smile and goes surfing on the weekends.

In short, our lives kept grinding along, and the rest of the world did, too. ISIS was in the news, doing unspeakable things in the Middle East. The new pope was making waves. Protests and then riots continued in Ferguson, Missouri, over the killing of Michael Brown. When the court decided not to indict the police officer who choked Eric Garner to death in Staten Island, a mere ferry ride away, the protests spread to New York, too.

Things got so heated that we started having long discussions about Black Lives Matter in Government class, and everyone took part in them enthusiastically, either because they felt passionately about the issue or because they were excited about the break in our usual routine. There were lots of personal stories about the NYPD and how they would stop and frisk you for nothing at all. For the most part, I stayed pretty quiet while Ms. Rathscott tried to wrangle the debate into some kind of teachable moment. And then, one day, feeling more talkative than usual or maybe just lonelier, I raised my hand and told the story of being with "a black friend," of being stopped by a cop and asked if I was "all right" while he systematically harassed my companion. "It was because I'm a white girl, obviously," I said. "I wish I'd said something, but I didn't. I don't know... it feels hopeless to me, too. I guess my only plan is to pay attention to how I'm treated differently and recognize that it's wrong and get better at speaking up when I see it." R. J. got up and walked over to my desk and gave me a fist bump, and the rest of the class laughed. The attention made my face burn, but from that point on, I felt like R. J. and I were friends by more than association, and he started inviting me to the astronomy club meetings.

———————

In the midst of the upheaval over the Eric Garner case, I went with my parents to a demonstration in Washington Square Park: a Sunday morning, a painfully blue sky, thousands of people waving signs and chanting "No justice, no peace!" Hull, predictably, opted out, but it felt good, actually, to be there with my parents, listening to them try to chant their way back to their raucous, dissident youth.

It was my mother who spotted him first, pointing to a clump of teenagers with their hands in the air. A girl wearing, inexplicably, a chartreuse tutu, a long lavender scarf, and sparkly white Michael Jackson–esque gloves was shouting "Hands up!" into a bullhorn, and the group was answering, "Don't shoot!"

"Look," my mom said. "Isn't that Tristan? Want to ask him if he wants to march with us?"

It was, indeed, Tristan, and while I pushed my way toward him through the crowd, I felt a twinge of irritation. He hadn't told me he was coming. I reminded myself to be reasonable; I hadn't mentioned it to him, either, because I'd thought of it as parent-daughter bonding time. But then, as I was calling his name, the girl dropped the microphone and with a strange, catlike leap, jumped onto Tristan's back and pumped her fist in the air. I called his name again.

If I was jealous (I was), the envy disappeared when he saw and recognized me. There was no guilt there, only joy at my sudden appearance. He dropped the girl's legs, depositing her back on the asphalt, and greeted me with a kiss.

"You're here," he said, as if it was a wonder.

"I'm here," I said. "With my parents. Do you want to . . . ?" I pointed toward them, where they were waving at us. They looked old in that moment, so out of place.

"Sure," he said, but then one of the kids with him, a big red-haired guy built like a football player, jostled Tristan with his elbow.

"Dude, you can't bail on us."

"It's okay," I said quickly. "No big deal."

"You're sure?" he asked, glancing again at my parents.

"It's fine," I said. "We're still studying together on Tuesday night, right?"

He assured me that we were and kissed me hard, in front

of everyone. Then there were some hurried introductions of the people I hadn't met before. He pointed to Miss Tutu and said, "Izzy, this is Dorie." I stuck my hand out like a robot.

"Isadora, actually," she said. "Isn't that funny? Almost the same as yours." And then she started doing a strange series of lunges and hops, ignoring my offered hand. I backed away, tried to turn it into an awkward wave to the whole group as I departed.

"Everything okay?" my mom asked, putting her arm around me.

"Yeah, totally. I didn't want to drag him away from the people he came with. You know." I did want to drag him away, especially from Isadora, with her stupid gloves, but I didn't, and soon afterward we started to march up Fifth Avenue and the crowd swallowed them completely.

I did see Tristan that Tuesday. He didn't say anything about the march or about Dorie, so I didn't, either. If I didn't mention her, maybe she would cease to exist.

THE KNIGHT

Izzy is only a borough away, a mere river between us, but without a car or endless money for cab fare, it can feel almost like a long-distance relationship. We still get to see each other, but it's in these tiny scheduled increments, and those long, beautiful nights seem like a distant memory. This evening we have a single stolen hour to study together at the coffee shop down the block from my dorm, even though it will take Izzy almost twice that long to get here and back on the train. She never complains about it; we take what we can get. But when I arrive, her pretty face looks worried, and I ask her what's up.

"A shooting down the street last night," Izzy says. "Probably drug-related, and the guy is in bad shape. There are police all over the place today. My parents are both really freaked out. They barely let me leave the house to come meet you."

"Anyone we know?"

"No."

"Hull's helping the situation, I bet?"

She allows herself a small smile. "All sanctimonious raised eyebrows," she says, and does an impression that makes me laugh, but then the corners of her mouth turn down again.

"It's not so bad, Izzy. There are always going to be shady characters, but they mess with each other, not with anybody else. You know that. Your parents probably know that, too. They'll calm down."

"It's not that," she says. Her eyes look wet. "I can't explain it. I worry that I've made mistakes that I can't fix. And I worry about you all the time."

None of this makes sense to me, but I rub her hand, bend down to kiss her knuckles. "Come on. You're the one who lives in the bad neighborhood," I joke. "I'm up here in my ivory tower. Safest I've ever been."

"Tristan, don't you think it's time to talk to Marcus?"

"What's he got to do with this?" My heart picks up speed. Izzy has told me time and time again that she was wrong about the gun, but I can't un-know the fear I felt the last time I saw him.

"Nothing. I swear—nothing. But he's been on my mind. You might feel better if you talked to him, don't you think?"

I doubt that. My feelings about Marcus are so twisted up

that there's no hope of unknotting them anytime soon. But to Izzy, I say, "I'll think about it."

"There's an astronomy club fund-raiser tomorrow, and I think R. J. talked Marcus into coming. You could come, too. An easy way to see him without having to talk very much."

"Why does it mean so much to you?"

"It would be nice to put it behind us. That's all."

"Look, I said I'd think about it, okay? Mark me down as a maybe."

It's not enough to soothe her, I can tell, but we decide to start studying, since time is slipping away. I'm supposed to be writing a paper about the French Revolution, but my mind keeps skipping around. I study Izzy's face, the little line between her eyebrows. I used to think I knew everything that was going through her head.

When it's time to go, we stand outside the coffee shop for a few minutes, neither of us wanting to be the one who turns away first. She weaves her arms inside my coat, under my arms and around my back, and rests her head on my shoulder. Even though I know we're almost exactly the same height, she feels small tonight. I bend my head down to kiss her, but she stops me.

"No," she says. "Keep it until next time. Keep it until tomorrow, when you come home to Brooklyn. Then it will taste sweeter."

It's a strange, flowery thing to say, especially from Izzy, and I think about it the entire walk back to the dorm, puzzling over whether Brooklyn is my home and what that word means. I'm still thinking about it when I unlock my door, turn on the light, and find, lying on my bed, Dorie.

"Jesus," I say, once I've managed to swallow my heart back down to where it belongs. "What are you doing here? In the dark?"

"Patrick let me in," she says, as though that explains everything. She makes wiggly ghost fingers around her face, drawing attention to those gloves. "Did I scaaaare you?"

"Um, yeah, you kind of did," I say, trying to laugh, but it comes out in a little huff, making me sound irritated. Which I am. Or tired, at least, and eager to be alone. It's definitely against the rules for her to be on this floor at this hour, especially in my room with the door closed, and I don't need trouble with the school administrators added to my problems. I like Dorie, I do, but she takes credit for convincing me to come here, and sometimes she behaves as though I owe her something.

"Don't be mad," she says, and pats the spot on the bed next to her. I sit. "I was lying here pretending to be you. You know, imagining what it's like inside your skin." She makes her hand into a little animal that looks around, sniffs the wind, capers across the bedspread and onto my knee. I grab the wrist. It turns back into a hand, and I return it to the space between us.

"Oh, don't be such a worrywart," she says. She rolls off the bed, lies spread out on Patrick's hypoallergenic rug. "I know you have a girlfriend." She stretches out the word *girl-friend* like it's an experiment her tongue is running. "Besides, it would never work between us. Opposites attract, and you and I, we're too much alike."

"We're nothing alike." It comes out sounding more severe than I mean it to. She turns on her side, props her head in her hand, looks up at me.

"Well, you said it, not me," she says with a smile that has too much in it to unpack. Then she does a kind of backward roll and hops up onto her feet. With her, it's always like having a conversation with a court jester. "You're coming tomorrow, right? Everyone else bailed on me. But I know you'll come."

It takes me a moment to remember that I'm supposed to go to a demonstration against police brutality with her. I'd forgotten when Izzy invited me to the astronomy thing. I have way too much to do; really, I should back out of both, stay home and study. Before I can come up with the words, though, Dorie has slipped out of the room, leaving me alone.

THE QUEEN

HERE IS WHAT I REMEMBER FROM THAT DAY, THE DAY of the full moon: three encounters.

1) On a whim, I stopped to say hello to Mr. K after school. I quit going to chess club after Tristan left; it felt too sad to be there, particularly because the entire team was depressed that Tristan was no longer leading them to easy victories. But that day, I was walking past the room where they met, so I stuck my head inside the door to wave to Mr. K and assure him that Tristan was doing okay and that they would surely run into each other soon at a tournament somewhere. Mr. K had thawed toward me after he came to believe that Marcus, not I, had been the one to interfere with Tristan's concentration at the beginning of the school year. His impressive eyebrows

twitched in a way that may have signaled pleasure when he noticed me in the doorway.

"And you are well, Iseult?" he asked me after I gave him my dutiful report. Until that moment, I hadn't been sure that Mr. K even knew my name. He pronounced it like someone who could speak French, and it made me think how little I knew of him and his life. So many people in the world, and you'll really only know a handful, and that's if you're lucky.

"I'm good," I said. "No complaints."

He sighed and turned to write on the chalkboard the topic for that day's meeting, a list of possible openings. "Beginnings, they are always wanting more beginnings," he muttered. "But so we go. Some say that in the opening, there is already written the endgame." In his shaky script, he added "Queen's Gambit" to the list. I didn't know who he meant by *they* or *some*, and I didn't bother to ask before I said goodbye.

You might see this as a missed sign, but the truth is that Mr. K was always saying stuff like that.

2) I had to be at the school that night to help with the fund-raiser, but because I had forgotten to bring a book I needed for the next day's AP Lit homework, I decided to dash home for a couple hours, work on the essay, and then go back. We had finally moved past the colonial era and arrived at Nathaniel Hawthorne, the *adultery and shit* that Alex had yearned for long before, on the day that Tristan and I had gotten in that stupid argument. I was sitting at the kitchen counter, trying to dream up something interesting to say about *The*

House of the Seven Gables, when Hull got home. He opened up the refrigerator and removed a plastic bag of baby carrots, started crunching them noisily as I sat there and stared at him. There was nothing strange about it, and yet there was everything strange about it, since the old Hull had gravitated more toward beef jerky and had always rolled his eyes at Mom and Dad's Meatless Monday dinners, their raw nut trail mixes, their homemade kombucha. He was looking much more muscled than he once had.

"Have you been working out?" I asked, incredulous that such a question would come from my lips, and even more so that it would be directed at my twin.

"Actually, yes," he said. "For weeks now, thanks for noticing."

"Sorry," I mumbled.

"No problem. A strong body begets a strong mind."

"Huh." I pretended to go back to my homework, but I couldn't concentrate over his crunching. "You know, I'm helping with this event at school tonight, a fund-raiser that I helped organize. I could get you in for free if you wanted to come."

"We'll see," he said, which I understood meant *no way.* "What are you writing?"

"A paper on *The House of the Seven Gables*. Escaping from the past and all that. Are you guys reading it?"

"Nah, *The Mill on the Floss*. Dysfunctional siblings. And all that."

"Ah."

"Well, I need to go meditate now."

I should have let it end there, but instead I asked, "Do you think it helps? The meditation stuff?" Hull stopped midstride and looked at me with an expression I recognized from his old self: snobbish pity.

"It makes of me a modern warrior," he said.

The old Hull would have been embarrassed to say something like that. He would have made fun of someone who said that. There were still times when I missed the old Hull.

It took a beat for me to realize that I must have uttered these thoughts aloud.

"I thought you knew that the old Hull is dead, Izzy," the new Hull said. And then he was gone, forgetting to put the carrots back in the fridge.

I suppose I might have taken this as a sign, too, but the truth is that the new Hull was always saying stuff like that.

3) The bleachers had been pushed back in the school gymnasium, and a big white disco ball hung from one of the basketball hoops. We were calling it a Full Moon Party, and it was a joint fund-raiser for a few different student groups, including the astronomy club and the Wiccan club (whose membership, as far as I could tell, consisted of Brianna and a group of freshman girls who wore a lot of eye makeup). A makeshift dance floor had been set up, and along the perimeter were some booths and tables where people could trade in

the tickets they'd purchased at the door. Brianna was reading palms, though she didn't look too happy about it, and directly across from her, I was working at the concession stand, selling MoonPies and sugar cookies in the shape of stars and planets. Someone had put together a lame playlist of songs about the moon, so people were mostly standing around in clusters in the half dark, talking and laughing instead of dancing.

Attendance was modest, but I'd seen Marcus walk in with Tyrone, and my eyes kept straying to the door, expecting Tristan to arrive. I figured that if he and Marcus were in the same room, some remembered way of being together would kick in and they could work out their problems. Or Marcus would punch Tristan in the face again. One of the two.

"Moon...river," Audrey Hepburn warbled as I watched Marcus wait in line at Brianna's booth. He offered her his palm, and they stood whispering to each other. Something had altered between them, I could tell, but it didn't look like the blossoming love that Brianna had once hoped for. Then they both turned to look at me, so I understood exactly whom they were discussing. I could feel my face turn red, and I fumbled a plate of cookies, sending a couple sliding to the floor. By the time I'd retrieved the broken pieces, Marcus was standing right in front of me.

"Hey," I said, flustered. "I'm glad you're here. I've been wanting to talk to you." The words were tumbling out much too fast, but I couldn't stop myself.

"Yeah?" He plucked a corner of cookie out of the hand I

was stupidly holding out in front of me and put it in his mouth. "About what?"

I'd rehearsed this part. "I told myself I wasn't lying to you, but I was. And I assumed a lot of stuff about you that wasn't true. And I'm really, really sorry that it messed things up between you and Tristan. Believe me, I never meant for that to happen." He looked at me for so long that I added, "That's all."

"Huh," he said. He looked up at the white disco-ball moon, stared at it as he said the next part. "I get so mad that I do some stupid shit sometimes."

It was the closest I was going to get to an apology or the acceptance of an apology from Marcus. I lifted my hand again, an offering this time, and we both stood there chewing the cookies I'd picked up off the gym floor.

"He might come tonight," I said.

"Nah," he said. "He's not going to show."

"How do you know?"

"You're supposed to be the one who knows him so well," he said. There was a sharp edge to the smile he gave me, but it softened after only a second. "Look, Izzy, you want to fix everything, but sometimes that's not how it is."

That was, actually, a fairly accurate summation of me and my relation to the world, so I didn't reply, just let it hang in the air between us.

"I still love him, though," Marcus said, so low that I thought I might have misheard, and then he turned and melted into the growing crowd, and before I could blink, another person had taken his place, impatiently demanding a MoonPie.

If I was going to recognize something as a sign, it would have been this, because Marcus never said stuff like that, not before, not after. But by then, signs were no use to us anyway.

THE KNIGHT

THIRD PERIOD, WHAT WOULD BE A STUDY HALL, IS AN independent study chess intensive for me at Westcroft. It's mostly an extra one-on-one practice session with our coach, Mr. Ippolito, and a few papers on the history of chess thrown in to persuade the administration of its validity as a class. Mr. Ippolito is one of the smartest people I've ever met: young and quick, with the darting energy of a flying squirrel. I still miss Mr. K sometimes, though, and today I look at Mr. Ippolito's face and hear Mr. K's voice inside my brain saying, sadly, "He has not *suffered* enough to understand the game."

Nevertheless, Mr. Ippolito is a good coach, and he's been giving me crushingly difficult chess problems to solve. Today, I surprise even myself in coming up with the right answer to one presented yesterday; all of a sudden, the solution is alive in front of me, like the teeth of invisible cogs have meshed together, making the whole machine whir and hum. The pawn gets promoted to a knight instead of a queen, and then it's mate in three.

"That's it," Mr. Ippolito says before downing the last of what is surely his seventh coffee of the day. "This one took me much longer than it took you. How'd you do it?"

"The answer came to me in a dream." I don't know why I say this. It isn't true, not in the slightest, but it makes Mr. Ippolito laugh.

"You're the most mystical chess warrior I've ever met," he says, and I can't tell if that's a compliment or not.

"I need to leave practice early today," I tell him. "Only twenty minutes or so. Something important to a friend."

He sighs. "Just this once. And only because you solved that puzzle."

I don't know when I cut out of chess practice alongside Dorie and Dan whether I'm doing it to go to the demonstration with them or to the fund-raiser with Izzy and Marcus. I walk my way into the answer, and as I arrive at it, it surprises me a little. Dan and Dorie expect me to follow them onto the subway going uptown, not the one headed to Brooklyn, and that's what I do.

When the subway car gets loud and crowded, Dorie

simply gets louder herself. "The thing is, it makes me roll my eyes when people ask how Gamergate could have happened. Misogyny in strategy gaming is as old as chess. Older, probably. Maybe I'll make a feminist chessboard, one that gives all women a subtle advantage." Dorie has been talking about the same magazine profile of a female e-sports star for at least thirty minutes now, attacking it from various angles, and I've lost the thread of her argument. Dan leaps in to relate *StarCraft II* to some Trotsky principle, so I'm saved this time, though I can tell that what Dorie really wants is for me to argue with her. She delicately nibbles the edge of one of her white gloves while she swings around the subway pole with the other arm. People glance at her over the edges of their phones or reading material, annoyed.

The reason I can't follow Dorie's monologue is that I'm distracted, wondering when and what I should text Izzy. I go so far as to pull my phone out and type *I'm not finished being angry at him*, but that feels melodramatic in a way that isn't quite true. The closest I can come to figuring it out is that I want to learn how to think of myself in some way that isn't in relation to Marcus, but every time I try to squeeze the idea into a few words, it sounds stupid. I drop my phone back in my pocket as the train pulls into the Forty-Seventh—Fiftieth Street station, resolving to text her later. I pen a small *I* on the base of my left thumb to remind me.

Dorie didn't mention that this particular demonstration was planned to coincide with some free pop concert at

Rockefeller Plaza. The sidewalk is awash in people, tourists trying to find the plaza, businesspeople heading home after work, a smattering of protesters carrying signs under their arms, all of them bewildered by the police barricades that are set up on seemingly every corner. There's no current to the crowd as people go one direction and then another, trying to find a way across Sixth Avenue. Dorie stops and asks several of the omnipresent police officers which way to go. They all give her different answers: six blocks north, nine blocks south, recalcitrant shrugs. By the time the third one brushes her off, she steps closer, gets louder: "This is ridiculous. You're all trying to stymie a peaceful protest. Because you're scum."

I don't want any part of this. Maybe Dorie can get away with saying stuff like that, looking the way she looks, but I definitely don't want to be standing next to her when she does. The policeman only sneers at her, and Dan hooks his arm through hers and drags her away, south down Sixth Avenue. I stick my hands in my pockets and follow them, keeping my eyes cast down toward my Chucks. Nobody—Mr. Ippolito, Aunt Patrice, the Westcroft dean who took a chance on me, and least of all me—wants to hear the word *police* whispered in conjunction with my name. But here I am.

From farther down the avenue, we can hear people shouting "Hands up!" Dorie bristles like she's picking up a scent, follows the sound like a bloodhound. The more ground we cover, the more I can feel a drift developing in the crowd, the mass gaining momentum, and around Forty-Sixth Street, it slows and piles into an embolism. We're body to body now, the crowd thick enough that we're barely moving forward, Dan, Dorie, and I packed into a close little triangle and the larger knot of people tightening around us. I'm tense, but I tell myself that I'm overreacting, because even though elbows are knocking elbows, everyone is calm and good-natured. Dorie is happily chanting, giving big smiles to the people around us. I stay quiet, wanting her to get her fill of rabble-rousing so we can get out of here.

Some jolts of electricity run through the crowd, and my eyes look for the source. There, down on the next block, people are pushing against the police barricades and the police are pushing back. The garbled bark of a bullhorn reaches us, though I can't see it and can't make out the words.

"That's where we want to be!" Dorie crows. She reaches down and grabs our hands, starts to cut and shimmy her way forward. That's not where I want to be. I'm filled with a stab of longing to be in the Sagan gymnasium at the stupid fundraiser, to be with Izzy and Marcus, the people who know me. I pull down on Dorie's arm, like I'm a kid trying to get his parent's attention.

"I don't like this," I shout over the noise. "I think we should get out of here."

"It does seem like it's getting rowdy," Dan adds, though I don't hear the tremor of alarm in his voice that I'm sure is ringing in mine.

Dorie is pressed very close against me, and I'm looking

almost straight down into her face, the cheekbones, the eyes, the amplitude of her smile. "No problem. I'm going to stay." She tosses off the words as if they are nothing, as if they have no consequence, but I recognize them as the challenge they are. *If you're not brave enough for this, maybe you're not brave enough for this friendship.* She turns as if she actually expects Dan and me to leave her here alone. We glance at each other and wordlessly reach for her hands again so we can be pulled along in her wake.

The tension along the police barricade is stronger now. We're close enough that I can see the stony expressions of the police officers, can see the locked muscles of their jaws. We're only a few rows back from the barricades ourselves now, and when a middle-aged but still fit white woman, not all that different in appearance from Izzy's mom, starts to throw her knee over the top of one of the wooden sawhorses, I'm close enough to hear the policeman say, "Ma'am, I will arrest you if you come over this line. I will arrest you, do you understand?" The woman continues to scramble over, and I know that Dorie is watching this happen, too, because she stabs her fist into the air and issues an excited yowl. I don't think I could force sound from my constricted throat even if I felt like it, but other people yell and cheer the climbing woman as the policeman fastens handcuffs around her wrists. She grins as an officer drags her behind the line of police.

There are more police now, pouring in from somewhere, and their heads, bobbing above the fray, are wearing helmets and visors instead of the regular police hats. "Riot gear?" Dan shouts to me. "Unbelievable!" He says some other things, rights of assembly and so on, but we are swimming in a sea of distractions, and one of them has risen to the surface, commanding my attention. Over to my left, there's a black guy in short sleeves tussling across the barricade with a cop. They're shoving each other and yelling. The cop is not one of the ones in a helmet, and I can see that he's very young, I can read the fear on his face, and I can hear it, too, when he says, "Are you threatening me? Are you threatening to assault an officer?" The shoving is rapidly spreading to other cops, other people, the circumference of confused turmoil widening; someone knocks into me with his shoulder, and I hear a woman to my left gasp at the rapidly escalating scuffle.

I look again at the man at the center of the conflict. I know that it can't be Marcus—this isn't his scene, not at all— but I can't take my eyes off of him, the outline of him so familiar, the close-shaven head, the bare muscled arms. I lurch forward, half tossed by the crowd, half of my own volition, and grab the man's arm at the exact instant that it's cocking back, readying itself to throw a punch. The motion of his arm wrenches me farther forward, and when he glances in my direction, to see who's responsible for the resistance to his movement, I see that it's not Marcus, of course it's not, this man doesn't even look particularly similar to Marcus.

I'm about to turn and try to locate Dorie and Dan again when there's a punch at my rib cage, so strong, with something that feels like ice. Then it's red-hot. A sound registers in some corner of my brain, a pop. Too many sensations at once: the scrape of the pavement, someone saying "Back up, back up, back up," a feminine shriek that could almost be Dorie if Dorie were one to shriek. And then I'm not even here.

THE QUEEN

THERE ARE SO MANY QUESTIONS ABOUT WHAT HAP-
pened next, questions that will never be answered for me.
Officer Vallese, his second week on the job, fumbling, he later
claimed, for his Taser: What did he say to Tristan? Did he say
anything at all? When he realized it was his service revolver
that he was holding, what did he do and where did he go? The
people in the crowd: Did they try to stop the bleeding? Had
they read memoirs of combat medics the way I have? Did they
put a clean compress on the wound? The bullet itself: Did it
hit an artery, a bone, an organ? Did it remain lodged inside
him or did someone pick it up off the pavement later?

I asked all of these questions in the hours that followed,
and no one could give me an answer that would satisfy me.

Even then, though, I knew I was asking so many questions because there was one person I didn't want to ask about: myself. What was I doing at the moment it happened? Was I selling a stupid cookie? Was I talking and laughing? Was I being told by Marcus that I couldn't fix everything? And why couldn't I fix just one thing, just this once?

THE KNIGHT

A COLD LIGHT, THE BEEP-BEEP-BEEPING OF MACHINES, the overlapping rustle of voices. I can see but not see, I can hear but not hear, something is wrong with my brain, with my voice, with the world. There is pain, but I cannot sort out what part of my body it is coming from.

Izzy, I think, and I guess my lips manage some sort of movement, because a face hovers over me as if in answer.

"I'm here," someone says, but it's all wrong somehow, it's not the person I want.

Izzy on the swings, her hair flying behind her. Izzy standing beside the telescope in R. J.'s room, her face so close to mine. Izzy bending down to wrap my ankle, the sun setting behind her. My mind crawls further and further up the rope of time.

"Izzy." My brain is reconnected to my mouth now, and I can feel myself say it this time. "Tell her to come."

And then another wave of cold light pushes me backward.

A chessboard, black and silver. I am standing on it, square b1, the white knight. I think of what I told Izzy about the knight—he is smart and wily and can dodge the enemy like no other piece. I will find my way out of this. The black pieces move, their smooth faces impassive. The opponent is clever, but I see the endgame already. I will march off the edge of the board, to where nothing is square.

I come to again, and this time the pain is insistent and it sharpens me. It is a physical alarm bell going off in me, and I can do nothing to quiet it.

"Izzy," I say, and the same face looms over me. I feel the rough sequins of her gloves on my arm, and it is all wrong.

"You'll be okay, you'll be okay, you'll be okay," she whispers.

"Izzy," I say again. "Is she coming? Is she almost here?" The gloves lift, the face tightens, drifts to a square of darkness that I recognize as a window. There is still the clamor of pain, a piercing whistle, a body-shaking gong. A nurse is standing by the bed, suddenly. She moves my arm, and the whistle becomes a scream.

"This will help," I think the nurse is saying, though I can barely hear her over the cacophony of pain. Besides, I know that there is only one thing that will help.

"Is she coming?" I ask.

The face by the window is carved of ivory, even the tears that are running over it are hard, crystalline. Who is she? My mind flails, trying to remember. She has a small, small voice, but it reaches me like an arrow. "No. No one is coming. There's only you and me in all the world."

Impossible that Izzy is not here, when she is the only thing that matters. A tide of panic rises in me. She has to be here.

Then there's the prick of a needle, and a blanket is thrown over the alarm, muffling the noise. I close my eyes, window shades being drawn. It's dark now, quieter, and I can think. Another chessboard stretches before me, disappearing into the distance, more like a road. The panic slowly drains, and I feel that click of satisfaction, of certainty, that I get when a game is a few moves from being over.

I've been silly, wanting her to show up here. She doesn't belong here, so it isn't important to wait. I will always find my way to her. I will go to her now.

THE ROOK

It's a full moon. Izzy and I are walking home from the fund-raiser, and, embarrassingly, I don't see it coming at all. The information descends out of nowhere, in the speed of the car, in the squeal of the brakes as it pulls up alongside us, and it's only when I see T's aunt looking at us through the open window that I know something is wrong. She says, "Get in," and her face is hard, and that's when I know *how* wrong this something is. Izzy is ahead of me, as always, maybe she's the one with the gift now, and she climbs into the back seat without asking a single question. I manage to jump in after her in the second before the door slams shut.

There is traffic on the bridge, taillights like red eyes, car horns like angry shouts. This gives us time, too much time, to hear the few details that T's aunt knows. A protest gone wrong, a single shot fired by the police, the police department not saying anything yet, and why was he there in the first place? She is talking in the way of someone who cannot take silence. Izzy says very little, though I can see a deep shiver in her, a tremor running through her whole body.

When we arrive at the hospital, Izzy tumbles out of the back seat while the car is still in motion, and this time she's far too quick for me to follow. Patrice gives a small cry of alarm and hits the brakes hard, but Izzy is already long gone, and the two of us sit for a moment, stunned, watching her streak across the small parking lot by the ambulance bay. Her long dress is pale gray, but in the darkness it looks white, and I wonder what she must look like from all those hospital room windows facing the street. A ghost, an angel, the rippling sail of a ship.

T's aunt throws the car into park, not caring that we're blocking in another car, and as we speedwalk toward those startlingly bright doors, she takes my hand. We have never spoken to each other, not directly, but there we are, hand in hand like I'm a little girl, or she is.

He has already been moved out of the overcrowded emergency room and into critical care on the third floor. God, the terrible smell of hospitals, even inside the claustrophobic elevator.

And then there is the room. Like a photograph that cannot be understood no matter how long you stare at it. Like a photograph that can be understood at a glance. There is the bed and what it holds, a form that was so recently human and now so clearly is not. There is Izzy on the bed, too, her body curled around that still form, her limbs stretching over it, her head lying upon it, her mouth open as if she is speaking, though I hear no sound. There is Patrice, crumpled on the floor next to me. There is the girl in the window, the one I think I am imagining at first, wearing a prep school uniform and crouching in the corner like a terrible gargoyle, like the old man from the Hermit card of my tarot deck. The whole scene, the whole terrible collage, it could all be titled "Too Late."

THE QUEEN

HE DIDN'T FEEL ANY DIFFERENT, AND THAT WAS MAYBE the worst part. He wasn't cold or stiff. He was perfectly himself. On his hand, written in pen, was a small *I*, and I pressed my lips against it.

I laid my head on his chest where it had been a thousand times before, and I waited for the soft bump of his heart against my cheek. It's only a muscle, contracting again and again; there's nothing magical about it. Someone who wants to be a doctor wouldn't forget that. But I did. I spoke to his heart as if it had a mind of its own. I whispered to it. I cajoled. I sang its praises and criticized its intractability. I begged.

And when it wouldn't listen, I begged my own heart to stop.

THE ROOK

THERE IS A FUNERAL, OF COURSE, OR A HOMEGOING ceremony, as the people in this neighborhood sometimes call them. I've never known Tristan to be religious, but the funeral is planned in one of the huge old churches that are all over Brooklyn, this one a few blocks from where he lived, and when I arrive with Hector and my parents, I realize that it has probably been chosen for its capacity.

Marcus is here, we see him almost as soon as we walk in the door, and Hector walks over to hug him, and though his face is stony and stoic, I can see the shock waves still coursing through his brain, I can feel them all the way across the room. I used to believe that Marcus could fix anything, used to fantasize about him making all my small troubles vanish once we fell in love. I stare at my shoes while Hector talks to him; touching Marcus is more than I can take right now.

We sit in a pew about halfway back on the right side, and I have a clear view of Marcus, who has now taken his seat in the front row. His arm is wrapped protectively around his aunt Patrice, who looks shrunken and shriveled, as though some internal layer of her has been sucked dry. There's a man on the other side of her, and I don't know him, but it has to be T's father; they have the same light brown skin, the same slightly square head, and he is weeping noisily, shamelessly, into a handkerchief, sounding as if he might never stop. It's painful to behold, so I force my eyes away from him, and I make a list of the other mourners to keep myself from thinking.

Everyone is here. Near the front, there are the other members of T's family, some of whom I recognize, like Marcus's mother and his sister. Farther back, there are dozens of people from school: R. J. and Roxanne and Tyrone and Kevin and even Frodo, whose eyes are so red that it looks like he hasn't slept for days. There are people from Sagan who I know only by sight, not by name, and there are teachers, too, and the principal, Mr. Price, who offers a tissue to a girl I've never seen before. The coach of the chess team, that old Russian guy, is here, looking pretty much as he always does, though maybe a little more stooped. There are some well-dressed white kids who are all sitting in a group; they take up several rows, and I guess that these must be people from T's new school, though I don't see that gargoyle from the hospital. Izzy's parents are here; her mother is wearing a black scarf in her hair, another around her neck, and even her brother is here, with an empty expression on his face.

Farther back still are the people who surely never even knew T, who have only heard what happened to him and have shown up here tonight, their faces twisted with anger and indignation instead of sadness. They take up some of the back rows, but there are too many of them, and they flow out of the church, onto the steps and into the street, and there are police here, too, for crowd control, I guess, or maybe as an act of courtesy to T's family, most of them looking like they'd rather be anyplace else in the world.

There is one person who is not here, and that is Izzy.

It's not until the funeral actually starts, when the pastor goes to the altar and starts to speak, that I remember that T is here, too. There's a coffin, almost buried under an avalanche of flowers, but I'm relieved that it is closed so that I don't have to see him again. Imagining him in there, looking like he did in the hospital bed, is bad enough, and I shiver, and my mom reaches down and holds my hand and whispers a Hail Mary, maybe to me or maybe to herself.

The pastor speaks, a few other people speak, but it's all a senseless garble. No one is getting it right. There's only one person, really, who has the words to explain who T really was, and she isn't here.

After the service, there's a reception in the church base-ment. Too many people want to talk to me, and I know it's because they've heard I was there, in the hospital, and they want me to tell them what happened. They want me to explain why she isn't here, but the truth is I don't know, except that Izzy, sturdy, practical Izzy, will never exist in the way she did before. They want me to tell them how we all go back to our lives now, and they want me to tell them what happens next, but there's no tarot deck that could help me answer that one. And besides, I know now that grief doesn't have a what-happens-next. It just goes on and on.

EPILOGUE

Port Anthony Mental Hospital.
Three years later.

IF LIFE RAN ACCORDING TO THE RULES OF THE MIND instead of the rules of nature, my heart would have stopped beating while I was lying next to him in the hospital bed. There would have been a graceful ending, a dying-of-a-broken-heart ending. We could have gone to the grave together, and everyone would know that the story was over and would understand what it all meant.

But the heart, that tough muscle, keeps beating, even when you wish it wouldn't.

There are ways to overcome the heart's persistence, you

might be thinking, and you'd be right. I haven't forced my heart to stop, though, not yet. Here are the reasons why: 1) It would kill my parents. Or, more accurately, it wouldn't kill them. I cannot trust their healthy hearts to stop beating, even if they are thoroughly broken. 2) I am a coward who can no longer bear to think of the body's workings. Me, the former future doctor, goes queasy at the idea of blood and guts now, and I can't think about the heart as an organ, even for long enough to tend to the problem of how to stop my own. And 3)... Don't you know what the third reason is yet? Think about it, for a few moments longer, a few more relentless heartbeats, and you can probably figure it out.

After Tristan died, my family was patient with me. The school was patient with me. Everyone was patient with me. They didn't hold it against me when I collapsed into a sobbing, vomiting, unfit-for-public-consumption mess in the hour before the funeral, and they didn't hold it against me when I couldn't force myself to go back to school. So I don't blame them for misunderstanding. "When you're ready," everyone said, which implied that I would someday, in fact, be ready to go back to being the person I was before. I already knew that to be impossible. Even Patrice came by a few times and told me that Tristan would want me to keep going, but I could see for myself that she would never truly get over it, either. I spent over a year in my parents' house while everyone waited for my mourning to be over and I waited for my heart to stop beating. I couldn't think, I couldn't read, I could barely eat and breathe and talk. My parents are big believers in paying for good mental health support after Hull's remarkable turnaround, so they decided, finally, to send me up here, an excellent inpatient grief program of indeterminate length. The loony bin, some might say.

Brianna has occasionally come to visit me here. Once, she burst into tears and confessed that she had long ago said something to Frodo that she shouldn't have. That and something about a love potion that surely only Brianna could believe. She seemed relieved but also confused when I was not angry with her. Anyway, she graduated from Sagan and got a full ride to Fordham and now is thinking about graduate school, where she will write a thesis on medieval literature and the occult. She showed me a picture of her fiancé, who looks a little like Marcus but so much softer. I am, honestly, happy for her.

Marcus himself has gone into business with Brianna's brother. I know that she's the one who arranged it, even if she's modest about it. Marcus is great at knowing every potential customer in a ten-mile radius, and their store becomes more successful every year.

Philip comes down from Cornell a couple times a year, and it is a small reprieve to see someone who barely knew Tristan. He tells me funny stories about the plays he's been auditioning for, and he never acts like we are sitting in the visiting room of a hospital or references why we're here. But before he leaves, he always leans down and whispers in my ear, "I know you're still in there," as though I have fallen into a coma. Maybe I have.

My parents come to see me often, of course. They bring me treats from the city—bagels from Brooklyn, knishes from the Lower East Side—hoping to lure me back to the land of the living. They worry about me, and I worry about them, but they stand on one side of a canyon, I on the other, and not one of us remembers how to walk the tightrope between.

Hull has never come, even on his vacations from Stanford when he must be back in New York. I don't know why. I admit that it stings. If there were anyone who would understand that the old Izzy is dead, it would be the new Hull, but he is far away, on the opposite side of the country, and I cannot know how often he thinks of me, or even if he does.

Mostly, my time here has been a river of moments, all the same, but here is one remarkable thing: When I first arrived, one of the nurses, the one with the sparkly blue reading glasses that are always perched in her hair, squinted at my name on her clipboard and gave a little murmur of surprise.

"Another Izzy?" she asked. "Never knew another one in all my years here, and then we had another one six months ago. Not this unit, though," and she gestured up the hill to the secure building where they keep the real crazies. "Poor girl," she clucked, then stopped herself short, as if she'd already said too much. I know who it must have been, even if she used to shorten Isadora to Dorie instead of Izzy. I don't know what became of her.

Eventually, I suppose, the money will run out, and I'll go somewhere else. Or maybe Hull will get that CEO position and send money and I'll stay here until my heart really does stop beating. And then there will be an ending.

The third reason, of course, that I haven't called it quits yet is that I can still remember Tristan. I can still imagine him. I can still conjure him, and in that way, he is still here with me. It is an admittedly pale version of him, but that is better than nothingness. I remember and remember. I imagine and imagine. I remember what it was like for me to live those months, and I imagine what the world must have looked like through his eyes and through Brianna's eyes, too. It doesn't matter that surely some of the details are wrong; it is all true anyway.

It was the doctors who first suggested that I write it all down. I think, though, that they now regret the advice, that they feel a little sheepish for having mentioned it, since I write for hours every day, finishing and then looping back to the beginning to start again. They now tell me that it might be advisable to stop this project and move on to other "avenues of healing." But I can't simply give up writing and replace it with attending another support group or painting watercolor landscapes; to do so would be to abandon him.

"So many twists and turns in your story," one of the doctors said to me while he was taking my pulse and giving me a reassuring smile. It is my opinion that they don't really need to take my pulse; they do it because some patients find it comforting. It makes them feel cared for. It makes them feel as though someone sees them. "It could almost be a novel," the doctor said.

When he was done, I buttoned the cuff of my shirt tightly over my wrist, hiding my implacable heartbeat away from anyone who might be looking for it. He had it all wrong, of course. This is not a novel. It's a romance.

Acknowledgments

While it's impossible to acknowledge everyone who helped me become a writer, let me single out my teachers and colleagues from the Creative Writing Program at New York University for sharing with me their sharp minds and their warm friendship.

Thanks to the Maribar Writers Colony for the space to think and the camaraderie I found there.

I owe special gratitude to two of the earliest readers of this manuscript, Jason Leahey and Dominic Romany, who were so generous with their advice and encouragement. You really are the bee's knees.

Kerry Sparks, my agent, is the stuff of legends. She's the champion that all writers dream of finding, and I can't thank her and her colleagues at Levine Greenberg Rostan enough for their work in bringing this book into being.

Farrin Jacobs and her team at Little, Brown are incredible. I'm so grateful that they graced *Izzy + Tristan* with their immense talents.

High school is full of more hope, transformation, and

uncertainty than a Star card in a tarot formation. My deepest thanks go to those who loved me through it: Llalan Fowler, Mignon Miller, Rachel Barnette, Dave Humeston, Jay Goyal, Stephen Kennedy, Tom Hankinson and most especially, my patient family, Dwight, Nancy, Dawn, and Ryan.

And finally, my endless devotion to Jason and Nora: You're the kind of big love that most people don't even dare to imagine.